The Washashore Murders

A Nor'easter Island Mystery

Judy Tierney

Cover photo & book design by Lara Andrea Taber, 2design art co.

Published by BookBaby 2024

ISBN: 979-8-89372-643-5
FIC0220400: women sleuths; FIC022100: amateur sleuths
FIC0221409: holidays and vacation; FIC00221070: cozy

To Ron, of course.

Washashore

A washashore is a person who has
moved to an island from the mainland.
The term is not usually meant as a compliment.

Table of Contents

Prologue: The Sea

They could have been in a painting. Two men wearing jeans and waxed jackets, watch caps pulled over their heads, fishing rods in hand, seated in silence on the benches of a small boat shrouded in wisps of dawn mist. And then, a line tightened, a rod arched.

It was Joel's. He sprang up. An experienced angler, he relished the fight, and he leaned back to reel in what looked to be a good-sized bluefish. It struggled against him. The blue flipped out of the water, and then it turned and pulled Joel forward trying to free itself. That was the moment the other man slipped behind Joel, extended his arms and shoved, hard, sending Joel overboard. The boat lurched as he hit the water and sank. The blue disappeared, trailing the line and pole.

Without wasting time, the man in the boat reached over and gunned the motor. Joel surfaced, gasping for breath. He grasped a gunnel and struggled to roll himself over it to get back in, but the man pried his fingers away and pushed his head under again. The whine of the engine as the outboard sped away drowned out Joel's screams as he swam to catch up. The man driving the boat did not look back. When he reached the vessel waiting for him, he turned off the motor and climbed out onto a rope ladder. He let the small blue boat drift away into the blood orange dawn.

Two weeks passed before the blue boat and the body were found on the west side beaches of Nor'easter Island. It wasn't that people weren't searching for Joel Berliner once they realized he'd disappeared, but he was a fisherman. The waters off Nor'easter Island can be treacherous, and he was not the first to be lost at sea.

Part One – Before

Chapter One

On the Monday evening when Columbus Day weekend ends, the bar crowd on Nor'easter Island considers it a tradition to gather on the beach and throw a moon at the last ferry leaving for the mainland. Never mind that it is already dark in the short days of October and no one on the boat can see them. They're celebrating because the holiday marks the end of the tourist season on the summer resort. The streets and hotels empty out, the year-rounders regain their island for themselves, and they look ahead to a quiet winter with cash in hand from working three jobs servicing the needs of the summer tourists. Glad to have their money, glad to see them go.

Joel Berliner was one of those islanders gathered on the beach. Everyone recalled he was there. But only a handful would admit to seeing him the next day, Tuesday, when he disappeared. Edith

"Dita" Redmond did. She said she saw Joel twice. She remembered because it was a special day in her household.

Early that morning, instead of sitting down for a leisurely breakfast, she and her husband Sean stood across from each other in their small kitchen. Edith, whose childhood nickname Dita had long replaced her given name, leaned against the speckled counter, her pink chenille bathrobe loosely tied at the waist. Sean, already dressed, was propped against the butcher-block table. Each held a mug of steaming coffee. Sean was trying to gulp his like a beer, rushing because he didn't want to miss the boat to the mainland, although they had plenty of time to get to Nor'easter Island's ferry harbor. It was a straight run to town and there was no traffic. While the island's summer population could swell up to 20,000 tourists a day, causing traffic jams on the narrow roads, once cool weather hit the island there might be more over-wintering birds than people. Dita and Sean were among a meager thousand or so year-round residents of Nor'easter Island, more of a summer resort than a place to pursue a life and a career.

Sean plunked his cup down in the sink and smiled at her. "Done," he said.

"How do you do that?" she asked, not expecting an answer.

"Practice," he said, opening the kitchen slider. "Let's go. The boat won't wait."

She followed him out, taking her coffee with her. Their goofy golden retriever, Tuffy, tagged along to the truck, edging himself in front of Dita as she opened the driver's side door. She motioned him in and he leapt up, then squeezed through the seats to the back bench.

It looked to be a good day for a crossing to the mainland, twelve miles away, but on Nor'easter Island that could change in a matter of a few hours. Out to the west, beyond Sailors Pond, which was across the street from their house, an angry black band cut across the sky with dark cloud cover behind it, marking the edge of a storm that might right now be raising Cain over Long Island, some twenty miles off to the west. It could be a mere thunder burst that would peter out before reaching them and not a gale; and, Dita hoped, not a Nor'easter, the storms for which the island was named. Those rose out of the North Atlantic, forming cyclonic rotations like tropical hurricanes, angry sea monsters that could hover over the island for days, pounding rain and punishing waves that eroded the beaches as though the storm was gobbling them up. This morning the weather directly overhead looked to be good, at least for now just a few light clouds.

"I hope the weather holds," Dita said, thinking Sean's ride home might not be so calm if a gale moved in.

He shrugged. "As long as the ferry runs, I'll be on it," he said. "Doesn't bother me."

She thought he seemed nervous, but not about the weather. He had scheduled appointments with loan officers at the two banks close to the mainland harbor. He planned to apply for financial backing to start a business on the island, a fitness center. Without a loan, he wouldn't be able do it. Dita had listened to his presentation before they went to bed last night. She thought it sounded good. He seemed ready, and today, he looked ready. He wore real slacks, and a shirt with a collar, clothes that usually hung in the closet ready for weddings and funerals, instead of the everyday jeans, tees and sweats that bespoke island life. Dita had actually run an iron over them last night. She kept one for these rare occasions, and used the window seat in the front room as an ironing board. The couple had debated the value of a tie, but landed on the side of, too much. Who among the mainland bourgeoisie, especially the banking world, would really believe an islander with a tie? They viewed the year-rounders from the summer resort like feral creatures.

Dita looked Sean over one more time. "You look nice," she said.

He smiled. "As do you. I love you best in your chenille robe. All you need are rollers in your hair." He leaned over and kissed her, and reached out to grab a piece of her.

"Stop. I have to drive. And you rushed me so I didn't have time to dress."

They headed down Founders Road toward town and the harbor, a five-minute ride today. She pulled into the parking lot and he gave her one more kiss before he opened the door and stepped out. She rolled her window down.

'Good luck," she called.

He turned toward her, and she saw faint worry lines crease his forehead.

He called back to her. "Yeah, let's hope. Don't forget to meet me at the five and please, get the recycling to the dump."

The five would be the boat that left the mainland at five and arrived back on Nor'easter Island at six.

She watched him stride through the parking lot. His height made him easy to spot as he joined the small knot of other islanders toward the bottom of the hill, all making their way toward the dock, forming a line at the ticket office, then climbing the gangplank and disappearing onto the boat. She hoped this day went well for him over there. If not, if he couldn't get a loan, they might have to leave the island. They weren't earning enough money to pay their bills. In the summer, she waitressed in addition to working part time as a reporter for the newspaper, *The Island Gale*, but neither of those jobs brought in enough money to pay their mortgage. Sean did small carpentry jobs and filled in on construction crews; but again, that wasn't a real living. They would have to go to the mainland if their business plan to start a fitness center did not get financing. She could understand why Sean was worried. Dita was also, but had promised herself she would remain optimistic.

She restarted the truck and drove through town, past all the white, wooden Victorian buildings, then turned toward home. She loved the stretch of road between the business district and their house. Sand dunes lined the ocean side for over a mile. In spring, they were covered with rambling pink rosa rugosa in flower. On fall mornings like today, the sun, hanging low in the sky, lit the tips of the beach grasses to gold.

She pulled into the parking lot just past the Beach Dune Restaurant, where the surfers parked their vans. The dunes were smaller there, and she could see the ocean. It was calm, which explained the fact there was only one other car in the lot. She parked facing the water, enjoying the view, and waited, checking her email on her phone while she sat there. It was a delight not to need to rush off somewhere, to open the windows and breathe in the salty sea air. Finally she heard the ferry's horn sound twice and she knew it was leaving the harbor. She watched until it passed by, making its way along the island to open seas, and then she started on her way home again.

When she got there, Tuffy jumped out and disappeared into the brambles that surrounded their yard. Dita showered and dressed before she went back to the truck. As she left the house, she let Tuffy, who was now sprawled out on the deck waiting for her, inside for his morning nap. She and Sean had already loaded the vehicle's bed with the trash the previous evening. Usually recycling was his job, but the dump, as everyone called the recycling center, was open two half-days a week, and this was one of them. She drove toward it, two miles up Founders, but pulled into her friend Rachel Berliner's driveway to visit her first.

Rachel's cottage leaned as though it were hovering over an oceanside cliff debating whether or not to take the plunge. Fifty years of storms with gale force winds had shifted the structure. Fifty years of sea air, salty and damp, had eaten into the siding, fading the cedar shingles from brown to the soft gray that tourists loved. Dita sometimes wondered if there were extra lines chiseled into islanders' faces, extra sprigs of gray hair on their heads. Maybe, islanders aged like their houses. If so, she thought, she'd better move off before it was too late. She liked her smooth skin and honey blond hair the way it was.

Nor'easter Island's harsh North Atlantic climate was a far cry from the frequently touted warmer climates of other tourist resorts like Key West, Oahu and Myrtle Beach. Still, there were enough stellar summer days to bring boatloads of tourists; and this year, city people awash in money looking for big second homes. Houses were being grabbed up as though there was a fire sale at New York's diamond exchange. Even Rachel's falling-into-neglect cottage caught their attention. Passers-by looking for an inexpensive summer place would slow down wondering if the price would be "the one" they could afford. Those looking for a Hampton's-style estate would wonder if there was enough land to demolish the cottage and build a mansion.

But Rachel's was not for sale. Her life was here. Dita knew that. A longtime widow, Rachel would not leave as long as Joel, her son, who was mildly disabled, lived with her. And her daughter Addie Morton, Dita's best friend, lived down the street with her husband and small son.

Dita rapped on the peeling wooden door and let herself into the front room.

"Hello, Rachel. It's me, Dita," she called. "Are you home?"

"Be there in a second," Rachel called from somewhere in the back of the house. "Make yourself comfortable."

Dita already had. She settled into the sagging couch and put her feet up on a small tattered hassock.

Joel stuck his head out from the kitchen. "I'm making some pancakes. Would you like some?"

Not having eaten, Dita was enthused. "Sure would, thank you."

Joel disappeared for a second, and returned with a cup of coffee for her.

"You're the best," Dita said.

Then she heard him beating batter with a spoon, wooden she

guessed, and oil sizzling in a pan. Not half a cup of coffee later, he stuck his shaggy head out again and beckoned her into the kitchen, a room last redone in the fifties. A highly polished, but cracked, blue and white patterned linoleum covered the floor. The one modern feature in the room was the white color of the metal cabinets, which had old-style glass knobs for handles. The sink was a real farm sink, white porcelain, chipped on the edges. The ceiling was discolored from the vapors of cookpots. Joel was griddling pancakes on top of a 24-inch four-burner stove.

Unlike Sean, who topped off at 6'4", Joel was 5'8," a stocky man, who despite his heft did not give the impression of strength. Dita came in and stood behind him, looking down over his shoulder. She, like Sean, was tall, a full 6 feet.

"I added blueberries. That okay for you?" Joel asked, as he flipped them over.

"Now they sound even better," she said.

When she'd first met Joel, earlier in her friendship with Rachel, he'd avoided her when she visited, and averted his eyes on the street when their paths crossed, uttering a quiet hello and moving on. But she'd become close to Rachel, and even closer to Rachel's daughter. Now Joel interacted with her, and with Sean, as family.

"I just left Sean at the ferry," she said. "You know he's trying to get a loan."

Joel turned to look at her. "I'm hopeful for him. I hope he comes home early, though. It looks like that storm out there is going to move on in and it's going to get nasty. That's why I'm making breakfast instead of out fishing on my boat."

Later, after Joel vanished, she would insist he couldn't have gone out on the water that day.

Rachel appeared, toweling her hair dry, wearing a pair of gray sweats. She flopped into a lumpy easy chair and Joel brought her a plate.

"I'm on my way to the dump," Dita said. "Want me to take

anything? Have Joel throw it into the truck."

"That would be nice. Did you hear that, Joel?"

They heard his "okay" from the kitchen. Then the back door opened as he went outside to get the trash.

"Did you notice how much better he is?" Rachel said under her breath to Dita.

"I did. What's going on?"

"Carol," Rachel said. "He's been seeing a lot of her lately."

Dita nodded. She'd seen them together once, but hadn't thought about their being a couple.

"Nice," she said.

They heard the back door again and Rachel put a finger up to her mouth to shush Dita.

Rachel changed the subject. "I hope things go well for Sean today. Why didn't you go with him?"

"He felt he had to do this on his own. It's okay, but instead I'll just be nervous here. I decided not to go to work. I can't concentrate," Dita said.

"After the dump, go home and relax. Read a book, snooze."

"I think so," she agreed. She stayed a while listening to Rachel talk about the customers who'd been in the store over the weekend; the couple who bought a Buddha fountain, the teenaged girl who picked up bracelet bangles, and the wealthy mainlander searching for the bird carvings she brought from Central America.

As it grew closer to lunchtime, Dita stood up. "I better go before the dump closes. It's only open until twelve. Thanks for breakfast. I'll help box up the shop this week if you want." Then she shouted toward the kitchen. "Bye Joel!"

She heard him shout back.

When she left the Berliner house, she drove to the transfer station, remembering to slow down when she turned onto the unpaved washboard that the town called a road. While she tossed her bags into the dumpster she gazed out over the rolling sea, thinking how lucky she was to live in a place where even the dump was scenic. In her white sweater, she looked like an egret about to take flight. She finished in no time. As she drove out, she revved up her engine hoping to hurry home. But she'd forgotten about the washboard, and the truck careened in and out of ruts like it was bouncing around in a pinball machine. Dust flew through the rolled down window. She coughed and swore under her breath as she closed it and eased her foot off the gas pedal. When she got to the main road, the paved Founders Rock Road that they all called Founders, the expected storm began. Rain, pushed by strong gusts, pelted against her windshield. The truck shuddered as the wind hit it. She felt like the vehicle would blow off with the gale, fly over the cottages and into the roiled sea.

When she reached her house, she sat in the truck and waited for the rain to let up before making the run inside. Her cottage was shingled, and as she looked at it, she thought it looked a lot like Rachel's, both dwellings clad in cedar. Her shakes weren't as ancient as her friend's. Yet, they were already graying in the sea air. A salt box cottage with the angled side in front, it was larger than Rachel's, but small compared to the mansions starting to go up around the island. Charming is how a visitor from the mainland might describe it.

When the rain finally tapered off, she ran out and sprinted up the eleven steps to the deck. She didn't mind getting her hair wet. She wasn't a woman with a coif. But she didn't want to be sopping wet either when she went in. Tuffy was waiting for her at the slider, head cocked so he looked as though he was asking where she'd been.

She brewed herself a cup of coffee, real coffee, not that coffee in a capsule in the expensive dispenser la-de-dah stuff, and settled into the window seat that overlooked Sailors Pond, the ocean inlet across the street. Tuffy settled on the floor close by. Pulling her legs up under her, Dita pushed her hair off her forehead and opened a mystery novel. It was not more than twenty minutes before the deluge began again with an even stronger wind. The rain pounded sideways of course, this time onto the window glass, pushed across the Pond by the strong gusts. Two months ago, that harbor was filled with pleasure boats; stinkpots, sailers, yachts, and even one or two small fishing vessels. Now few remained, just a decrepit cabin cruiser and one 36-foot black wooden sloop. Dita thought they must be on heavy moorings to stay tethered in this wind which was straightening the flags flapping above them, a sign of at least a 30-knot blow.

A blur of people hurried past on the other side of the street, umbrellas held in front of them, of no use in the gale, raincoats trailing behind like kite tails. That was when she recognized Joel. She recognized him by his shape and uneven gait. She jumped up and ran to the door.

"Joel," she called. "Joel! Come in out of the rain."

But the wind carried her words away from him and he continued south, toward town. It looked like he was pushing and shoving with someone as he went, but it could have been the wind blowing their coats that made it look that way. She could grab her raincoat and dash outside to pick him up, but she really didn't want to go out in this storm again. She also knew when men started doing that, you stayed out of the way. So she told herself soon he'd be closer to the beach pavilion where he could take shelter under the eaves and call the police station if he was in trouble. She thought about calling it in, but she imagined Sean's reaction, that she was babying him like his mother did. Addie, Joel's sister and Dita's best friend, agreed with Sean, who felt Joel needed space to become more independent. Now that he might have a girlfriend, maybe they were all right. Besides, he must have already walked the half-mile from home. She shut the door. Tuffy brushed up against her, and she stopped thinking about Joel as she leaned down to pet the golden. Had she known it would be the last time she would see the man, that he would disappear and die, she would have expended the energy. But she did not; she went back to the window seat with her book. It wasn't as soft as a hammock, but it was comfy, and she drifted off into a deep sleep.

Sometime later, a car pulled into the yard. Dita vaguely thought she heard the door open when someone walked in, and then the dog bounded across the floor. She opened her eyes and saw Sean with Tuffy, who was wagging his tail. Sean, a six-footer plus with a basketball player's build, stood over Dita and shook the raindrops off himself like a big puppy. Sprinkled with cold water, Dita jumped up.

"Did you call me?" she asked.

"Yep," he replied in his gravelly ex-smoker's voice.

"Oh, I am so sorry. I guess I fell asleep." Leaving a spouse waiting at the dock, especially in the rain, was a big no-no on Nor'easter Island. It could even be used in a divorce hearing. She hoped Sean wouldn't hold it against her. "How'd you get home? Taxi? Funny, Tuffy didn't bark. I would have woken up."

"It's okay you forgot, *this* time," he said. "When you didn't answer I grabbed a ride with Karl Schultz. His car was on the boat, so I didn't even have to cross the parking lot." He bent down and kissed her. "You might be interested in what he told me on the way home. The police department's been trying to find a way into a drug ring on the island. They know from the rumor mill that heroin use is up, but they can't get anyone to give them a lead as to who's bringing it in, or even who's using. Maybe you ought to meet with the police chief or Karl for a story?"

"Karl. That's why the dog didn't bark. He knows the sound of Karl's car," she said.

Karl Shultz, a local police officer, was their neighbor. He lived several lots beyond them. Their two families were the only winter residents in the cluster of homes on their dune.

"You told me the gossip, but not about the loan. I guess that news isn't good, is it?"

"Probably not. Neither said no, but neither said yes. We have to wait to hear from them."

Dita tried to contain her disappointment. "I'm sorry," she said. "I wish I could help."

"Yep. Nothing we can do." He looked away from her. "And, by the way, I don't want supper. My belly's churned up like the seawater out back of our house."

The Redmond's house was on a spit of land between the sea behind and the salt pond out front.

Sean continued complaining about the trip. "They almost cancelled the boat. It was a lousy ride back."

He went into the bedroom and got into dry clothes. He was about to plop himself down in the recliner to watch a hockey game when the landline phone rang. He was close, so he grabbed the receiver.

"I have it...Yeah." He listened for a moment, then called to his wife.

"Dita, have you seen Joel? It's Rachel. He hasn't come home for supper." He raised his thick hedgerow of eyebrows, wrinkling his forehead, a signal that told Dita *so what*?

She took the phone and listened to Rachel. Then she told her she would call Addie, and invite her to go to the Washashore Pub to see if Joel was there. She knew Rachel called her instead of Addie because Addie would agree with Sean and tell her to chill out. Dita picked up her cell phone and decided to speak instead of texting.

"Addie, your mother called. Joel didn't come home for supper."

"So what?" Addie responded, in agreement with Sean. "He's a grown-up."

"Come down to the Washashore with me. We'll ask around. Sean's too tired."

"Girls' night out? If so, I'm in, though I'm not concerned about Joel."

"I'll pick you up soon." Dita hung up the phone.

"Nothing happened to him, Dita," Sean said. "Rachel babies him too much. He might have been a bit crazy a long time ago, but he's been fine for years. Nothing's going to happen because he stays out late and forgets to tell his mother."

"I know. And I knew you would say that. But I should have gone after him and given him a ride. Then I'd know where he went, and who he seemed to be messing around with. What if it wasn't just jostling and he's in trouble?"

"Okay, you should have picked him up, and you should have given me a ride," he said, his face breaking into a grin. "That's two misses in one afternoon. Did you at least do the garbage run?"

She nodded.

"I guess it tuckered you out," he said. "Okay, Washashore Pub for you and Addie. Take the truck. Their driveway is going to be a muddy mess."

He was already stretched out in his recliner. She knew he'd be sleeping in minutes. Before she went out the door, she leaned down and ran her fingers through his hair, still thick, though salted with beginning gray. He reached up and pulled her closer for a kiss. She had loved him from the start and still did.

"The driveway," he repeated.

"Right," she answered.

Chapter Two

The turnoff to Addie and Mel Morton's house was so close Dita wouldn't need to shift out of second gear before she got there; and she would stay in that gear especially because their long, unpaved driveway kept returning itself into a wetland when it rained. It was a rough ride. A slow and low gear was best. Every few years, Addie and Mel had sand and gravel poured onto it, but the pace of its erosion was way faster than the pace of their ability to collect funds for the repairs. Sometimes Dita walked over there after a rain, forgetting that small ponds pooled in its hollows and the ground turned to mud. Faced with getting wet and mucky, as well as snagged by the rosa rugosa prickers that overgrew the track's sides, she would give up and go home.

This evening she was glad to have Sean's truck to *sploosh* through. She beeped when she got there instead of texting, an old habit from the time before cell phones.

Addie bounced out of the house, her long red curls flying, excited to go. "Did you eat yet? Tonight's the fish taco special," she breathed as she slammed the door shut.

Dita often wondered why Addie was not more than *zaftig*, a Yiddish term for pleasingly plump. Almost every conversation began with a food group.

"Actually, I haven't. I fell asleep and Sean woke me up when your mother called. I didn't even hear him call me to pick him up. Or come in."

"The cook there is really good. In summer, he's the Gustamente Chef."

Dita let that simmer a moment. In summer he was a chef; in winter, a mere cook. She smiled. Oh, well.

"Might as well eat. Sean won't be hungry tonight. His belly took a beating."

"Did he get the loan?"

"We don't know," Dita shrugged. "He didn't say much about it because he was so sick. He has to sleep off the trip."

Besides, she knew he didn't want to think about what would they do if they didn't get the money. There weren't many ways to bring home a paycheck in winter on a resort island with no bridge to the mainland, and almost no businesses in the off-season.

"The parking lot's puddling up already," Addie noted as they passed the beach pavilion. "It'll be totally flooded in no time if the rain starts again."

"Mmhmm, but since no swimmers are expected in this storm, it doesn't really matter," Dita answered. "And everyone surfs a little further up."

Clam shells crunched under her tires. She thought of this piece of Founders as the gulls' dining room. It was the spot where seagulls flew off the estuary across from the beach and slammed their shellfish catch down onto the road to crack them open. She passed a tourist bar that was closed for the season and slowed down at Bridgegate Square, really just an intersection with four stop signs, and no bridge nor gate. It was not even square, its roads being slightly askew from each other. Nevertheless, people claimed that in the old days, whenever that might have been, there was a bridge. She turned the corner and pulled into the parking lot next to the Washashore Pub. Finally, she thought, an apt name. A Washashore is a person who moves to Nor'easter Island from any-where else, unless their family had island roots. Almost everyone she knew was a "Washashore," for better or for worse. The term was somewhat pejorative and people dredged it out of the lexicon when someone got picked up for drunk driving, for brawling, or larceny. Or ran for public office and was disliked. Or sat at a bar and drank a lot.

The Washashore was in a plain rectangular three-story building with a covered front porch. It shared the first floor with a taco takeout. Unlike most of the buildings in the center of the town, it was not white, not Victorian, and it was shabby.

"Shall we make a run for it?" Addie jumped out and took off for the front door. Dita followed, pulling up her raincoat hood. The deluge had tapered but not stopped completely.

Inside, a clutch of people surrounded the pool table. Even in the dim light, Dita recognized all but one. She knew the people on the bar stools as well. In winter, this was a local watering hole, one of two that stayed open through the off-season. It was not just dark, but dank, at least until the heat was turned on; and it wasn't on yet.

"Why does this place always smell so bad when the weather cools?" Dita groused. A faint ammonia odor rose from the wood-en floor boards next to the rest rooms. "And it needs a makeover. Even the stool cushions are tearing."

Addie took her arm. "It greets you like an old friend." Her cheeks dimpled as she smiled at Dita.

"An old friend who doesn't wash?" Dita asked.

Addie laughed. "Let's have fun, tonight. No more complaining."

Dita did want to have fun, so she didn't argue. Sometimes you had to let things go.

Everyone looked up as they made their way to a table, but only for a second as they were recognized. Someone new would have rendered more scrutiny. Neither of them spotted Joel. He wasn't here now, though he might have been earlier.

Harry, the blonde and tattooed owner, was bartending today. He was a friend of Addie's and she went right over to ask if he'd seen Joel. Dita approached Sonny, who was nursing a beer at the bar. A transplant from Maine who came to work as a waiter one summer and stayed on, he spent his winters pickling his liver with alcohol. Dita figured he'd been here all afternoon, drinking on a tab, nursing that considerable habit. Despite his being a sot, he was a nice fella, most of the time.

She hoped today was one of those times.

"Hey, Sonny," Dita sat on a stool, leaving an empty between them so as not to smell his breath. Also, she didn't want to tower over him too much. He was a tiny man, often unshaven, and unremarkable in his features, someone who could melt unseen into the background of the bar.

"Dita. How ya' doin'? How's Sean?"

"Both good. Addie and I are looking for Joel. Seen him today?"

"I think he was here for a while." Sonny looked around. "He left."

"Do you know where he went?"

Sonny took a swig of his beer. "Maybe I saw him leave with Trent, you know, that new guy that's been living out on the West side. Yeah, I think he did."

"You wouldn't know where they were headed, would you?"

"Nah." Sonny turned away from her and focused on his bottle. It was almost empty, and Dita knew he was thinking about his next one. She wouldn't get any more information from him. She wouldn't feed his alcohol habit either, though.

"Thanks," she said. "Rachel is worried. If you see him, tell him to call her?"

Dita joined Addie and Harry, and ordered a sandwich for Sonny. She did believe in feeding him food. She wondered if he ever ate anything besides an occasional bag of potato chips. He seemed to get thinner and thinner during these drinking jags, his face more pinched. She feared he wouldn't make it to 45.

"Shall we eat?" Addie asked. "Harry says the cook got fresh cod from Steve."

Ah, yes, Dita thought. The cook who was the chief at the Gustamonte in summer.

"I'm surprised Steve was out today in this storm," she said, "but then again, he's usually out at dawn, so he probably came in before it hit. Sure, I'll take the special. And I'd like a hot spiced rum and cider with it."

"Make that two," Addie told Harry. They often drank those together in the fall and winter, the combination of the cider and the hot rum warming them after a cold walk in the wind.

They chose a table away from the door, but not close to the rest rooms. They didn't want to ruin their appetites after all. They got comfortable in their chairs before Addie broke their silence. "Harry says Joel was in earlier. Maybe he'll come back while we're here."

"Sonny saw him leave with some new guy, Trent. Addie, I thought he was with a bunch of people when he passed the house." Dita did not want to tell Addie he might have been fighting, but she did.

"And?" Addie asked. "So, maybe he was hanging around with some of the guys."

Addie pushed a red curl from her forehead. Dita noticed worry lines forming, though she had denied any doubts that Joel was okay. Then Addie thought aloud.

"There aren't many places to go. It's wet outside, so that leaves here, the guy's house and ours, or maybe a covered porch at one of the closed hotels. Or, he could have gone to Carol's. They've been seeing each other a lot lately, although according to my mother he's never stayed overnight with her."

"I'll call your mom if you want."

"Please. If I do, she'll guilt me into riding all over the island to search. You know he's fine and we should stop thinking about him."

Dita nodded. "As Sean would say."

Harry shouted for them to pick up their plates. No wait service for them.

"So, Dita, have you decided yet?" Addie asked as they sat down again and Dita had made the call to Rachel.

Dita knew what Addie was talking about, since they'd already picked up their food. It was about getting pregnant, having children. Dita didn't really want to discuss this with her friend right now. How could she say that she knew she and Sean would not make fit parents at the moment? That they, unlike their friends in high school and college, and even unlike Addie and Mel, were untethered, like seaweed in the surf, so to speak, not advancing in careers, and sometimes not able to pay their bills. They were not financially stable, along with everything else. But, despite her reluctance, she took the bait to try to explain.

"Addie, Sean and I are in our mid 30's, still at odds with the middle-class world, hanging out, working out, probably drinking too much and smoking pot, living day to day," Dita said.

"So?" Addie asked.

"I work part time and Sean doesn't even have a steady job. You know that. He subcontracts to other builders. We have to pick up extra money bartending, waitressing, or house watching."

"What about the fitness center?"

"That might be more like a fizzled firecracker than a go right now if he can't get financing," Dita said. "Sean is one of those guys who can't sit at a desk all day. Some of them rise to the top of a business, where they can flit from meeting to meeting and idea to idea. You know, you've seen those self-important puffed-up dudes on the Internet. Or they flounder. Sean has brains and brawn, but he's not yet settled, not like your Mel. I know you find Mel a little boring sometimes, but he's steady."

"I think you're exaggerating," Addie said, taking a bite of her taco.

"And look at me," Dita continued. "Am I any better than Sean? I haven't pursued my writing career beyond working for a small weekly paper, reporting the almost non-existent news in winter."

She let that sit a moment, and then she gave Addie the rest of her negative self-evaluation. "I chronicle monotonous town meetings, and write the monthly column showcasing summer people's mega-mansions, some of them monstrosities I abhor. Other island writers spin poems about the sunsets, trill about egrets in flight."

Dita waved her hand in the air, then leaned in toward Addie. "Some of them even engage in not-so-secret liaisons with famous visiting poets. Then they use metaphors and similes and splashes of color. I churn out artless articles at pennies per word."

"Wow. I didn't expect all that," Addie said. "Chill out girl, don't be so hard on yourself. Babies don't care about momma and poppa's careers, especially here. There's a whole community to catch you if money gets tough. Kids just want your love. And you're getting older. By the time you decide, it might be too late."

Addie leaned forward. "Don't act like you don't know that, indecisive Dita." She smiled into her friend's face, tapping her finger on the table as she sipped her rum and cider and bit into her fish taco. "The time is now. You're 35."

"Indecisive?" Dita asked. She thought to herself, *is that what I am? Maybe, but I'm not about to be pressured by anyone, not even Addie.*

Dita stopped eating and drinking for a moment. "I thought I was quite decisively saying not now, Addie, I'm not ready. We, Sean and I, will make that decision when the gym is up and running, if it gets up and running. Keep your eye on this tummy and that should give you the news if there is any. Until then, zip up."

She was feeling angry. Addie was questioning her like her mother did. She'd been waiting more and more impatiently for Dita to give her a grandchild ever since she'd married Sean. Having children was not the only reason for life, was it?

"My Danny's getting toward the age when he could babysit," Addie said, trying a softer tactic by bringing up her little boy, who was ten. "I'll need to keep him off the beaches at night when the summer kids are partying."

"Really! So that's why you keep asking," Dita took a potato chip, which she was glad they supplied with the tacos, even though they didn't really go with them. She thought they must have run out of corn chips.

Addie changed the subject. "I'm going to call Loretta and tell her to come join us."

Dita thought Addie noticed how angry she was, and just wanted to clear the air. "It's too late," Dita said. "She's stretched out on her couch watching one of those singing talent shows."

"I'm texting anyway." Addie's thumbs tapped on the glass of the phone. "There."

They continued to eat in silence until their plates were empty. "I'll take these up to the bar." Addie slid Dita's plate under hers. "Be right back."

Dita watched her friend thread her way through the tables, angling toward Harry, who was wiping glasses at the kitchen end of the bar. She sighed. Instead of leaving the dishes on the bar for Harry, Addie was carrying them into the kitchen. With a flick of his fingers, Harry signaled Brenda, his helper, to take over the service; and before she even got there, he followed Addie and disappeared into the kitchen. Dita hoped Loretta would show up. Otherwise, she would be spending the evening alone, waiting for Addie's brother, without Addie.

"Don't look so glum." Loretta was standing in front of her. "I got here as fast as I could."

Dita was startled by her friend's rapid appearance. "How'd you do that?" she asked.

"I was coming anyway. I was almost in the parking lot when Addie texted."

"I'm glad you're here. I saw that guy Brian Martin glancing over at me, debating." Dita shuddered. She crossed her legs, as though closing up in defense. Though she was not a man magnet like the red headed, cherubic-looking Addie or the mermaid-shaped Loretta, she was attractive. "I'd hate to be a single chicklet like you on this island, Loretta, especially in the winter, prime for the on-the-make bar dude," she said. "One hour I'm alone here and that guy is already weighing the benefits of hitting on me versus the damages of Sean coming after him."

"Where's Addie?" Loretta asked. "She didn't go home, did she?"

Dita nodded toward the kitchen.

"She's in the back with Harry? What's wrong with her? Everyone knows Harry's a bad boyfriend, even on the side," Loretta said, and then she lowered her voice to a whisper. "I think he might be into heroin these days."

Loretta removed her scarf and hung it on the back of an empty chair with her jacket. She flipped her long blue-streaked hair onto her back.

Dita was surprised. "Heroin? Really? Hmm," she said, thinking of Sean's comments earlier.

Loretta put her hand over her mouth. She shook her head. "Forget I said that."

Dita nodded, but tucked the information away to think about later. "Okay. By the way, that's a particularly nice one," she said, reaching out to touch the trailing scarf. Only in the heat of a mid-summer's day was Loretta without a scarf; and even then, one might be tied around a straw hat.

"Yes, it's from Lyon...France...I bought it when I was there with Jake. Remember him? It's fine silk."

Dita did not remember Jake. There were many ex-boyfriends in Loretta's past, and only one or two were memorable. But the scarf was memorable, and she mouthed the word, "Nice." She lifted the trailing end off the floor and doubled it onto the chairback. "Wouldn't want anyone to step on it then."

Loretta responded with a shrug. "I suppose you're right. You know, I could use a new wool one—navy blue maybe? I already have a red one."

Dita had knitted the red one. "When I finish knitting Sean's new watch cap, I'll have enough yarn left over. Want a stripe or a seashell on it?" she asked.

"Yes," Loretta said. She stretched out her legs, clothed much less elegantly than her neck in gray cotton sweats with a rip in the right knee. She was the picture of paradox, not quite ready for the fashion page of any newspaper. Still, her clashing couture never worked against her. She took a sip of Dita's hot cider and rum. Drinking someone else's liquor didn't bother her even in the age of transmissible diseases, when a winter flu was hopscotching around the island.

"You can have it," Dita said. She signaled Brenda to bring another two. "Hey, Brenda changed the TV channel from sports."

"Jake's nephew is on that game show again tonight. Didn't you know? He might even win. Notice no one complained that they turned the basketball off."

Dita did notice. None of the guys went to switch it back. No one seemed to miss Harry either, as Jake's grandson took the stage and the bar noise subsided.

"That's him," Loretta said. "I think I've seen him at the town beach hanging around the lifeguard chairs."

Brenda placed their drinks on the table and stood behind Loretta, watching. "I seen him there too," she rasped.

Another smoker, Dita thought. Dita knew Jake, but did not recognize his grandson. "He's fast on the buzzer," she commented, leaning over toward Loretta.

Brenda was still standing there. "Yeah," she agreed. "Coming in tomorrow, Loretta, for lunch shift?"

Loretta nodded.

As they watched, Addie slipped back to the table, and when the competition ended, it was Addie who stood and cheered first, leading the rest of them as though she'd never left the table. Brenda backed away to the bar.

The noise picked up, and Loretta hissed at Addie. "What's wrong with you? Harry? No, not a good guy for you. Stay away."

"You don't really believe all those nasty rumors people pass around this island, do you?" Addie asked.

Loretta answered. "Not all of them. But I do believe the ones about him. Is your life with Mel that dull?"

Dita wondered if that meant Loretta believed the rumor about Harry and heroin.

Addie's face was turning red. "I'm ready to leave. Joel's not coming."

Dita could tell her friend was furious.

"You have to wait for me since you asked me to come, and I'm not ready," Loretta said, ignoring Addie's obvious fury. "They'll be picking the winner soon."

Jake's nephew won. The bar erupted in cheers. Money was passed, as bets had been placed on the contest, and Loretta rewrapped her scarf around her neck. "Now I'm ready to leave."

"Let's go," Dita ordered.

Addie and Dita didn't speak on the way home. Dita dropped her friend at her house.

"When does Mel go back over there?" she asked.

Mel, Addie's husband, worked as a town planner, but with two part-time jobs for two different towns. He spent half the month on the mainland and half on the island.

"He leaves tomorrow on the first boat. Dita, I am your best friend, right?"

Dita nodded.

"Then you need to treat me that way. Believe me when I say extramarital sex on kitchen counters with codfish bits under my butt was not on my menu tonight. You are so wrong. And so is Loretta."

Dita was quiet. She was doing her best not to burst out laughing. She should be contrite. Since Dita didn't apologize, Addie continued with her rant.

"She sounded like those gossips that go around the island spreading dirt about everyone, and you didn't defend me, so I assume you agree with her. Those gossips make it sound like winter on Nor'easter Island is a big orgy just because there's nothing else to do. Let's think. Which would be worse? Me having a little fling or you turning into a yenta."

"Okay, okay, I get it, codfish butt."

Addie glared.

"Why did I disappear with Harry? You want to know why?"

Dita really didn't, but she just sat there with her mouth shut.

"I asked him to come to the clinic tomorrow to get a flu shot, a blood pressure check and a health screening. I am the nurse there, remember? He and his stool sitters have been real holdouts, and I figured if I could convince Harry to go, I had a shot at the rest of them, excuse the pun. To my surprise, Harry did me one better. He offered to let me run a clinic in the bar. We'll try to sign people up tomorrow and I'll screen them next day.

"I want you to understand this, too. As the island's nurse I do try to retain a bit of dignity."

Thoroughly admonished, at last Dita felt ashamed of herself for even thinking Addie was in the back having sex.

"Dita, I think your journalism job's getting to you. You report on so many sordid things, you're beginning to think the worst of people, even me. How could you think I would do that? Me, the person you are closest to in the world, except perhaps for Sean, and men don't count for that."

"I don't know how I did. I was wrong, and I regret it. And I so wish I reported on sordid things, unless you call someone being denied a building permit, sordid."

Addie got out, slammed the truck door, and disappeared into the darkness. Dita could hear her steps pounding up the staircase to her porch. She felt like the jerk that she was.

Chapter Three

Dita was home now. She glanced out the window toward Addie's. The second-floor light was on. Addie was still up. Should she call and make a full apology? Or wait until morning, when Addie was calmer? Better to wait.

She could hear Sean snoring upstairs. That ferry ride home must have been a real rocker in the squall. He was definitely sleeping off his seasickness. As she climbed upstairs and into bed next to him, she wondered whether she would get any sleep with that racket. That was her last thought before the telephone woke her up at 7 a.m. the next morning.

It was Addie. "Dita, my mother just called. Joel didn't come home last night. She's frantic, and I have to say, I am too. I wasn't concerned about him missing dinner, but this is not like him. At least it's not like him since before, you know, when he had psychotic episodes.

I am going to speak with Carol. It's possible he spent the night with her, although, as I said last night, he hasn't up to now."

"I'll ask around at the office, for sure. And I'll talk to your mother." Dita hesitated before changing the subject. "I was going to call you anyway when I got up. I want to apologize again for what I said last night. I did not spot any codfish on your butt." Even then, Dita could not resist a jibe. "Was there?" she asked.

Addie laughed; and then Dita, knowing it was better now, burst out in guffaws too. "You sure know how to put things when you're angry."

"I guess so. You know, I thought about it before my mother called, and realized if you had ideas about me and Harry in the kitchen, I imagine everyone in the bar had even worse ones. I'm going to have to straighten the record by doing the clinic. And I admit I do flirt a bit with Harry. I'm lonely when Mel goes off to jobs on the mainland." She confessed to Dita that she sometimes wondered if Mel was fooling around over there. Dita hadn't known that was a concern for Addie. Mel was not known for flirting up the tourist women in summer like a lot of the island guys, nor did he play around in winter there. Not that he wasn't attractive. But maybe, when he was somewhere else, he became someone else. Dita shook her head in disbelief. Not Mel.

"But I have a more important thing to focus on right now, finding Joel," Addie said. "I doubt he has his medication with him. Let me know if you hear anything, Dita, would you?"

"I will, and I'll sit down with your mother in the shop and make a list of people who usually see him, just in case we need to look further than Carol."

Sean was awake, and listening. "Joel? Not back yet?"

Dita shook her head again.

"Maybe he got lucky. That could be a good thing. Boy, I'm starving. Let's have breakfast. Pancakes today?" he almost leapt out of bed.

"Someone's feeling better," Dita quipped. But, she thought, does anyone think about anything but food? Food from the Gustamonte Chef for Addie, pancakes for Sean. And his take on Joel being missing was at the opposite end of the spectrum from hers and Addie's.

Sean smiled.

"What exactly happened at the bank?" she asked. "You passed out so fast I never got to ask much."

His smile turned upside down to a frown. "I probably won't get the loan. One was a flat out no; and the other, well, he didn't give me a definite no, but he wasn't encouraging. We just have to wait."

Dita sighed. "Okay."

"Look, if we can't get the money there, maybe I can get one of the bigger businesses on the island to partner with me. Or the town. It would be good for people to have a place to work out, especially in the winter. You know, a place to go besides the two bars and the grocery store. Let's not give up. I really want to do this."

Dita hugged him. "I'll start the pancakes."

"No, it's my turn," he said. "After we eat, we can both look for Joel. I'll drive over to Carol's, and if he's not there, I'll search as I do my house checks."

One of Sean's winter jobs was to look in on houses for summer cottage owners, either weekly or biweekly, whichever they paid for, to make sure there were no leaks in pipes or roofs, no mice scuttling around eating holes in the lamp cords, and no break-ins. Every few years, groups of teenagers would decide the empty houses made for fine partying, and they would get in through an unlocked window or push in a flimsy door and camp out late at night for a few weeks. Eventually they would get caught and get stuck with community service sentences. The break-in parties would stop for a year or two and then start up again with a new clique of kids.

House checking did not take Sean a lot of time, but neither did it pay enough to keep them alive either.

Dita hoped they wouldn't have to leave Nor'easter Island. She loved living there and she loved their salt-box cottage. Yes, the living room was the size of some women's walk-in closets. And there wasn't much actual closet space. Each time Dita bought a new item of clothing, she gave one away. It was that tight. What did she really need to wear on Nor'easter Island in winter anyway? Sweats, jeans, sweaters, sneakers, rubber boots, hats, jackets and gloves. And wool scarves to protect her face from the wind. No runway clothes necessary for this life. A small closet was good enough.

She'd take the views over closet space any day. Sailors Pond across the street, and from the rear windows of their bedroom upstairs, the Atlantic Ocean; the sound of the surf lulling them to sleep; the Milky Way lighting their nights; storms that sent the house groaning like a wooden boat.

Dita loved to sit in the extra bedroom reading a good book while the house made music in the wind.

She would leave if she had to, but she so wanted to stay. She threw on her robe and joined Sean downstairs. The sun was shining into the kitchen. She sat in a warm swath of light. The slate blue floor tiles reminded her of the sea in spring. The light blue counters, the sky. The butcher block table served both as a place to eat and a surface to prep food. She'd had Sean pull out the double sinks when they moved in, and replaced them with one deep and large, stainless-steel sink that could hold a lobster pot. What good is living on an island if you can't cook lobsters and steam clams? The refrigerator was large enough but not ginormous. She'd noticed all the newer summer houses had fridges that were the length of one of her walls. Who needed that anyway, unless you were storing a whole cow? And on this island, where fluctuations in electrical power were great enough to kill appliances and often did, it was better to have inexpensive ones. The power company called these murders 'acts of God' that their insurance did not cover.

The kitchen, like the rest of the house, was small but service-able; and what's more, she liked it.

They ate their breakfast with Tuffy under the table, presumably hoping something edible would drop. When Sean finished, he put his plate in the sink.

"Don't clean up," Dita offered. "I'll do it, since you cooked,"

"All right then. I'm off to check a few houses," he said, giving her a quick peck on the cheek.

He put on his leather jacket, the one he'd worn since college, and was about to step out the kitchen slider, but Dita stopped him.

"You said you would stop at Carol's to ask about Joel. Could you just pull into a few extra driveways on the West Point and see if there are any cars with New York plates? Joel was last seen with some dude from New York who's staying out there. Trent, I think that's his name."

"Sure. I met that guy a few days ago. Beat him at pool at the Washashore. He's an art dealer, you know, high end stuff. I don't know what brought him out here."

"All of our high-end art?"

Sean chuckled. "We do have some good artists, but high-end, I'm not so sure."

With that, he gave her a quick hug and disappeared out the door.

As she cleared the dishes, Dita heard his truck start up and pull out of the yard. She was glad they were almost matched for height so they didn't have to fool with moving the seat back and forth every time they switched drivers. When she finished, she went up-stairs and pulled on her jeans and the white sweater, grabbed her own beat-up leather jacket from its hook in the dining room, and started for the door. But she did not get out. A large blonde dog blocked her way.

"Yes, Tuffy, you can come." The two of them got into her Toyo-ta Camry, one she and Sean had bought used from a friend who ran a body shop on the mainland. It was a car that aged but never died. There was no gloss to the maroon paint, which had faded into a flat matte finish. Patches of rust pocked the bottoms of the doors and the rocker panels. But everything mechanical worked. They drove to town, and she let the dog wait outside when they got to The Island Gale office, the newspaper's suite of two rooms over a real estate business on the main street.

"Don't go anywhere," she told him. Everyone on the island knew the dog, and more likely, at one time or another, had thrown a tennis ball into the waves for him to retrieve. She wasn't concerned about losing him if he wandered. He knew where he lived. It suddenly hit her that Joel did also. Maybe something had happened to him. Deep into that negative thought, she caught herself as she tripped on the curb.

She left Tuffy in the doorway where he would wait for someone he knew to come along and give him a treat, especially now that Columbus Day weekend was over and the tourists had all gone home. While there might be new names for that holiday, on Nor'easter Island it was a day that marked the official end of tourist season and the onset of slumber season.

Dita climbed the stairs and went into the office. The editorial room, where the writers and editors were squished in at desks crowded together in two rows, was empty. She walked through to the front to find her bosses.

"Where is everyone?" Dita asked Jane, the accounts administrator, and the only person she found.

"Assignments, mainland, overslept," Jane said. She went back to tapping on her keyboard with her long, lacquered fingernails. They made a clicking sound unduplicated by any other Dita had ever heard. Dita detested it and swore to herself she would never get fangs for nails.

Dita updated Jane on Joel, but Jane had not seen or heard anything about him. Would she have said so anyway? Dita didn't know.

Jane had heard about Dita, Addie and Loretta at the Washashore though.

"The talk is that you had a really good time, especially Addie," she said with a half-smile, not quite a smirk, but on its way.

Dita could not believe the rate of speed of island gossip. Addie was right.

"We were looking for Joel, hoping he would show up there," she said, ignoring the inuendo about Addie. "How about putting out the word for people to keep looking. The longer he's gone, the more we'll worry."

The woman annoyed her on any day, but today Dita found her unbearable.

Before heading over to Rachel's shop, she stopped to take out coffees from the Books and Bakes where the owner, a former editor at a large publishing house, served up books, newspapers, puzzles, coffee and homemade muffins, croissants, and scones, each on a different day of the week; and also, sandwiches and salads for lunch. Today the breakfast treat was scones. But Dita, having already had that big breakfast with Sean, just ordered coffee to go, one for her and one for Rachel. The usual early morning crowd was there, including Mary, her editor, not on assignment after all. They were talking about Jake's grandson winning the television contest. Dita said hello and asked about Joel. No one recalled seeing him. Then she drove over to Chapel St. where Rachel rented a storefront. She parked in the driveway as she knew no one would be coming or going in this season, and after Tuffy lapped up a drink out of the water bowl placed outside for passing pets, she took him with her into Rachel's Lorelei Shop.

Chapter Four

The bell jangled when Dita opened the door, but Rachel was nowhere in sight.

"Hello, Rachel?" she called. "Hello, it's Dita."

"I'm back here," came a muffled reply.

The shop was not large, just one medium-sized room and a small curtained off back space more aptly described as a closet. Rachel was bending over a cardboard box in that closet.

"I'll be done with this one in a minute," she said. "I'm packing up and I really need Joel to help. I wish I knew where he went."

Dita heard the annoyance in Rachel's voice. She was still more angry than fearful for him.

Tuffy found Rachel before Dita, and he pounced, crashing into her. Rachel careened over onto a pile of boxes while the dog licked her face. She gave him a hug and Dita pulled him off.

"Well, that was some hello," Rachel said, not without good humor as she unfolded and righted herself. "I'm glad you two stopped in to see me. Be careful, Dita. I know how you trip over things sometimes.

"Only when I'm thinking about stuff, and I'm not doing that right now," Dita answered, and then she laughed. "Besides, you're the one trying to get up off the floor."

Rachel straightened up as much as she could, given her arthritis, and went into the sales area, sweeping strands of gray hair from her face. Today she looked her sixty years. Wrinkles creased her cheeks, and her eyes were puffy. She hadn't bothered with makeup or lipstick, though most island women eschewed those in the off seasons anyway except for Jane.

"So he's not back," Dita said, handing her friend the coffee she'd brought her.

"No. Thank you for the coffee."

"Let's talk about where he might be, or who would be most likely to know where he went," Dita suggested. "And while we do, I can help you pack up."

Rachel had not made much progress with her leftover stock. The shop was overcrowded with crafts and chatchkas in summer. Now the unsold items still filled it, even the nooks and crannies. Shelves were stocked with boiled wool baby slippers from India, stone Buddha statues, and fountains ranging from small to tall from India and Nepal where Rachel had travelled the previous winter; turquoise earrings and bracelets from the Southwestern United States, bright, embroidered vests from the Andes Mountains in South America, fluffy alpaca rugs from a mainland farm. The walls were hung with paintings by local artists and tapestries from Central America. Mexican sandals were piled in a corner, and on the counter, necklaces, rings and tiny jewelry boxes. There was barely a comfortable patch of floor for Tuffy to curl up on because even that was stocked with a tower of oriental patterned throw rugs, the tower too tall for him to climb onto.

Rachel pointed to the counter. "I'll just cover that jewelry later, not pack it. Dita don't think business was bad because I have so much left over. I ordered more stock in mid-August. I'll have this when I open in the spring. Hand me those vests, please."

"Okay. Rachel, Sean is on his way to talk with Carol. Even if he isn't there, she might know where Joel went."

Rachel shrugged as she took a few folded vests from Dita. "Addie spoke with her on the phone just now. She had no idea where he might have gone. If you think he left the Washashore with that Trent guy from New York, maybe I should call him. He called me the other day and said he'd like to see some of the paintings I have here from local artists."

Dita thought that was a good idea, so Rachel found his number and phoned. He agreed to drive over that morning, though he denied being with Joel. When the bell on the shop door jangled, both women thought Trent had arrived, but it was Loretta, come to chat. The sound awakened Tuffy, who had pushed aside some packing paper and made a spot for himself. He barked and raised his head for Loretta to pet.

"Yoohoo, I thought I'd stop in," she called as she let herself in and reached down to the dog. "You still have a lot of packing to do." She fished in her jacket pocket and pulled out one of the treats she always carried for Tuffy.

"Are you here to help or critique?" Rachel asked.

"I'm here to tell you what I found out about Joel," Loretta replied.

Rachel dropped the sandals she was boxing up and gave her full attention to Loretta, who had a different silk scarf on today, a turquoise one she'd found earlier in the summer in Rachel's shop.

"He's been going out fishing every day. I met the sailors from that black boat out in the Pond, and they see him leave in the morning," she said. "They talk to him at Happy's Boatyard sometimes when they row over there to kibbitz with Happy."

Dita was quick to remind Loretta that she'd seen Joel walking on Founders, he was at the Washashore in the afternoon and he wouldn't have been out fishing in the squalls.

"But if you know those guys, would you ask if they saw him last night?" Dita asked.

"They sailed early this morning. Usually, they don't come back for a few days," Loretta said.

"Where do they go? Do you know?" Dita asked.

"No," Loretta answered. "Maybe Joel went with them. Did you try his cell?"

Rachel glared at Loretta with the same ferocity as her daughter Addie had the evening before when Dita angered her.

"What do you think?" she retorted. "I never heard him mention that sloop. What's its name?"

"Good Days, Better Nights."

Most pleasure craft and even working boats had names in addition to their requisite registry numbers. Sometimes the names indicated companies also owned by the vessel's owners. Sometimes the names indicated where the money to buy them came from, like Twenty-one and Arbitrage. Less creative types named them after spouses and mistresses and children, like the Katyloo and Cory; still others their dreams, Moonlight, Heavenly. Never had Dita heard a name like Good Days, Better Nights.

"That's a mouthful," she said, repeating it.

Loretta shrugged.

"When Joel passed my house, it looked like he was arguing with someone," Dita said. "I almost thought that he was getting into a physical fight, pushing and shoving with a couple other people. I called to him but he didn't hear, and they moved on toward town. I debated getting into my car to follow them, but the weather was so bad, I decided it was probably just the usual back and forth guys do."

She lowered her head and murmured, "Now I wish I had."

The other two women didn't reply. She wondered what they were thinking. She looked up again, but both of them were just folding embroidered blouses.

Tuffy was standing at the door, tail wagging. "I'm going to walk him for a few minutes. Text me when Trent gets here," Dita said, glad to step away before they processed what she had just told them. She opened the door for the dog and followed behind him.

Traffic was sparse, as were pedestrians. Dita let Tuffy sniff his way along Church Street, then led him down to the empty ferry harbor. No boat was expected for several hours, so the parking lots were not busy. A couple of guys were loading freight onto dollies in expectation of shipping the boxes out that day, and they waved. Dita went toward the commercial fishing vessel docks, and stood at the railing along the water. It was a deep sapphire blue today, like the stones in several of Rachel's rings. She pulled her jacket closer around her. The cold chilled her, but clarified the air. She could see across the Sound to the mainland, including the suspension bridge between Stratford and New-burgh. She wondered if anyone she knew was crossing it now. Maybe even Joel.

Right in front of her, a dolphin cavorted, swimming in circles, leaping and diving, all by itself. She snapped a few pictures with her cellphone. If the *Island Gale*'s photographer didn't get here in time to take a picture with a better camera, at least they would have hers. She texted the shots to the paper. Then she leaned on the railing and watched the creature for a while, until she thought perhaps Trent would have arrived at the Lorelei. She called to Tuffy, who'd wandered off to explore the scents by the gutting ta-bles. Though empty, they still reeked of fish. As she was about to start back to the shop, her phone chimed. It was Rachel, texting to alert her that Trent had indeed arrived.

She let Tuffy into the Lorelei first, and immediately wished she hadn't. He didn't know the man leaning against one of the window sills, gesturing at Rachel, and he let out a low growl. The man stiffened, and Tuffy went into a watchdog crouch. Dita rushed to him and held him by his collar.

"Easy boy, easy. Not an enemy."

Dita supposed that man was Trent. Loretta laughed and asked if Trent had a house full of cats that Tuffy smelled on him.

"I have no cats," Trent said, with a discernable shudder. "You've been to the house. Have you ever seen one?"

Dita's antenna when up. Loretta had been to his house and more than once? She took a closer look at Trent. He was too old, too stringy and angular for Loretta, and he was most probably not into women either. If Loretta had been to his house, it was not to pursue him.

Rachel had already questioned him about Joel and she brought Dita up to speed. "Trent got here a few minutes ago. He says he wasn't with Joel. They may have left the bar at the same time, but not together."

"In fact, I don't know him at all," the man said. "Someone did walk out when I did, but I don't know if it was your son or not."

Dita wondered if he was lying.

Trent stepped carefully around the rugs and boxes, and made his way along the perimeter of the shop to look over the artwork Rachel had hung on the walls. He stopped in front of one, a painting of the golden fields off Founders Road.

"Do you have more by her?" he asked.

Rachel shook her head. He took out his pocket notebook and wrote down the artist's name. Then he continued his journey around the perimeter of the Lorelei.

"You should come out to the house," he said to Rachel, almost as an aside. "You might find one or two things to sell."

He was moving toward the door but stopped at the counter on his way to look over a tray of gold rings with semi-precious and precious stones.

"From India?" he asked, picking one up and examining it closely. "Nice ruby."

Rachel nodded. "I picked the stones myself at the factory when I was in India last year."

Trent left his card on the counter. "Call me," he said.

As soon as the door shut behind him, Dita asked Loretta when she had been at Trent's house.

Loretta unwound her scarf and retied it. Dita was beginning to wonder if this was a so-called tell, something she did when she was nervous; or even lying.

"Actually it's not his house," Loretta said. "He's staying at the Bradley's out on the west side cliffs. You know, the gargantuan gray one that looks like four condos stuck together?"

She started picking at the wool on a baby slipper. Dita thought she was trying to avoid facing her.

"They called and asked if I would clean while he is there," Loretta said. "They pay good, so I said yes."

"How good?" Dita asked. She knew Loretta cleaned houses but usually it was only in summer. Realtors hired her when renters left a house and it needed cleaning for the next people coming in.

"$175 a pop."

"I would say that's worth it," Dita said.

It was enough to make Dita consider taking jobs. "Are there more of those?" she asked.

Loretta stopped picking at the merchandise. "No, not in winter. I need to go," she said, tightening her scarf again. "I'm working at the Washashore for lunch shift. Remember, Brenda asked me? Bye, bye."

"Say hello to Addie," Rachel said. "She's running a clinic there today. And keep asking for Joel, please."

Dita did not want to leave Rachel alone. It was almost time for lunch, so she asked if she would like to go to Books and Bakes for a sandwich. Rachel thought she should stay at the Lorelei in case Joel returned; but if Dita wanted to bring something in, that would suit her. Behind the Lorelei's counter were two folding chairs which they could use while balancing their meals on their laps. Dita knew where her food would be - all over her clothes - so she cajoled Rachel a bit harder.

"We can post a note on the door for him. We'll be right down the street."

So, they set out for the Books and Bakes, Tuffy in tow. They were the only customers. Most island workers would be having their lunches at the Washashore and the office workers at their desks, as they'd been here for breakfast earlier. Since they were alone, Dita brought Tuffy in with them. They chose a table near a window that overlooked the harbor. The dolphin was still swimming laps. Dita pointed it out to Rachel, who smiled for the first time that day when she saw it leap and flip.

"I wish we all could find joy in small things," she said. "Let me treat you. You boxed this morning and helped me cope, and I know you haven't a lot of extra money for lunches and frills."

Dita was embarrassed, but Rachel was right. She shouldn't keep spending money on lunch.

"And," Rachel continued, "let me tell you some of Joel's history. You haven't been here long enough to know how he was before, you know, before he accepted treatment."

Dita listened. According to Rachel, his illness became apparent during his first semester of college. Away from home in a setting with strangers, he started to hear voices, imagined plots against him, stayed up all night. When he wandered the campus and the dorm talking to himself, the Dean contacted Rachel and her husband. Since then, he'd been hospitalized three times and his college career ended. Rachel picked at her salad, today's special, a Waldorf with pecans and hardboiled eggs.

"The reason I get so worried when this grown man doesn't

come home for supper and stays out all night without calling is that years ago when he did that, he didn't reappear for months," Rachel said. She stopped to sip her coffee before continuing. "And then I would get a call from a hospital in another city. Once he walked in front of a car and got hit, once he threatened a young woman and followed her, and once he was found under a bridge, nearly dead."

Though he hadn't disappeared or had a psychotic episode in almost ten years since his current medication routine, Rachel told Dita she worried that this could be the start of another episode.

"I don't watch him anymore to make sure he is taking his medicine. But, Dita, I checked the medicine cabinet and he didn't take it with him."

Now Dita could understand her anxiety over Joel's sudden disappearance. She'd never thought about Joel's past. He was just part of Addie and Rachel's family, someone included in their lives who was somewhat immature. She wondered why she'd never asked. Maybe she hadn't wanted to know, and just wanted to accept him as he was now.

"Those years must have been so difficult for you," she said.

"Yes, and for my husband. He had heart disease and I think his worrying about Joel contributed to the attack that killed him. Addie was away at college, so Joel didn't affect her so much. That's why Addie thinks I'm over-reacting."

"I get it, Rachel. If he doesn't come home or call by tomorrow, maybe the police should start to look," Dita said. "On the other hand, think about this. If he left because he got into something with those guys on the street, and is hiding, it would be better not to search. It's up to you. I could write something for Friday's paper if you want, or not."

"Do it, please," Rachel agreed. "He wasn't in trouble with anyone."

Dita wasn't so sure.

"And without his medications he might have difficulties again," Rachel said.

"But maybe he would be all right without them now," Dita tried to reassure her.

"I hope so."

They walked back to the Lorelei when they were finished. Rachel's grandson, Danny, was standing outside waiting to go in.

"We got out of school early today so I thought I would help box up, Granny," he said, running to give her a hug. He waved to Dita and gave Tuffy a quick pat.

Rachel brightened. She opened the door so he could run in, and murmured good bye to Dita over her shoulder with a thank you. Dita thought Danny looked just like his mommy, Addie, even down to the unruly red tendrils framing his face. She was quite fond of the boy and often spent time with him. Today she felt a longing for the day she would have a Danny or Danielle of her own.

"Keep me in the loop," Dita said, leaving them to their task, while she returned home with Tuffy to finish hers. She needed to write the article she'd been putting off all day, one about a meeting that didn't deserve one line of copy. She wished she had something more interesting to look into. Maybe she would take Sean's advice and call Chief Gomez about the island drug problem.

Chapter Five

Two weeks passed without news of Joel. Addie no longer dismissed her mother's concerns. She told Dita she too was certain something terrible had happened to Joel. Chief Gomez declared him officially missing. If he showed up at any hospitals in a psychotic condition, Addie told Dita, they would be notified. If he was not psychotic, notification would require his permission.

"A moot point," Addie complained, "since he hasn't turned up."

"I'll call the chief and do an article," Dita said. "Maybe more publicity will help."

Her guilt was turning into a tsunami wave. Now she was sure that if she had caught up to him that rainy day as he passed her house, he might not have disappeared. She would do everything she could to help find him.

Gomez told her the police had checked Happy's Dock where

Joel kept his outboard motor boat and fishing gear. The fact that both the boat and gear were gone, but the trailer still sat in a corner of the yard, was an indication that Joel left by sea. Dita already knew that, as the family had previously gone there themselves. Still, it could be mentioned in the article. Plenty of summer visitors subscribed to the paper to keep up on island news. One of them might spot Joel somewhere on the mainland.

There was nothing the police could do, according to Gomez, as he also previously had told Rachel. It appeared to them that Joel left of his own accord.

Then on a Saturday morning after a 48-hour Nor'easter finally moved out to sea–it had seemed to want to become a permanent washashore–Dita and Sean invited the Mortons to join them on a hike at Periwinkle Beach. They were at the Mortons' house, waiting for Mel to finish getting ready, when Addie's phone chimed. Addie put it on speaker mode. It was Rachel.

"You're on speaker mom. Sean and Dita are here, too," Addie said.

Usually, Rachel would have given a big hello to Sean and Dita, but today her call had a purpose. "Addie, they found Joel's boat."

"Where?"

"It beached on the West side, by Oyster Cove. George came to the house himself to tell me. He's on his way there now. He thinks it must have come up in the storm."

"And Joel?" Addie asked, her voice quavering just a little.

"No."

They heard Rachel sob on the other end of the phone. Dita felt relieved that Joel had not washed up with his boat; but then, where was he? She looked at Sean and took his hand.

"Please," Rachel said. "You go look at it. Talk to the police. They want someone from the family to take it back to the dock."

Addie sat down and took a breath. Mel took the phone from her.

"We're heading there right now," he said. "We were going on a hike anyway. We'll go to Oyster Cove instead."

He reached out for Addie and Danny, who were throwing on their hiking jackets and boots. Dita and Sean were already out the door. They all jumped into Mel's SUV and headed down Founders. The storm, far offshore now, still pushed the sea. Big rollers were breaking on the beach across from the Beach Dune Restaurant. The parking lot by the restaurant was filled with surfer vans. They spotted their friend Teddy struggling into his wet suit, on his way to join the other surfers, black specks riding the waves like frigate birds. They honked at Teddy, but didn't stop. Dita saw Teddy beckon to Sean. Next, she worried, he'd be surfing too, and he'd never be home. If so, she'd have to take up the sport in order to see him. There were women on the island whose husbands left for months following the big surf to Central America and Hawaii. Dita knew that didn't leave a lot of room for fatherhood.

They turned right at the corner, passed the Washashore and drove west to Oyster Cove Road. Then they turned again and headed for the dirt track that led down to the beach. When they reached the end of the road where the track began, they bumped along until it narrowed again, into a path. They left the SUV and jogged the rest of the way on foot, Danny bringing up the rear with Addie. There were carve-outs where the storm had eaten away portions of beach. Dita knew these often filled in again, but not always. Global sea rise was taking a toll.

Dita saw Chief George Gomez, Sgt. Karl Schultz and Happy further up into the cove huddled together like seagulls during a blow. The Mortons and Redmonds hiked up to join the men, who were bundled up in watch caps and waxed jackets, standing with their backs to the wind. George took Addie and Mel a few paces off. Dita and Sean, with Danny, stood close enough to hear the conversation if they strained. Dita took notes. George was saying he and Karl went over the beached boat for traces of blood, but hadn't found any yet. The hull was damaged. George estimated it had been drifting in the water for some time and got battered on the rocks around the island before finally coming in on a swell, crashing in and out until the tide turned and it beached. He could only conjecture that either Joel had tied it at a dock somewhere along the coast and it came loose in the storm or, their worst scenario, that he'd gone overboard. The waters to the west of the island were particularly rough without a storm; and in a storm could easily capsize a small boat.

Karl returned to the boat again and shouted back to the group. He suggested Joel's disappearance could have been suicide. "I hate to say this, Mel, Addie, but with his history, you know."

Sean and Dita looked at each other. "Did Karl even know much of Joel's history?" Dita whispered to her husband.

Sean whispered back, "I don't think so. He's just trying to make like he's important."

They had forgotten Danny was standing with them.

"He's a jerk," the boy sputtered.

Dita agreed, but she put her finger in front of her mouth and said quietly, "Shh."

George cleared his throat, and caught their attention. "We contacted the Coast Guard to start a search. Happy was on the mainland for a few days. He wasn't at his dock when Joel took the boat out. He doesn't have any idea where Joel might have headed."

Happy nodded. "I wish I did," he said.

The adults walked over to the motor boat together. Struggling to hold back tears, Danny wandered down the beach by himself picking up rocks and shells.

"Is there any gas left in the tank?" George asked.

Karl and Happy checked. It was a quarter full. Though the boat was damaged there were no obvious holes in the bottom. It looked like it might stay afloat, so they pushed it into the water and watched. It did not sink.

"Let's see if she starts," Happy said. He was a wiry, emaciated old man, but when he pulled the starter rope he did it with the strength one would expect from Sean.

The motor turned on the third try.

"I can bring it back to the dock," Happy said. "Little enough I can do for Joel."

First, George had a question. "He still had gas. Couldn't been out there too long, could he? Ten, twelve hours?"

Happy shrugged. "Less."

"He wasn't out there for two weeks," George was almost thinking out loud. "He must have turned the engine off or it would've run out of gas at some point."

"He might have been drifting while he fished to save gas," Happy suggested.

"Still, it's a bit odd," George said.

"Ready?" Karl asked Happy. "I'll go with you." He got into the boat.

Dita wondered why he seemed to be in such a hurry. And Mel had planned to bring the boat back to the dock. But Happy pushed it to deeper water and then got in. Karl opened the throttle and they motored off slowly. The boat was damaged, but still operable. Danny was skipping rocks in the surf. Dita and Addie joined him and they watched the blue boat disappear around the curve of the cove.

"I hope they find Uncle Joel," Danny said. "Maybe he went over to the mainland and the boat got loose in the storm. He could just be visiting someone."

"He could," Addie said. She put her arm around him. "Let's go home."

The next morning, a birder reported sighting a body on Laughing Gull Beach. Addie got the call from her mother while the five of them, she, Mel, Dita, Sean, and little Danny, were sitting around the kitchen table at the Mortons' finishing up brunch, playing a fierce game of Scrabble and eating apple crumb cake with Tuffy at their feet. Dita and Sean had been keeping their friends company while they waited for more news, expecting the jangle of the phone at any moment. When it came, Addie jumped to answer it. Though it was expected, Dita still felt surprised.

She watched the color drain from Addie's face as she listened and hung up quickly, walked over to Danny, and stood behind the boy, laying her hands on his shoulders. Dita expected the worst.

"I'm afraid they think Uncle Joel has washed ashore north of where his boat came in," Addie said, her voice quavering. "They've found a body. They want us to go over there and confirm that it's Joel. My mother doesn't want to. She wants me or Mel to do it."

"I'm so sorry," Dita said.

Mel volunteered. "I'll go," he said, taking another piece of crumb cake for the ride. He was a stocky guy, matching Addie's *zaftig* figure for heft, but pleasant looking, with an open face framed by thinning brown hair, and dark brown eyes. His mouth, curved upward, always looked ready to smile. He was the kind of guy who could be counted on in a crunch. He could manage fraught situations, a rare quality that helped him deal with townspeople in his job as a planner. He stood up, wiped his face with his napkin, and took his keys from the counter before going over to his wife and embracing her. Then he leaned down in front of Danny, who had begun to sob, and held him. Danny had been the closest to Joel, who took the boy with him fishing, clamming, and biking. Of all of them, Danny was the one who had really believed Joel would return.

They tried to console each other; but then Addie told Mel he needed to get going. There was still a slim chance that the person lying on the beach was not Joel. Sean offered to go with Mel, and Dita decided she needed to go to get the story. She was a reporter, after all, and if that was Joel, she wanted the piece written with compassion. Addie decided to be with her mother. She would wait at Rachel's with Danny. They all put on their coats and went outside into the bright sunlight. Sean beckoned for Mel and Dita to get into the truck. Mel opened the front seat door immediately. Dita thought he seemed glad to let Sean drive, to ride shotgun instead.

"C'mon, Tuffy," Dita opened the back door of the truck to let him jump in and got in with him.

"I'll swing into the driveway so you can let him out," Sean said.

Dita's stomach was churning. Though she had expected the worst, now that it was happening, she was consumed with guilt. Could she really have prevented this if she had reached out to Joel that last day in the storm? Perhaps it was easier for her to focus on her perceived guilt rather than her sorrow over the fact that Joel was dead. He was not just Rachel's son and Addie's brother, he was also a friend to her and to Sean, frequently stopping in to bring them a seabass or a flounder he'd caught. Sean would join him out on the water sometimes, both of them walking in afterward with salt caked hair, their clothes stiff, reeking of the sea.

Covering the identification was not an assignment Dita wanted, but one she felt she had to do, for Joel and for Rachel and Addie, Mel and Danny. As always, she had her reporter's pad in her bag and a pen. Her cell phone was in her pocket. She would snap a photo of the police, but not of Joel. If the paper's photographer showed up, she wouldn't let that happen.

She knew, of course, it was going to be Joel who washed up. The police knew him, the rescue squad knew him, everyone on the island knew him. They would not have called if they had the slightest notion it was someone else. Yet she held onto a slim hope that it was not Joel, or anyone else she knew.

It didn't take long to get to Laughing Gull beach. No destination was more than twenty minutes away on Nor'easter Island. They left the truck at the end of the lane where the path began. Most of the gulls had flown south already. It was quiet except for the sound of the surf. In summer, the eerie laughter of the birds, who always seemed to be sharing a colossal joke, made this a noisy place to sunbathe. She didn't come here much; and if this body was Joel, she probably wouldn't in the future. She trailed behind Sean and Mel who were moving at a brisk pace. She was used to seeing the corpses of gannets and gulls, or sometimes half-eaten bass. But she'd never seen a human corpse, especially someone she knew and cared about, like Joel.

She expected Karl would dismiss the death as one waiting to happen due to Joel's past. She gathered her strength and followed the men, thinking that the testosterone that led them into trouble also helped them wear a cloak of courage when it was needed, no matter how they felt inside. Next to them, she was a coward. She caught up when they were close to those already on the beach, Gomez, Karl and Happy also, who had wandered down from his cottage when he saw the police arrive. On the mainland, he might have been told to leave, but on Nor'easter Island, his knowledge of the sea and boats was well regarded. Later, when giving Dita a quote, Chief Gomez said he appreciated Happy's knowhow.

The body was below the storm high tide line, surrounded by desiccated strands of seaweed, and empty clam and oyster shells that had come ashore along with small reminders that trash was still discarded at sea, pieces of broken rope, pop-tops, bits of paper and plastic.

Gomez and Schultz were waiting for Mel near the body. Dita hesitated as Mel and Sean joined the small group. She stood back from the men, who now circled the corpse. She forced herself to glance through the space between Mel and the Chief. She was close enough to see the body splayed out on the damp sand, bits of tattered clothing hanging here and there, the skin wrinkled and ripped from being battered about in the surf.

"Where are the oilcloth coveralls he wore in winter?" she wondered. She averted her eyes, not wanting to see the head or the face, and then looked down. She dug the toe of her sneaker into the sand, pushing over a small tower of slipper shells nestled into each other.

Mel moved away from the other men, closer to her. She heard him speak into his phone. He must have called Addie. "Joel," she heard him say.

Oh, no, she thought, for sure, Joel.

Sean laid a hand on Mel's shoulder, and Dita stood closer. Mel was in tears as he clicked off his call. Dita willed herself not to be sick. Her stomach turned over and her breakfast coddled. She regretted coming along to witness this.

"I can't imagine what happened out there," Sean said. "I've been fishing with him enough to know how careful he is. He never goes out when a storm is due and the waves are up."

"I know," Mel said. "I feel that way, too. How could this be?"

The chief and Karl, with Happy, came over to talk. The chief surmised that Joel's body might have come in on the high tide the night before, but Happy said he also could have washed up there in the storm like his boat. Or, since few people walked that area off-season, he could possibly have worked his way up the beach for days.

"I'm so going to miss that fella," Happy said. "Always ready to give me a hand when I need help around the boat yard." He raised a gnarled hand and wiped his eyes. "My friend, summer and winter. He could have run the yard without me. It just don't make sense." He turned his face away from them so they couldn't see the tears run down his cheeks.

The tide had turned hours ago, and soon water would cover the corpse. Then the current would carry Joel further away. They couldn't wait for a medical examiner to fly in from the mainland. The chief called dispatch to find out if Doctor Bennett was on his way. Because there was no official medical examiner on the island, Dr. Bennett, the director of their medical center, had to come, as did the rescue squad with their motorized, mobile stretcher that was designed to drive over sand and difficult terrain. But Doctor

Bennett arrived with the rescue squad as the chief was on the phone. He went over the body looking for injuries that might have occurred before the drowning. Being dragged over the rocks coming to shore had obfuscated any that would have been obvious, so he gave the okay to load Joel onto the stretcher, and they all followed it to the ambulance. Mel, even more broken up now, spoke to Dr. Bennett and climbed into the front seat of the ambulance with the driver, who was a friend of his on the rescue squad. He would go to the medical center with Joel's body.

"Call me when you're ready to go home," Sean said.

Dita and Sean were left on the beach with Karl. Sometimes grief makes a person numb, there is a disbelief and a distancing that protects our hearts from cracking. This is how Dita felt, as though she were floating above herself watching the scene that had just unfolded. Karl stood close to Sean, his hands folded across his chest. He drew up to his full height. With his police hat, he was still shorter than Dita, though he often tried to use his big-boned body to carve out more space for himself. He cleared his throat. Dita waited for the pronouncement that would follow.

"Either fell in or jumped," Karl said, facing Sean. "It's a shame."

Dita heard his voice as though it was miles away, drifting in on the wind. She thought he was talking as though Joel was a stranger, without any feeling for the life that was lost.

Karl's voice continued to fill the air. "There've been a few in the Pond, climb into their boat at night, drunk and fall off the ladder." But, Dita realized, Joel knew how to fish from his boat without falling in. He didn't drink. And he had been satisfied with his life, not suicidal.

"I don't agree with you Karl. That's so cold," she said, drawing closer to the two men as she wiped tears from her face.

"I'm sorry, Dita. I know you guys were friends," he said, turning toward her now, shrugging. "I'm just speaking the truth."

"Your truth, not mine," she retorted, drilling her gaze into his bloodshot eyes. Either this call had gotten him out of bed, or he'd already been drinking. Dita suspected the latter. She wondered if the chief had noticed.

Sean backed away from Karl to be with Dita. She put her anger at Karl aside for now and leaned against Sean, feeling his body against hers.

"I'll miss him," she said. "He was always at the Lorelei, showing me something interesting that had come in or offering Tuffy a treat."

Joel had been a fixture in their lives.

"Mel's right. Danny will be devastated. He loved fishing with his Uncle Joel," Sean said. "As did I."

Dita and Sean trekked back to their truck and started home. They passed Happy's boat yard where he was already going into his office, a wooden hut with room inside for only two people on either side of a small desk that was always piled with stacks of papers. The yard was filled with vessels wintering over, standing on trailers and covered with tightly bungeed off-white canvas tarps. There were no boats in the water. The docks were also all pulled and stacked next to the office until the spring weather returned. Joel had been one of the few with a small motor boat to use the yard, and one of the only ones to use his boat in winter. She could see the battered blue hull sticking out behind Happy's office.

As Happy had said, Joel was a friend, and he was always welcome there to keep the old man company. Dita doubted he had ever charged Joel for the bit of space his boat used.

They avoided going past the Washashore Pub, turning off on a side street that connected to theirs. Most of the white houses along it were empty for the winter, their owners gone to their city homes or Florida for the winter. Only one was inhabited by a year-round family. She looked to see if anyone was outside, so she could throw the obligatory wave. There was no one.

Dita realized her anger at Karl was somewhat misdirected. She was really angry at herself. Had they all treated Joel as just an add-on connected to Addie, Rachel and Mel? Could they have folded him into their lives more closely, so he would have had them watching over him? Tears welled up in her eyes, tinged with guilt along with the sorrow. Dita tried to compose herself.

"Shall we stop at home for a minute before we go on to Rachel's?" she asked.

Sean nodded. They drove down Founders Road past the empty dunes. There were but a few surfers left. Even the crows had flown off somewhere else. Dita called Addie.

"Can we bring something? I have leftovers, and sourdough bread," Dita said.

"No, we have cold cuts for lunch. Just come," Addie said.

"Ready?" Sean asked.

"Yes. Shall we bring the dog?"

"I think Danny would like that," he said.

They drove past the empty summer homes, and pulled into Rachel's yard. Dita knocked once and walked into the living room. Rachel sat in a small easy chair with her face in her hands, a tower of tissues balled up next to her on the side table. Addie, on the couch, held Danny, who was sobbing, shaking with grief. The sun shone in the front windows, throwing patches of light on the worn green rug.

Danny let go of Addie and crossed the room to Sean. "We, we won't be going fishing with Uncle Joel, anymore," he said.

Sean reached down and tousled Danny's unruly hair. He leaned over and promised in a low voice, "We'll have to go together, Danny, and catch the fish for him. Right?"

Danny nodded and put his arms around Sean. Dita felt her heart ache. Tuffy pushed his nose into Danny's face, and the boy took him into the kitchen and filled a bowl with water. He kept treats for the dog in the cupboard, and he opened it and gave him one.

"At least I still have one friend," Danny said. "Tuffy."

They stayed several hours, making themselves useful by answering the phones, both landline and cells, for the family. Word was spreading, and the phones rang incessantly as people found out. Mel came. Instead of calling, he said, he had decided to walk, but then Harry came by and picked him up.

When Sean and Dita were ready to leave, Dita murmured the usual platitude, if there's anything we can do, call us, but Rachel interrupted her.

"I still think this wasn't an accident or suicide. Dita, please keep looking for information," she pleaded.

Addie stood up. "Mom, you need to stop this. Dita, let's wait for the coroner's report."

Dita could tell Addie was angry by how her face flushed. She had a redhead's white skin, and emotions colored her like a rising sun. Dita reassured them both she would do what she could. Then she and Sean left their friends to their grief.

They shed more tears together as they drove home. When they got there, Dita opened a bottle of red wine. She sat in a chair by the front window, watching the bufflehead ducks fish near the shore in Sailor's Pond. Sean grabbed a beer and pulled a chair next to hers.

"To Joel," he said.

"To Joel," she echoed.

"Sailboat's gone," he said. "Those guys are in and out all the time."

The pond was empty now, except for the ducks and an abandoned cabin cruiser that looked about to sink. Someone working in one of the restaurants had lived on it all summer. Now he'd gone home to the mainland, and left the vessel out there to rot. If it stayed afloat until next summer, someone else would move in. If not, it might drift half submerged until the harbormaster dragged it ashore or it beached itself in another storm.

"What a day," Dita said, slipping out of her shoes. "Red sky tonight."

It was as though the emotions of the day had risen, inflamed the sky, and then the water too. Dita and Sean watched, transfixed, until the fiery sky faded to black and the sun shrank to a mirage upon the pond, and disappeared under it.

"Poseidon returns to his underwater home," Sean said. "It feels like this little island of ours suffers more than other places. ..." Dita broke off. She'd had that conversation with Sean before. Was it the bad luck of the island, or just that it was so small that they all noticed and felt every loss? She felt this one to her core. This one hurt more than the others.

Part Two – After

Chapter Six

Dita poked her head into the Lorelei looking for Rachel. The coroner had not yet released Joel's body, and Rachel tried to stay busy while she waited by continuing to box up her inventory.

"Looks like you're almost finished," Dita said.

Some of the shelves were empty, there were spaces to walk through on the floor; the crammed Lorelei had yielded to Rachel's efforts. Whereas Dita might have considered this an achievement before Joel's death, now she thought it reflected the loss in Rachel's life.

Rachel looked up and said, "Danny has been a big help. He comes in every day after school. I'm lucky to have such a caring grandson."

Dita nodded. It was hard to watch Rachel blink back her tears. Dita noticed new wrinkles on her face, sagging skin under her eyes. Her black sweater, once a tight fit, draped a bit around her midriff.

"Have you heard anything?" Rachel asked. "You know, about who he might have gone off with."

"No. I wish I could say yes," Dita replied.

"They're releasing his body tomorrow, and we can have the funeral. The coroner's report will take longer. Dita, I think they're going to call his death a suicide because of his illness. Unless there are bullet holes, knife wounds or damage to his head that looks inflicted by someone, they'll sweep him aside and move on to the next body. I hear they have quite a few waiting for reports.

"But I know my Joel," Rachel continued, "and he was happy, not depressed. Carol told me they were talking about him moving into her place; he made enough with his jobs here to support himself. I don't know if you're aware that he had so much kitchen experience he was to be sous chef at the Gustamente next summer. And he loved fishing. He'd made a life. Why would he jump into the middle of the sea? I think something happened out there. Someone murdered him, Dita. Someone pushed him in."

"Not suicide, I agree; but why murder? Why would someone push him into the sea?"

Dita thought both were illogical conclusions to Joel's life. She and Sean had talked at length about it, and neither of them could think of any reason for Joel to plan a suicide. But Sean had also talked to some of the contractors and guys at the Washashore, especially Karl, who felt certain it could not have been foul play.

"I only know what Sean says Karl told him," Dita explained. "If it was murder, someone had to have a second boat nearby to pick them up and then let Joel's boat drift away. It would have had to have been planned and more than one person in on it."

Dita asked Rachel if Joel had been feuding with anyone. The island had its share of family feuds that lasted generations, but they were usually over land boundaries, even a few feet. With a limited amount of land and buildable lots, squabbles erupted between brothers and sisters, best friends, neighbors, business owners.

"Joel didn't own anything but his boat and fishing gear. What kind of argument could he have? He didn't even run lobster pots," Rachel said. Lobster fishing was highly territorial, with ownership declared for fishing holes where pots were dropped.

Neither woman could come up with a motive for someone killing Joel and the police had not been able to either. Still, Rachel was convinced someone had wanted him dead. She asked Dita to pursue that for her, to search for someone who might have hated Joel enough to kill him.

"Can you do that for me, for Addie and Danny, and for Joel?" Rachel asked.

"I'll keep digging, but as far as the chief is concerned, his case is closed here unless the coroner finds something. I doubt I'll uncover much of anything." Dita said. "In the meantime, after his obituary runs and you've had his funeral, I'll sit for an interview with you, so you can make your points."

Rachel reached out and hugged Dita. Tears ran down her face.

"I appreciate it," she said.

Dita left and went home, mulling over human mortality, the fact that we all think we will live forever, but in a moment our flame can sputter and go out. She realized anyone could lean over the edge of a boat and plunge, or step into the street without noticing an approaching car. She felt what happened to Joel could happen to any of them. And she knew it was time to talk to Sean about the rest of their lives.

He was out front, sawing some planks by the basement door.

"This is for the Kelly porch," he said, stopping for a few seconds.

Dita could wait until he finished. She didn't like to break his concentration when he was using power equipment. She said hello, gave him a quick kiss, and went back into the house. She could catch up on some housework until he was done. When she heard the slider open and Sean's keys jangled as he took them out of his pocket and dropped them onto the kitchen table, she was upstairs in the bedroom changing their sheets. He called out hello and she shouted back. She heard his shoes tread upon the wooden steps. "Did you make any calls today for the gym?" she asked, flapping a fitted sheet and letting it drop onto the mattress.

"I did. We're not going to find money to start a fitness center. That's it. We'll have to figure out another way to earn a living here," he told her, lifting the mattress as she fitted a corner of the sheet. "The banks won't loan money to us, none of the hotel owners want to partner up, and the town won't subsidize memberships for year-round residents."

"Nothing from the town?" Dita asked, not convinced. "That's terrible. It's wrong. People need a place to exercise here in winter especially. Maybe we wouldn't all drink so much if we had a place to exercise and stay healthy."

Sean shrugged his shoulders and grimaced.

He looked so beaten. Maybe one more idea would help.

"How about trying Bill Murphy or Cal Rittenhouse?" she suggested.

Those summer residents were both New York bankers and from the size of their so-called cottages they must be wealthy.

"That's might work," he said. "I'll try them, but don't set your heart on it happening."

They finished the last corners and sat on the bed.

"We might end up having to move, Sean."

"I don't want to, and I don't think you really do either."

"But I do want to be able to pay our bills. And, I thought we agreed it was time to start a family," she said.

"Let's wait and see what Bill and Cal say. I could also try a couple of the other summer people. Let's not cut and run yet."

"Okay," she agreed, but only halfheartedly. Then she changed the subject.

"When the funeral is over, I'm going to try to interview Carol. Rachel asked me to find out if anyone thought Joel was unhappy or suicidal before he disappeared, so I'll check that with Carol."

"You do know the guys at the pub all think Joel's death was suicide."

"I do. You told me. I want to talk with them too. I want to find out why they think Joel killed himself. Because he had a mental illness, or because he indicated he was unhappy, or threatened suicide? It's important to me and to Rachel."

"To us all. I miss Joel too," Sean admitted. "I need to drop those boards off. You want to come?"

"Sure," she said. "It'll be good to get out for a ride around the island. Let's bring Tuffy and take him for a walk afterward."

They grabbed their jackets, called the dog, and left the house. They rode up Founders Road toward the dump. Patty Milford was in her front yard with a hose, spraying the water into a tub. She motioned for them to pull over.

"I'm cleaning sand out of clams we got this morning. We have a lot. Want some?"

"I have a soft cooler in the truck," Sean said. He jumped out and pulled it from the back seat floor, and Patty spilled the clams into it.

"Stuffies tonight?" Dita asked Sean as they pulled away.

"Steamers with these!" he said. "But not enough for all our friends."

They dropped off the boards at the Kellys' and went on to Cottagers Beach. It was high tide, so they couldn't walk toward the North point. Instead, they turned toward their house. It was several miles away. Today they would only do one mile and then go back to get the truck. The land bordering the beach consisted of small grassy dunes. Last summer a piping plover couple, a rarity these days, had burrowed a nesting hole into one of them, just above the storm high tide mark. The island birders had quickly built a fence fenced around them to keep dogs out. They watched the nest until they saw eggs there. The great mystery of the summer was whether or not those eggs would hatch. That is, until the day Joel washed up and created a new, more macabre mystery.

They walked until the line of dunes disappeared and striated clay cliffs rose from the beach, topped by summer homes built precipitously without thought to the erosion below them. Then they turned around and headed back toward their truck. And they had their talk.

"Dita, plenty of people have children without a lot of money. I love hanging out with Danny, and I can see us having a few of our own. We don't have to wait for jobs or a gym," he said.

"But Sean, they do cost money. We can barely pay our bills. We need health insurance. We don't have any."

It was an old argument Sean couldn't accept.

"I'm sure I'll find something. Let's move ahead with our lives," he said.

"Soon," she said. "Let's at least have health insurance first."

"If I can't start a gym, I'll try to get a job with the town. Road crew, inspections, something. This is a great place for kids. Look at Danny. He has the run of the island all winter. Addie and Mel never have to worry about where he is, he's outdoors a lot. It's like going back to another century."

"I know this is a great place for kids except in summer when they get introduced to a lot of stuff that's bad. Then they party on the beach with the older college kids that work here and turn their parents' hair gray. But yeah, until then, it's a good place to grow up," she said.

They held hands now, walking in step, breathing in the salty air. A seal had come ashore to sun itself against the cliff. It looked like a pup, just taking a rest, not ill or injured.

When it saw them, it flopped back to the water and swam off.

"Let's wait until spring," Sean said. "Our lives should be more stable by then."

She was not so sure that would happen, but she could wait, at least until then.

Chapter Seven

The morning of Joel's funeral Dita rolled out of bed at dawn. She raised the window shade to check the weather and looked out over the dunes toward the water. A fiery disc of sun lay flat upon the sea, then stretched into the sky. A freighter beyond the horizon seemed to float in the ether, a school of fish rippled the water into a vee, like geese in flight, speeding past in the shallows.

She felt a need to get out on the beach before breakfast, so she put on sweats and sneaks, not waking Sean but nudging Tuffy, who was curled up on Sean's feet. The dog followed her downstairs; she threw some kibble in his bowl. He gobbled it down, as dogs do, in two gulps, and then they went outside and ran next to each other toward the beach. The air was still, scented like fresh laundry. The crows woke and circled over the dunes calling to each other. A small herd of deer loped toward her neighbor's house, taking a route along the beach they'd used for years before that behemoth was built. Dita jogged along the water line; Tuffy splashed through the surf. She felt like maybe she could face the difficult day ahead. On their way back, they followed the high tide wrack line. The waves had frozen into a scalloped ridge of snow. Her feet molded it into small piles as they jogged through it.

When they reached the house Sean had the coffee ready. Dita took off her shoes and he held out a full cup.

'Mmm, that's good," she said, sipping. There was almost nothing Dita liked as much as her first cup of hot coffee in the morning. Maybe chocolate in her croissant.

"Almost time to go," Sean said. "Better put on warm clothes."

"Yep." Dita murmured, but she did not move and Sean didn't either. They were both avoiding the fact that this was the day Joel would be buried. Denial is a powerful protection.

"I hate funerals," she blurted out. "Why do we have to die?"

"I hope you don't expect me to answer that question, especially when I just woke up." Sean took her empty cup and put it with his in the sink.

"Come on," he said to her. "Get a jacket, at least, and more if you would. It's bound to be chilly at the cemetery."

"Right. We can stop off and change afterward for the reception."

Dita expected it would be worse than chilly by the time they got there. The wind was starting to kick up. Some days the stillness of early morning whisked into a brisk breeze by mid-morning. In those conditions, she found fleece useless. She took out her heat tech shirt and leggings, and then layered a sweater and wool leggings over them. A fake fur hat and scarf and mittens with her parka and boots, and she was ready. She felt five pounds heavier than usual when they drove off.

The cemetery was directly across from their house on the other side of the pond. They could see the hill from their front windows. To get there, they had to drive around the pond, toward town and then to the west.

A long line of vehicles preceded them at the entrance. They snaked upward and parked along the verge all the way in the back adjacent to an unmarked area. It was rumored that this meadow was where people of color had been buried. Dita found it shameful, that people were mistreated and set aside, in both life and death. If true though, at least they had the best view for the cemetery, had it not been a cemetery, would have been one of the most coveted pieces of real estate on the island. As she and Sean followed everyone back down the slope on foot to Joel's gravesite, Dita could see both the ocean and Sailors Pond far below. The waters sparkled and met the sky in an almost invisible blue seam, appearing endless. Dita felt as though one tiny tap could send her floating into the blue ether forever. She hoped the deceased spirits, including Joel, could bask in its comfort like she did.

When it wasn't to attend a funeral she loved going to the cemetery, especially on guided tours. Today she did not linger over history. She kept up with the line of mourners marching toward Joel, passing without noting the grave of the unknown sailor who washed up on their shores from a sinking ship or perhaps a fall overboard, never to be identified. At least Joel had come home. She looked straight ahead as she and Sean followed the other mourners to the gravesite. It was time. She could no longer deny the reason they were all here.

The family was gathered in a tight knot next to the urn that held his ashes. Dita was surprised by the size of the crowd. There were some extended relatives she recognized and a few island friends of Joel's, including Carol, and friends of Addie's and Rachel's. But there were many more she didn't recognize. She learned later that long-time customers of the Lorelei shop had made the voyage over to the island to support Rachel, as had colleagues of Addie's, summer medical interns and medical residents. Dita and Sean found their way to the front, and stood close to the family. Danny came to them and they nestled him between them. The wind swirled, making her feel frigid despite her layers.

The graves in the cremation section of the cemetery were smaller than those for full caskets, so Joel had neighbors close to him. Rachel told Dita he would have liked that. Dita barely heard the benedictions and songs. It was as though she entered a state of suspension; her way of dealing with grief was to go numb. Sean's arm was around her and Danny, steadying them; and then it was over. Danny returned to his family, and they walked to their truck.

"Are you alright?" Sean asked when they were inside.

"I guess. I'm a bit shaky. I seem to always tremble at funerals. And you?"

He nodded.

They were about to leave when Danny knocked on the window. Dita rolled it down.

"Can I come with you?" he asked.

"Of course," Dita said, and he jumped into the back jump seat. She reached over the seat and wiped his tear-stained face with a tissue. "We're stopping home for a minute first, though."

"That's okay. Mom and dad have all these people to talk to. I told her I would try to find you."

"Tuffy will be glad to see you," Sean said, turning back toward Danny.

"Will you guys find out what happened to Uncle Joel?"

Dita answered, "We're trying."

Danny decided to stay at Sean and Dita's instead of going to the funeral repast. That was probably his plan in the first place, Dita whispered to Sean while they were upstairs changing. She texted Addie to let her know, and she made a peanut butter sandwich for him with a glass of milk and two of her favorite chocolate covered chocolate chip cookies. He was curled up on the couch with Tuffy spread across him. The dog's big blond head was on Danny's shoulder. On a less somber day, Dita would have snapped a picture. Although on the mainland a child his age would not be left alone, on the island, children were more independent and capable of caring for themselves for a few hours. If there was a problem, the adults would be right down the street. Danny could even walk there if he got bored.

"I almost forgot my potato salad," she said, reaching into the refrigerator once more.

"Got everything now?" Sean asked. He turned to Danny. "See you in a while," and they went out the door.

"Wait," Dita said. "I forgot to lock the front door. I wouldn't want anything to happen to Danny." She went back and turned the key in the lock, something she rarely did.

Although they had dressed in better clothes for the lunch, they were still somewhat bundled in sweaters and boots. The reception lunch was being held at the Beach Dune. The Beach Dune used to stay open winters, but with a change of ownership in the past few years, it now opened only for the high season.

Sean and Dita remembered it as always drafty and cool in the winters when it was the island hang out. In those days, the Dune had a limited menu of five daily items, with one hot meal at lunch every day and dinner on weekends. They served bar food, hamburgers, fries, chili, clam chowder, hot dogs, and a rotating menu of one real meal a day, shepherd's pie, fish and chips, Salisbury steak. Today the new owner, a friend of Rachel's, opened the restaurant for her. She had restocked the bar and turned on the heat. But Dita and Sean knew the heat wouldn't have warmed the winter chill enough.

Cars were parked all along Founders Road almost down to the beach pavilion. There were no close spaces. Dita and Sean did a u-turn and headed back to a nearby driveway that belonged to a summer resident they knew would not be around until spring. They pulled in and parked. Property rights were only enforced if there was someone to claim them. Then they trudged the short distance back along the road. People were spilling out the door of the Beach Dune, gathering in small clutches on the long porch. Some, surprisingly, even sat in the wooden Adirondack chairs that overlooked the beach across the street. How many summer afternoons had Sean and Dita sat in those chairs holding a bowl of chili or clam chowder, watching tourists cavort in the water. One day they'd witnessed a couple unabashedly engage in sex in the shallows, oblivious to the sunbathers on the beach, traffic on the road, and diners pointing and laughing from the Beach Dune porch. But today was a different kind of day.

"The whole island's here," Sean remarked.

"Even some who weren't at the funeral," Dita added.

They squeezed through the door. Sean looked at Dita when they cleared the entrance and said, with a grin, "We squoze in successfully,"

"You're joshing me, aren't you? Is squoze a real word?"

"If it isn't, it should be. Like we always say we squoze the lemons."

"Point taken," she said.

He took the potato salad from her and found a spot for it on the buffet table. "There's Karl," he said, pointing to a group of people standing at the bar. "I should go talk to him."

"Hmm, he's not high on my list. Look, he's out of uniform today. If he drinks too much and lets out some information, I approve of you hanging out with him. I see his boss. Maybe I'll talk to him," she said, smiling and nodding toward the chief.

"I think you're trying to one up me, but go ahead. It'll be a while before we can get close to Rachel, Mel or Addie anyway."

Dita elbowed her way over to the corner where Chief Gomez was nursing a drink. He, unlike Karl, was still dressed in his uniform, which surprised her.

"Hello, George. How are you today?" She looked him up and down. "Not expecting trouble, are you?"

"Just paying my respects like everyone else. Sad day."

He pulled a chair out for her with one hand. "Have a seat. Let's chat."

"On the record?" she asked.

"Maybe some of it."

"Okay," she said, pulling the reporter's notebook and pen she always carried out of her bag. "Tell me when it's not."

"I know you and Rachel are convinced someone murdered Joel," he said, "and I want you to understand that I didn't dismiss that right away. However, no one's come up with a motive or a grudge or any remote reason to explain it. And we can't find physical evidence. He's too banged up from the rocks and whatever else he might have hit out there in the water."

Evidently the chief had spoken with the coroner, Dita surmised. "So, you're giving up," she said. "Suicide, you think."

"I didn't say that, Dita. The coroner said there's water in his lungs, which indicates he was alive when he went in. Do you know how many people drown falling off boats?"

"No, can you tell me?"

"Cruise ships lose about 25 to 30 every year, that we know of. There could be more."

"Joel wasn't on a cruise ship," she said.

He took a sip of his coffee. "Even fishermen go into the drink," he told her, looking officious. "Over 200 of them had fatal falls between 2000 and 2014 in the United States alone."

Dita tried to look impressed, although she was only feeling angry that George was attempting to justify Joel's death using statistics she already had looked up herself. "You don't say. Sounds like you researched this."

"I did," he said. "You're not the only one who knows how to surf the Internet for information. Fishermen, they lean over to fix a line or pull in a fish, and maybe they lean too far. Especially on nice days not everyone wears a life jacket."

Dita knew that. She'd spent years living next to Sailors Pond.

People on sail boats and stink pots that come in there almost never have life jackets. Sean had a telescope set up so they could watch the stars, but they also checked the names on boats they liked, and Dita sometimes watched people move about their decks when she was bored.

"And then there are the drinkers," George said. "We've lost some right in Sailors Pond. They get soused out there and topple over. Or they get soused on land and can't find the rung on the ladder getting back onboard in the dark."

Dita recalled one like that the previous summer. Karl had mentioned it also when Joel's body came in. She realized she wouldn't get anywhere trying to convince the chief that someone had pushed Joel into the water.

He took a forkful of beans from his plate, chewed them and then, after he swallowed, he wrapped up their discussion, his voice a little kinder. "It's easy to have an accident on the water, Dita. I think Joel had one. I have no way of proving otherwise." He put down his fork. "The fact that there was gas left in the engine tells me he turned off his boat. That makes me lean more toward suicide than an accident."

She bit her tongue to keep herself from retorting that in her eyes, the case had never really been open. He apparently had said all he was going to say about Joel.

"Can I quote you?" she asked.

"Of course," he said. "Would you like a picture?"

Dita forced a smile. "No. We have plenty in our files."

He shook his head. "I feel just as badly as you and the rest of the community about Joel. It affects all of us."

"Me too," she nodded, wiping a tear from her cheek. "I should find Addie now." She packed her notebook and pen into her bag, and left his table. Her appetite was ruined.

As she pushed through the throng of townspeople, she spotted Loretta flirting with Bob Mankawicz, a summer cottager from

New York whose former wife was a frequent customer of Rachel's Lorelei. Bob was newly single, having divorced after a long separation, and he was a decent-looking guy, with grey streaks in his black hair, and green, piercing eyes. Dita figured he must have gotten the island house in the divorce agreement since he was here today. She silently cheered Loretta on, but she knew Mankawicz only hung with the millionaire cocktail crowd. Loretta could be but a one-night stand for him, if even that. In fact, she wondered why he was here at the funeral, and then she remembered Joel had taken him on some paid fishing trips.

Nonetheless, she decided not to interrupt Loretta's flirting, and just gave her friend a slight shoulder tap as she moved past her in the crowd. Loretta nodded at her and quickly returned her attention to Bob. Dita admired her friend's ability to attract men. She was one of those women Dita called a man magnet. They trailed her like the tails of her long scarves.

But not Bob. He moved on past Loretta, elbowing his way through the crowd to another summer cottager, a Wall Street banker who often flew in weekends on his private plane. Dita, still watching, caught Loretta's attention again. Loretta rolled her eyes.

When Dita finally spotted Rachel and Addie, she was close to the buffet table. She took a plate and filled it, having put George's pronouncements aside and regained her appetite. There was roast turkey and island venison stew, the latter she thought from Carol, a raw bar with oysters on the half shell and clams in their shells, all harvested from the pond. Harry stood behind that bar, covered by a white apron, knife in hand ready to shuck. Further down the buffet there was clam chowder made by the Beach Dune, the island's best; a cobb salad she recognized as Addie's; fish tacos, an island staple; mashed potatoes, pastas, baked beans and string beans. The desserts were not even out of the kitchen yet! She took her plate of food to Addie's table, balancing it on her palm with her arm bent, a move she learned during her waitressing summers at the old

Beach Dune. Addie was sitting with their mayor, a stout, cheerful man with catalogue clothes and severe gray hair. The mayor said he was just getting up and gave Dita his seat.

"That's special. He gave me his seat."

"Don't feel too special. He didn't want to be here anyway. He's off to chat with more important people," Addie said.

"Hmm, I didn't realize you were out of sorts with him."

"We always struggle with him over health and safety inspections. He never wants to hurt businesses. Always thinking of reelection."

Dita laughed. "Not too many people want his job anymore, Addie. Do you really think that's the reason?"

Addie shrugged. "Look over there. He's working the crowd. I think he has his eye on a run for state rep."

"You could be right. Anyway, I wanted to let you know Danny seemed very comfy curled up on our couch with the dog. I left him lunch. He's my favorite island boy."

Addie smiled. "Thanks. This is too hard for him. Mel is off island so much with his planning jobs over on the mainland, having Joel around filled in for him."

"I know. I think Sean will try to help. He's quite attached to Danny."

"It might be time to nudge him a bit toward, you know, having one of your own."

Dita's food didn't taste so good anymore. She tried to ignore the comment. "It looks as though your mother's free right now. I'll just take my plate, jump over there for a few minutes."

"Running away?" Addie asked, but Dita already had her back to Addie and was threading her way through the crowd, her plate resting on her crooked arm and palm again. This was not a day to discuss maternity plans.

Rachel reached out for Dita when she spotted her. "Come talk with me," she said. She was standing near the drinks bar, the crowd of men with Karl and Sean having moved off to a table.

"I needed to stretch my legs for a bit," Rachel explained. "I saw you talking with George before."

"Yes," Dita replied. She set her plate down on the mahogany bar.

"Did he tell you it was an accident?"

"He did."

"Dita, are you convinced?"

"The more important question is, are you?"

Rachel grimaced. "Of course not. My son knew boats and he knew fishing. He wouldn't fall off like a dummy. And he wasn't suicidal either. Please believe me, Dita."

"I do. I'll keep digging around, but I haven't yet learned anything that would back up your conviction."

"Thank you, my friend," Rachel said, and she reached over to give Dita a big hug. "But be circumspect around Addie. She wants me to drop this."

"Really? I was just with her and she didn't say anything," Dita said.

"She will, I'm sure. Now I need to sit again."

"Okay, I think it's time for us to go home anyway." She had finished her food and felt like she didn't need any of the desserts which were now spread out across the bar. "I'll try to find Sean."

He was waiting for her near the door. He'd had his dessert, two slices of apple pie, and with his belly satisfied, he was ready to go. They walked in step to their truck.

"I have a full stomach," Sean said, "but an empty heart."

There were times that Sean could drop his island macho man act.

"Yes, food does not fill a heart, does it?"

Danny was playing a video came when they got home. His plate and glass were both empty, and Tuffy was now at his feet snoring.

"Everything okay?" Sean asked.

"Yep," Danny challenged him without looking up.

Sean picked up a controller and sank onto the couch next to him.

"You can't beat me," Danny said.

"I can and I will."

Dita slipped upstairs to read her email and relax. She took off her shoes and her layers of warm clothing and stretched out on the bed in her heat shirt and leggings. She fluffed her pillow just so and pulled the extra fleece throw over herself. She tuned out the bings and buzzes from the competition being fought downstairs, and opened the book she was reading at the moment, a thriller set in Wyoming, letting it transport her to the world of the heroic but flawed sheriff. When Dita read a good novel, she immersed herself.

She did not hear Addie and Mel pull into the driveway or come through the door. Addie called out to Dita when she was halfway up the stairs, and startled her friend.

"Oh, it's you. You scared me," Dita said. "I didn't know you were here."

"I guess not. You didn't hear us downstairs, the commotion of the dog and Danny and us?"

"Nope, I didn't. Guess I was half-asleep reading." Dita yawned. "Take a seat." She patted the bed.

"Don't mind if I do. I'm wiped. Long day." Addie climbed into the bed, dropped her shoes to the floor and stretched out next to Dita as she spoke. Her face was tear streaked, like a windshield with worn out wipers in the rain. The mascara she'd applied for the funeral was smudged on her cheekbones instead of her eyelashes. Dita had never seen her so distraught.

"Yup. What are you reading?"

Dita showed her.

"Oh, can I have it next?"

"Of course, but I just started, so it might be a bit."

"That's fine. In the meantime, Dita, I need to ask you a favor. I mean, you need to do a favor for me. Look at me because I'm serious about this."

Dita put her book down and turned to face her friend. "I take it it's not about the book."

Normally, Addie would have smiled at the half joke, but not today. She said, "I need you to accept that Joel fell off his boat, whether it was by accident or an act of suicide. You need to stop hunting for a murderer."

Dita felt stunned. "And you're sure there wasn't one?"

Addie put her hands on Dita's shoulders. "The coroner's report will tell. But this is what I am sure of. My mother is going to go to pieces trying to prove someone killed my brother. She needs to stop. She needs to grieve and go on. You both need to accept that if the coroner's report say's Joel's death was accidental, it was."

"What if it wasn't?" Dita asked.

"She'll never pull herself together if the two of you keep pursuing a theory you'll not be able to prove. I am begging you to stop, for her sake and for mine."

Dita knew she couldn't stop, not even for Addie. Her need to know the truth might have been seeded by guilt, but that need had grown into something else inside her. Call it an anger at the way people mistreated the Joels of the world, or call it a growing sense of justice, Dita was changing from happy-go-lucky post-college hedonist into an adult, an ethical one. Always indecisive and non-committal, now that she felt that sense of righteousness, she was going too far for Addie.

When she did not say she would stop, Addie took that for what it was, a no, and she continued to press Dita.

"If it was murder, and I am not agreeing it was, it happened at sea, no witnesses, no traces, no evidence," Addie said. "Please, our friendship is important to me, but if you keep on with this, we won'thave one. I need my mother. Danny needs his grandmother."

Dita sat up straighter, pulled her pillow up higher behind her head.

"Addie, you know Joel hasn't been suicidal in years. I don't remember his psychotic episodes because they happened way before

Sean and I came here."

"I remember them, though. Those were terrible times for our family."

"I'm sure they were. Your mother told me some. But lately, he hadn't mentioned wanting to die. He seemed happy. And, not for nothing, I think he's been fishing at sea long enough not to tumble over the side of his boat and drown."

Addie shook her head. "He could have slipped and fallen, hit his head on the gunnels and gone over. It happens. Dita, the point is, I can't rescue him, but I need to rescue my mother."

Addie reached down and put her shoes back on. She stood up. "Please tell me you'll stop writing about it and you'll stop questioning people. I appreciate your efforts up to now, but it's done. Okay? Let him rest in peace."

Dita stood also. "But Addie," she started to protest.

Addie raised her voice. "No, I'm telling you to stop." She fled the room and raced down the stairs. "Danny, Mel, we're going home."

"But we're playing a game," Danny protested. "And I'm ahead."

"Put on your coat," she shouted, and she slammed out of the house.

The tears that had been leaking from Dita's eyes all day cascaded out, tears for Joel, for Rachel and for her friendship with Addie. The only way she knew to solve problems was to dig out the truth behind them. She realized now that was why she became a reporter, to lay out the truth in front of people, to make the world a better place. The force of Addie's anger cracked her open. She realized some of it was fueled by grief. But grief was not pure sadness, it was imbued with anger from the helplessness we feel in the face of death. Dita understood that. Still, the fury Addie directed at her hurt. She didn't want to lose their friendship.

Chapter Eight

Sean must have heard Dita sobbing. He went to her and wrapped her in his arms. "What happened up here?" he asked.

Dita told him what Addie said.

He tried to reassure her. "She didn't mean it, Dita."

But Dita knew that Sean was wrong. She was close enough to Addie to know when she was speaking from her heart. "She did. I know Addie. What a miserable day."

"Maybe she's right about dialing back your investigation," Sean said, as gently as he could.

"You, too?"

"I'm not saying you're wrong, just that if it upsets the family, it might be better to drop it, or go about it quietly."

Dita sighed. "I don't know how to do things quietly," she said.

Sean reached over to the tissue box on the night table and

pulled one out. He wiped her face. He agreed with her that she didn't know how to tiptoe around an issue. Then he did something many significant others don't do. He just listened as Dita talked.

"If it was any other fisherman who didn't drink or do drugs, they wouldn't call it an accident. They would wonder what happened. But because Joel had a history of mental illness, they think he threw himself overboard or was too stupid to stay in the boat or even to swim back to it. You and I both know he was a strong swimmer."

Sean worded a careful reply.

"I hear you, but they aren't saying that. They're making the point that freak accidents happen, especially at sea."

"Sean, they're mostly saying it was suicide. Joel and Rachel have lived with prejudice against the mentally ill for a long time. No one looks at psychiatric problems with the same compassion they have for people with heart disease or kidney failure, even though mental illness is also biological."

Again, Sean did not disagree.

"Let's try to think of this logically. What reason did anyone have to kill Joel?" he asked.

Dita admitted she hadn't come up with any.

Then Sean hit a nerve. "I think you are still feeling guilty that you didn't rescue Joel from the rain and that group you saw him with. You think this was your fault."

Dita winced. She knew he was right. "True. If I hadn't been so lazy, so self-indulgent, Joel might still be here."

"It's not your fault. Sure, you could have run back out into the rain and gotten drenched, and tried to get him into our house, but maybe he wouldn't have wanted to go anyway. And who wouldn't have decided to stay dry? You need to stop punishing yourself."

"Maybe, but all of us could have spent more time with Joel, made him more a part of our lives."

"Okay, we could have. But that doesn't mean he wouldn't have died."

"I guess," she agreed, but not wholeheartedly.

" Dita, not to change the subject, but I will. Both George and Karl have each told me separately that there's a drug ring operating on the island, and the people in it are a closely-held secret. Didn't your boss assign you to do a story? Although, according to Karl and George, you won't crack their wall of silence either."

Dita harumphed. "Come on, Sean, you know how few secrets get kept on this island. I'd say, none."

"All I know is Karl claims he occasionally overhears a conversation at the Washashore alluding to heroin use, but he's never able to get a name."

"Maybe Joel stumbled into that without intending to," Dita said.

"Maybe."

Dita wondered if she could pry a little harder.

"Please, be careful," Sean told her. "If you're right about Joel, it's all the more reason to be careful."

"You think reporters fit into the expendable category too?"

"I do. And I want to keep my reporter around."

He got up, walked over to the window, and looked out. "We still have an hour or so of good light. I think I'll stretch my legs, take the dog for a walk. It's low tide."

"Me too. Give me a minute to get my shoes and a jacket on."

They headed down, Tuffy following, and went out the door. They decided to go across the street to the beach at Sailors Pond.

"So did I tell you George offered me a job on the police force, but Karl warned me against taking it?" Sean asked.

"What?" Dita stopped in the middle of the road. With the funeral reception finished, they could have lain down and slept there without getting run over.

"When?" she asked.

"The other day. You were busy running around interviewing people so I didn't get a chance to tell you."

"I didn't know you wanted to be a cop," Dita said.

"I didn't. I don't." Sean laughed. "It was a surprise to me. I bumped into George at the café one morning, and we started to talk. You know how George is, always making small talk to get a bead on the pulse of the island."

"I do," she said. "Except he never finds out who the dealer is despite his chit chat. Maybe he's just nosy."

"Don't be snide. He asked if I might be interested in the job. I told him I'd think about it. Dita, I know how anxious you are to get started on a family. The gym proposition isn't panning out, so I said, maybe."

"Hmm, Officer Sean."

They both laughed.

"But why did Karl warn you not to take it?"

"Well, it wasn't really a warning. He just said I would have to go to the training academy on the mainland for the same course they give the city and state police over there. I'd be away from home for a while. That would be hard on both of us."

Dita didn't disagree. She also could not picture her Sean carrying a gun.

They passed through the parking lot and reached the boardwalk to Dinghy Beach, so named because boaters who anchored out in the pond rowed their dinghies to shore here when they wanted to go into town. Before the boardwalk was built, the marsh between the beach and the street was a muddy tidal mess, pockmarked by the footprints of boaters, a perfect breeding ground for mosquitos. Back then Dingy Beach was named Mosquito Beach.

Dita and Sean tromped over the wooden boardwalk as Tuffy dashed ahead of them, happy with his romp.

"Maybe you could find some other town job if policing isn't for you," Dita said. "Do you really think you'd be happy doing that work?"

"Maybe. I don't know. You don't think I'd be able to keep up with Karl?"

Dita smiled. "Hopefully never with his drinking. He keeps the Washashore profitable."

"Are you implying the job drives him to it?"

"Are you?"

When they reached the end of the ramp, they stepped down onto the sand. Dita picked up a few shells for her collection and dug around for sea glass. It was becoming rarer since plastic replaced glass bottles. Sean took a tennis ball out of his pocket and threw it down the beach for Tuffy to retrieve.

The sun hung low over the pond. Crows began to gather across the street, cawing and calling to each other in raspy voices as they circled above the dunes, getting ready to settle down for the night. There were not a lot of trees along that stretch of Founders Road, and Dita wondered where they built their nests. As the pond lit up, they watched for a few minutes, and then meandered back toward their house.

"I thought I'd make one more try to raise money. That guy Loretta was flirting with today, he might fund me. I'll call him in the morning and try to get together with him."

"You do know he just got divorced," she said.

"Yeah. Word among the guys is he had a prenup and didn't get hit too bad. Snobby as these summer titans are, they like making money and my gym will."

"Hmmm."

"If it's nice out tomorrow after I talk with him, I might go clamming. Those we had the other day just whetted my appetite."

"Mmm, maybe stuffies," she said. But her hope was tomorrow would bring a different kind of stuff into the picture. Mankawicz was a pretty buttoned-up snob, but maybe he would like the idea of investing in "his" island. The wealthy thought of Nor'easter as theirs, though to the year-rounders, they merely migrated like the birds and didn't put down roots.

Chapter Nine

Dita and Sean stopped in at the Books and Bakes for coffee and muffins Saturday morning, hoping to mingle with neighbors to catch up on the week's gossip. Dita's editor Mary was there with a full table, Paul from the summer day spa; Gail and Bonnie, a retired couple from the Southwest corner; Johnny, the furnace repairman; and Doug, one of the construction contractors. It was a glum group, Dita noted to Sean. They were huddled around two tables pulled together, their voices low, tears visible in a few eyes. Even Ellie, who was working the counter, had pulled up a chair behind Bonnie. Sean and Dita did the same, behind Mary. Dita leaned in and whispered to her editor.

"What happened? Why is everyone so upset?"

Mary spoke in a low voice, but loud enough for all to hear. "It's Sonny. He didn't go downstairs to get his coffee this morning so

Gladys checked on him."

Dita knew that Sonny rented a room from Gladys, who made ends meet with boarders.

Mary continued. "She banged on his door and then she went in. Dita, he was dead. Cold. No pulse. Gone."

Dita let out an involuntary, "Oh, no," and covered her mouth with her hand.

Shock registered on Sean's face. "Sonny's dead?"

"It was too late to revive him," Mary said. "Gladys tried to do CPR, and when the rescue squad arrived they injected Naloxone, but...." She did not finish her sentence.

"I knew his drinking was way out of control, but I never heard he used heroin," Dita said. She turned to Sean. "Did you know? He was your helper on some of your handyman jobs."

She looked him in the eye, hoping he would say he did not.

Sean shook his head. "No."

Dita felt a wave of relief wash over her. Sean was still talking, though.

"What makes them suspect an OD? Most of the time, he couldn't even pay his bar bill."

Mary told them she had spoken with Chief Gomez. Sonny died with a needle still in his arm. Dita drew in her breath. Could this really be? And coming so soon after Joel?

"Poor Sonny!" Sean almost shouted. "I can't believe it. He just liked his rot gut whiskey and beer. I never heard him talk about drugs. I never saw him use any, other than an occasional puff of pot someone would pass to him. He was an old-timey drunkard, or so I thought. This has to be wrong."

"What happened to Joel was wrong too," Dita said.

Ellie got up and went to the kitchen. She brought out a large pot of coffee and set it on the table, then returned to get cups and spoons.

"Sugar's out. I'll get the milk pitcher. Grab a muffin or a roll, it's on us today," she said.

Of all of them, Sean knew Sonny best. "The other night at the Washashore Karl told me there're more addicts on the island than we're aware of," Sean said. "They're secretive, no surprise there. But he said that the chief can't get anyone to talk. Usually someone overhears a conversation and passes it on, you know how that goes. Sonny was sitting right next to me at the bar. He heard him too. Didn't say a word."

"I guess we know why now," Ellie said, folding her arms over her chest, glancing around the table.

It was quiet in the café, No one knew what else to say. They sipped their coffee and worked on their muffins. Finally, Mary pushed her chair back and stood to leave. She beckoned to Dita to follow her out. Once there, beyond earshot of the others, she asked Dita to write the obituary.

"Usually, a family member or friend submits one, but I don't know of anyone that close to him. Do you?"

Dita did not.

"You and Sean knew him better than a lot of us, though," Mary said. "I think he's from northern Maine somewhere."

Dita had been looking for a meatier assignment than meetings, but obituaries of people she cared about weren't on that list. She would do it, as she thought it was the least she could do for Sonny and maybe she could dig a little more into the workings of the island drug culture.

"Okay. But Mary, you'll have to talk to the medical center," she said. "Addie's angry at me, so I can't call her. They must have next of kin names there."

"I can, but what's with you and Addie?"

"A story for another day," Dita said. She didn't want to talk about it. She hoped it would blow over. And then Sean came out, ready to leave. He reached out and held her close. She could tell how shaken he was by Sonny's sudden death.

"This I did not expect," she said.

"I don't know what to do," Sean said, catching his breath as though he'd been running. "I thought he would drink himself to death eventually; but this, now...I don't know how to deal with it."

She put her hand on his arm. "Me too. I'm that upset also."

They drove home like zombies. It was fortunate no one else was on the road.

"Maybe I'll do a little work, do a few house checks. It'll calm me down a bit," he said. "On second thought, I need to talk to Karl. How could no one know?"

She thought someone should find out.

He dropped Dita at home and went on. She was glad he wasn't doing any carpentry because his mind would not be focused on a task like that and he might lose a finger. She let Tuffy into the house with her and called Rachel.

"Hey, any news of Joel's coroner report?"

"No," she said, "but you must have heard about Sonny."

Rachel told her Addie had been called into work to assist when the rescue squad took the 911 for Sonny. They had expected to transfer him there for treatment, not to get him ready for transport to the state medical examiner.

"I'm writing the obit," Dita said. "Do you know anything about his family?"

Rachel didn't.

"Pity," Dita uttered. "No one seems to."

She called Gladys, who told her she'd found his license and social security card in his room but not a birth certificate. Gladys claimed she had no idea he was using, though they lived in the same house. Dita wondered how that could be; but according to Gladys, she saw him mornings and not much more. She'd gone into the room a few times, but only when he'd been sick and needed help. She collected his rent and looked in on him occasionally, but they weren't friends. Dita spent the rest of the afternoon on the phone talking with people she knew had spent time around the island with Sonny. None of them had a lot to add. They were all heavy imbibers like him, their bonds with him formed around their bottles, not past lives.

It was typical of the island, she thought, that the daily gossip was focused on who went into the kitchen with Harry but not about the terrible things they saw but didn't want to face, like alcoholism, drug addiction, spouse beatings, and thefts, the island's underbelly.

Sonny's full name was Wilson Carter Ames. When Gladys read it to Dita over the phone from his driver's license, it sounded like he came from a branch of an old family tree. The fallen scion of a proud Yankee family, maybe. Sonny had mentioned to several people, including Dita, that he grew up in northern Maine, but he never told anyone which town. When Dita searched on her computer, she learned the state was full of people with the name Ames, but none with the first names of Wilson or Carter.

Dita wondered whether his mother would ever hear about his death, if she was still alive. Did she care about him? Did she think about him? Dita obsessed about it more. If no one had ever cared about him, how did he get the name Sonny? It was a term of endearment. She decided he must have at some time been somebody's beloved little sonny.

What happened in Maine, Dita wondered, to make him leave home, turn his back to his past, and become a drunken washashore? What tore the ties to his past? Nor'easter Island was a perfect place to hide out from a life you didn't love, or that didn't love you. She searched, but she couldn't find any information on poor Sonny in her internet search.

She knew so little about him, even after talking with his pals. Had he ever fallen in love, or had a dream for his future? It seemed no one on the island had a clue. Dita thought that was the saddest thing. She wished she had spent a little more effort asking Sonny about his past. It might have made a difference if she'd done more than just buy him a sandwich now and then. She felt ashamed that he'd slipped so far out of everyone's consciousness and become a cardboard figure with a bottle of poison in his hand. And now a corpse with a needle stuck in his arm. How easily we consigned people we knew to the dead persons file while they were still alive. Could she do better than that in the future? She hoped so.

After extensive research into old newspaper postings and telephone calls, she was able to compile a list of hotels and restaurants where he'd worked the last fifteen years that he had lived on Nor'easter Island, and she would include those in his obituary.

He was only 39 years old. Dita reflected on the fact she always thought he was older, but that's what heavy drinking will do. She started to write, and it made her cry. There would be a gathering. Harry would hold a memorial service of sorts at the Washashore for him next Sunday, but no burial unless someone claimed the body. Maybe, she thought, she and Sean should take his ashes and have him buried in the island cemetery where he could rest forever overlooking the ocean, instead of being thrown into the ground with other poor souls somewhere in the middle of the state on the mainland. It wouldn't cost too much, and people would chip in. She'd talk to Sean, and have Harry hold off on his service until they got his ashes.

Harry offered to pay for Sonny's burial. It was a small group that gathered the day they to buried him in the same area of the cemetery where Joel was laid to rest, the one reserved for cremated remains. A frigid wind was blowing in from the West across a wan sun. It stung Diana's cheeks. She shivered and was grateful it would not be a long ritual. She moved closer to Sean, who seemed to radiate heat no matter how cold the air.

Sonny's ashes were lowered, they all bowed their heads, and Bernard, who stood in as a rabbi for the few Jewish residents on the island, said a short prayer for his soul. Bernard had volunteered, his philosophy of benevolence extending to all people. Gail, an island folk musician, sang a shanty about being lost at sea, and Chief Gomez made a plea for information on who was bringing in the hard drugs circulating around the island. He was concerned that no one seemed to admit they knew Sonny used, or that they knew who supplied Sonny. There could well be more deaths, he told them.

Heartache is what Dita felt, and as she looked around, she could see she was not the only one. Impaired and struggling, Sonny was still one of their own. A humble life cut short. Tears for Sonny and for loved ones long lost were shed and froze into rivulets on many faces. Gladys brought flowers and placed them on the grave. His buddies from the bar put a beer mug there to hold the flowers. Sonny was at rest, Dita hoped. The mourners headed to the Washashore to toast his spirit and fear for their own. Sonny was but one among a throng of washashores cramped into small rented spaces on the island among the high and mighty who vacationed there in their palatial summer homes.

Dita felt a cloud hanging over her. They were back at the pub for yet another funeral lunch, so soon. This time the crowd was all local. More had come to the pub than the graveyard. Dita and Sean had to search to find a table with open seats. Then he went to the bar to order drinks and Loretta squeezed into his space next to Dita. She held a cup of hot spiced cider with rum in each hand. She put one down in front of Dita, the other in front of herself. She pulled her wool scarf from her head and let it drape down.

"There," she said, plopping into the chair and ruffling a few locks of the blue hair around her face.

"I talked to a lot of people about Sonny," Dita said. "Everyone liked him, but no one was close to him. Sad."

"Yes," Loretta agreed.

"So, how are you really doing? We never talk about that stuff." Dita was now concerned for all her friends. She didn't want to lose any more to eternity.

Loretta shrugged. "I'm okay, I guess. I bartend a few shifts here, dust off a few summer houses, and I make enough to pay my rent and almost get by. If I had one more house, I'd be better off. The Bradley job helps."

"I wish Sean could find a few more jobs. Then we'd be okay too."

Loretta clicked her tongue. "I didn't know you were short."

Dita nodded.

"I can ask around," Loretta said.

"Thank you. And now, let's get some food before it's all gone."

Plates heaped with food covered the bar, most of it from island homes, casseroles, pastas, potatoes, vegetable souffles, breads, and desserts of all kinds, apple pies, lemon squares, brownies, and cookies. It was a typical island funeral spread. They made their way to the end of the buffet line. Karl was behind them. He leaned over Loretta's shoulder and quipped, "If only Sonny was here to have some. It would be the best meal he'd eaten in many a month." Loretta rolled her eyes, nudged Dita, who was next to her, and gave her a small nod. When they had put some distance between themselves and Karl, Loretta whispered that he seemed to place himself in her space as much as he could.

"So annoying," she said.

"Just one of your many admirers," Dita said, meaning it.

Sean had returned with their drinks, and his own heaping plateful of food. "It's too bad Sonny can't be here for this. I don't think he'd eaten this well in years," he said, echoing Karl's comment; but his voice was not a quip. It was filled with compassion, and so the words took on a completely different meaning. To Dita, it demonstrated how different her husband and Karl were as people. Oceans apart, she thought.

Harry proposed a toast. He held up Sonny's bar tab, and ripped it in half. "I'll be lonely here without him. I'll miss his company every afternoon. I could rely on him to be here whenever I needed a hand to unload cartons with me, or bring the bottles out back. To Sonny!" he said.

As Dita held up her glass with the rest of crowd in the room, she wondered who among them was also using and who had supplied Sonny with the drugs that killed him? Would the rest of them be attending more funerals? She decided to talk to the chief this week, and she'd talk to Karl too, use it as a jumping off point to investigate drug use on the island. Maybe she could do a series, get some insight into how much of a problem it might be. When she'd interviewed Sonny's friends, she'd been looking for background for his obituary. She hadn't pushed hard enough about his drug use. She needed to go back and talk with each of them again.

But first she'd find Carol, then Trent. She would dig a little deeper into Joel's death, even though she risked alienating Addie more. Dita still felt ashamed that she had shown a lack of character, or perhaps selfishness, that day she saw Joel fighting on the street and she chose to stay dry instead of helping him. She couldn't just let his death go unexplained. Dita needed to atone for that day.

Chapter Ten

Carol lived out on the south side of the island, halfway up a hill. That hill eventually led to a cliff overlooking the sea, but at some distance past her cottage. She had no water views. She did have conservation land though, with stone walls, long grasses and trails abutting her yard. Open space was desirable, although second place to the sea on Nor'easter Island, and it added value to Carol's property. She'd had several unsolicited offers to buy, all of which she'd turned down. She knew what would happen to her house, which she loved, if she sold. It would be demolished and a huge monstrosity would replace it. She'd inherited that cottage from her mother who came, as they say on Nor'easter Island, from old island stock. Her forebears had the dubious distinction of being among the Europeans who'd wrested the land from the Native Americans. Now her best friend was one of the few descendants from that tribe remaining on the island.

Dita took the truck to navigate the unpaved track. When she reached Carol's, she noticed that it was in far better shape than Rachel's. Someone had been helping Carol with repairs. There was scaffolding along the side of the house where the shingles around a second-floor window were being replaced. No one was working up there today, however.

Carol heard Dita pull up and she opened the door for her. As Dita stepped in, air wafted out, giving her a whiff of something delicious. She looked around the cottage and located the covered stew pot on the stove along the back wall.

"I'm making venison stew," Carol said. "One of the hunters brought the meat over. They get to hunt on the conservation property this year only because the deer are overrunning it, killing all the vegetation. They have to cull the herd or there won't be many plants left. I wouldn't eat the deer if they were just killed for fun."

She took Dita's coat and motioned for her to take the easy chair near the door. The cottage's main living area was what modern house hunters call 'open concept,' a combined living room and kitchen. But it had been that way since the house was built in the 1800's because back then, the kitchen fireplace heated the whole house.

Dita had never been there before. Baskets lined the opposite wall, stacked behind a long table. She learned later that the baskets held Carol's jewelry-making supplies, wires, clasps, loops, sea glass she collected walking the beaches, and beads she bought. She was known as one of the better jewelry makers on the island, and her wrapped sea glass was highly coveted. Dita owned several pairs of the earrings Carol sold in summer at the Lorelei.

Carol was a rotund lady in her early thirties, with wide brown eyes and short brown hair. Her face was unremarkable, perhaps even plain. She was a serious person who did not join in the barroom revelry popular on the island. Even her slow, measured step evoked business.

Today, Dita noted, her eyes were red, tear trails lined her cheeks, and she looked ten years older than her age.

"I came to talk with you a bit about Joel," Dita said. "but also, Sonny."

Carol told her Rachel had called and convinced her to speak with Dita, though initially she hadn't wanted to.

"Rachel does not believe that Joel committed suicide," Dita said.

"I know," Carol said. "It's hard for me to believe it also. Did she tell you he was going to move in with me?"

Dita nodded.

Tears filled Carol's eyes. "I keep wondering if that was too much pressure for him. It was his idea, and he seemed excited about it; but maybe he felt he couldn't and didn't know how to tell me."

Dita thought that would be scant reason to jump in the sea and let yourself drown, and she said so.

"I keep thinking what was it like for him in those last moments? Wouldn't he have reached out for the boat? Wouldn't his instincts be to live?" Carol asked. "I think if you jump off a bridge there's no turning back, but the boat couldn't have drifted far from him."

She breathed back a sob. Dita waited before asking questions.

"Carol, had he said he wanted to die, made any recent attempts? Were there any hints? Rachel says he was happy, and not depressed at all, but mothers view their children differently than others do."

"He never expressed a wish to die. Not to me," she said.

Dita paused a minute, in case Carol wanted to elaborate. When she didn't, Dita asked if there was anyone who seemed angry at Joel or harassed him. The woman at once responded with an emphatic no. She was not breaking down again, so Dita pressed on.

"Please think for a second. Jealousies bubble up easily here. Someone takes a job someone else coveted, a guy sleeps with a girl another guy thought should belong to him, you know what it's like here in winter. Was there anyone else who wanted to be with you?"

"Of course not."

There was a more delicate part to this question. Dita lowered her voice and leaned closer to ask it. "How were you two getting along? Might you have had an argument about something that week?"

Carol replied with another sob. "I told you we were going to move in together. We had no arguments or troubles lately. We were close. I just can't understand."

Dita steered her to Rachel. "How about with his mother? Did they have a falling out?"

"Not that I heard. He was going to tell her about us this week, and he was sure she would be happy. Rachel and I are friendly. She sells a lot of my jewelry."

Dita knew Rachel was overjoyed that Joel had found a partner in life. She had one last question for Carol about him.

"Is there anyone who thought they should be sous chef next summer instead of Joel?"

Carol shook her head no.

"Can you think of any reason someone would want Joel dead? Anyone whose toes he might have stepped on?"

"I don't. But if I do think of something, I'll let you know."

"Okay Carol, I'm so sorry for your loss." Dita paused a second, waiting for Carol to gain her composure. "Before I go, I have a few more questions related to Sonny's death. I'm writing an article about drugs on the island. No one seems to have had any idea Sonny was using. I wondered if you'd heard anything among your friends because some of them drank with him."

"Dita, none of them knew. They were as surprised as we are. I'd seen people looking kind of like they were nodding out in the summer, but they were temporary workers who left."

"Restaurant kitchen help?" Dita asked.

"Yes, and shop help, too. I believe if owners staffed their own stores, they'd have a lot less shoplifting loss. You could almost see some of the help nodding off when they weren't on their phones," Carol said.

"Maybe I'll check with some of the shopkeepers," Dita said.

Carol put her hands on her hips. "If I could point you somewhere I would, but I was shocked about Sonny. So was Dorie, and she was the one who spent the most time with him drinking out back of the pub."

"Do you think Dorie would talk to me about Sonny?" Dita asked.

"She might. I'll call her."

"And again, I'm sorry for your loss."

Carol dabbed her eyes and opened the door for Dita to leave. As Dita stepped through, a black and white cat zipped into the house.

"Orca," Carol chuckled. "A barn cat from the farm down the street. He adopted us. Joel named him."

Dita turned to ask her one more question, as to who was doing the work on her house. It was, Carol told her, Joel. He'd borrowed somebody's scaffolding.

"I guess I'll have to hire someone now."

"Maybe not," Dita said. "I'll see if Sean can do those few for you. It wouldn't take him long."

Dita left feeling even sadder about Joel's demise. His life was unfolding, a new leaf opening for him in his relationship with Carol and in his work life. There was no justification for him to kill himself; and why would someone want him dead? Maybe it was just an unfortunate accident, where Joel leaned overboard and fell in, and the boat got too far away for him to reach. But Sonny, he was more of a mystery.

As she was driving away, Dita pulled over to let another car by on the narrow road. It was Brenda. Dita wondered where she was going. Brenda looked over at her, startled, like Dita was the last person she expected to run into there. And it was true, Dita did not often come up this back road. But seeing Brenda gave Dita an idea. She would stop at the Washashore, not because she needed a drink, but because she wanted to hear what was brewing there, particularly since Brenda wouldn't be eavesdropping. Maybe Harry would speak freely without his helper hanging over him.

When she got there, a few of the regulars were around. It was slow, though in summer it would be crowded at what was universally celebrated as happy hour. One of the drinkers doing shots and whiskey at the bar was Whitey Cairns, an old fisherman who had often helped Joel gut his fish. He was a wiry guy with a wild beard and straggly white hair. He wore an old black sweater and faded jeans, a pair of holey sneakers on his feet. Dita noticed the shoes because she usually saw him at the dock with his fisherman's slickers and boots.

She took the stool next to him. She liked Whitey, who spoke real offshore New Englandese. It was a language with misplaced r's, sometimes dropped into the middle of a word instead of at the end where it belonged, or placed at the end when it didn't belong there. He said paster for pasta and lobsta for lobster. It had taken her a while after moving to Nor'easter Island to understand that language, but now she enjoyed listening to people who spoke it.

She ordered a shot of Tia Maria, her favorite coffee-flavored liquor, over ice, from Harry, who seemed to be working alone. She didn't see Loretta and she knew Brenda was elsewhere.

"What are you digging into these days, Dita?" Whitey asked.

"Sonny and Joel. It's hard to believe Joel suicided. Seems like things were going well for him. And it's hard to believe Sonny was using." Dita thought Whitey might know something more. Maybe he even saw Joel go out on what turned out to be his last trip.

"I feel the same way about Joel. I was down at the dock with him the week before he disappeared. That was the last time I saw him. He came in with a load of flat fish. Told me they were hangin' around the wind turbines. Seemed happy. Didn't say a thing about checking out of the world."

"Did he say anything about anyone who might have had a

grudge, acted angry at him?"

Whitey responded with gusto. "Been at least ten years since anything like that happened with Joel. He's been steady. Gottar say I'm gonnar miss him at the dock. Seems like too many people are disappearing before their time, Sonny, him."

Dita nodded and waited.

"Sonny's the last person I'd of expected to overdose. How'd he pay for the stuff? No one would just give it to him. He ran a tab here, and some days all the money he had was the change janglin' in his pants pocket. It don't make sense."

Sean had asked the same question. How did he pay for it? Not for the first time, Dita wondered if Sonny's and Joel's deaths could be related? But how?

"Were Joel and Sonny friends?" she asked.

Whitey ran his hand through his hair, downed another slug of beer. He said he thought the two were friendly, but maybe not friends.

"Sonny's best friend was whisky," Whitey said.

Karl Shultz took a stool next to Dita. She hadn't seen him arrive, but he'd noticed her. He was in full uniform, Sgt. Shultz today.

"What are you doing here alone, Mrs. Redmond?" he asked. He smiled, but it reminded Dita of a predator about to snap.

She thought that was a hostile way to say hello. Did she not have a right to hang for a while, just like Sean sometimes did, or for that matter Karl?

Whitey answered for her. "She's doing your job, Sarge. Trying to figure out why Joel would kill himself out there in the deep blue. And how Sonny got H."

Karl shot him a malicious stare. "Really. And what are you doing, Whitey, second guessing everything?"

Whitey finished his beer and his shot and got up to leave. "And just so you know, Sarge, I'm not drivin'." With that, he walked away.

"So, it's just us," Karl said, looking her up and down.

What was it about that guy that always made her feel skeevy when Sean wasn't around, like she was a rabbit he wanted to skin and hang on his duty belt?

"I might as well ask since you're here, Karl. We already talked about Sonny. But why would Joel have wanted to die? Do the police have any theories?"

"Come on Dita. You know the guy was crazy. Okay, he didn't act it lately, but he was really out there. Throwing himself off a boat, that's not so hard to imagine."

But it was hard for Dita. "Karl, you seem to have adopted some false beliefs about the mentally ill."

Dita being tall gave her an advantage that shorter women didn't have with men. She looked straight across, eye to eye, or down at most men. This discombobulated them in an argument. Looking down at women, they were accustomed to dominating. When Karl looked at Dita, he had to look up. She had an advantage, and could tell from his pursing mouth, he was annoyed.

She continued to argue. "They're not all suicidal, and sometimes they get better. You know, just like people with pneumonia or cancer, some of them improve."

She tried to smile.

"Huh!" he harumphed. "I look at everyone, calculate what they might do. Joel had a past. That counts. But okay, if he didn't suicide, then he fell overboard like a lot of other fishermen."

"Then why was there still gas in his motor?" she asked.

With that, she slid her credit card to Harry, signed her slip and stood up to leave. She'd catch Harry another time without Karl watching her, ready to start a rumor about her and the bartender. She figured he was the one who'd started the gossip about Addie and Harry, and she also knew he pressured Loretta to sleep with him, though he had a good-looking wife at home.

"Say hello to Sean for me. Tell him to take a turn down here,"

Karl said.

"For sure," she said, as sweetly as she could.

She attempted to maintain civility with Karl, in part because he was one of their policemen, in part because he was their neighbor. And, the largest part, because he was somewhat of a buddy to Sean. She needed to interview him more to find out what he was doing to unravel the drug ring, but not at a bar. It was too suggestive for him.

She hadn't learned much that day, except that people who knew Joel had no inkling he would kill himself. And no one thought Sonny had money for heroin. And she already knew both those facts before.

Chapter Eleven

The next morning, Dita called the police station. She recognized the dispatcher's voice. It was Felicity, who rotated shifts with two others. The chief was in, Felicity said, and she put Dita through. He told her to come on over that afternoon, right after lunch.

She began to prep for her session. She would let him talk first, then ask her questions. Things she wanted to know: how long had he been aware there were more than a few local users? Did he think they all bought separately over on the mainland, or was there a supplier on island? If so, did he have any idea who it was? What was he going to do about it? Did he have a plan? Had he known about Sonny? Did he suspect Harry?

Gomez might not know all the answers, but maybe he could at least point her in a direction. And, because she had promised Rachel to continue to investigate Joel's death, had anything new come up?

Five minutes before one, she made sure her pad and pen were in her bag. She put on her coat, and drove over to the police station, which was right next to the fire department. It was a small brick building, like the Washashore Pub, one of the few non-descript boxes on the island. But like many New England municipal buildings, it was deliberately plain to demonstrate the town officials' frugality with citizens' money. Dita stopped in the entrance hall at the dispatch window, as the door that led to the actual rooms of the department was locked. Felicity wheeled up in her office chair to hand her the clipboard with the sign-in sheet. She was a matronly, middle-aged woman with frizzy gray and brown hair. Not a looker, but she had a friendly smile. She took the clipboard back and buzzed the boss. Then she hit the button to open the door for Dita.

"Go on in. He's in his office," she said.

Dita knew the way. She went through the door and turned left. Ahead of her was a small office, a bit larger than a closet, with room for one or two persons to sit on the outer side of George Gomez's desk.

"Hey, George," she said, as she knew the chief fairly well and was on first name terms with him.

He stood. "Dita, how can I help you today?"

Unlike the stereotypes of police figures, he was a pleasant-looking man without a receding hairline, and his eyes wore laugh wrinkles. Even more unlike the stereotypes, he was trim, no beer belly. George was one of the island's skin divers, a spear fisherman, which was one of his motivations for retiring after his twenty years on the mainland and coming to lead the six-person island force. His low-key personality allowed him entrée into the community, where he was regarded as a friendly acquaintance rather than an authority figure.

"You want to talk about Sonny and narcotics on the island. I'll be frank with you. I've heard rumors that there are some; but until Sonny died, I couldn't substantiate them. Sure, I have a lineup in my head of who they might be, but no evidence. Not even whispered names."

"You never suspected Sonny was using, then?" Dita asked.

He shook his head. "Of all people, not him. What about Sean? He hired Sonny, helped him earn a few bucks now and then. Did Sean have any idea?"

"He says he didn't," Dita replied, gulping down her fears that maybe he did. "I was thinking of interviewing the other people in the boarding house. Have you interrogated them?"

"As far as I know, Sonny was the only one there the night he OD'd. The others come for a few days every couple of weeks. Those sailors out in the pond. They left a couple of days ago."

"I didn't know they stayed there," Dita said, thinking about the fact that Loretta knew them.

"And Harry?"

"Maybe," George said. "I've got my eye on him."

He leaned back in his chair, in that way men do, balancing on the back legs. "This is an island, Dita, and islands are notorious for drug trafficking. Are we an exception? I had hoped so, although a few years back, before I took over, the feds dug up the lots near your house looking for buried money. I think they suspected someone of being a pilot for a South American cartel."

"I heard that too" she agreed.

"There's a history of nefarious doings, just like any other island. People are still searching for pirate treasure from Captain Kidd," he said. "Seems to crop up every few years. Dita, be careful in your search. If there is a drug ring operating here, it could be dangerous to get too close. We're doing all we can to uncover it."

"I'm sure you are, but talking to an officer of the law is a lot different from talking to a news writer. Maybe I can find some leads," she said.

"Keep Karl in the loop, then. You'll need him in back of you to keep you from getting in too deep. I've got him hanging around the pub to see what's going on there."

Dita was not thrilled that Karl was the one who would be her protection, as she thought he was shallow and lacked energy for his job. Sending Karl to the pub on the job seemed like a mistake also. He drank too much to notice much. But she couldn't turn down any offer of support.

"Is there no other information you can give me? Or a direction you can point me?" Dita asked.

"Keep your ears open at the Washashore Pub. People clam up around me and Karl. Maybe you can eavesdrop where we can't." he folded his hands on his deck, signaling the interview was ending. "At any rate, be careful."

"Of course. Before I leave, I promised Rachel to ask if there's anything new on Joel."

The chief shook his head. "You need to give that up. There's nothing, and there never will be. I'm sorry, and I feel for Rachel, but I have no witnesses coming forward. We don't have the coroner's report, but we know what it will say."

She left with her next step clear. Find Karl.

When she got home, Sean and Karl were outside, lying on wooden dollies, their heads under Karl's car. It had moved from his yard to theirs despite being broken. Sean wheeled out when he heard her drive in. His face was streaked with grease.

Dita laughed. Karl pushed out too.

"You're just in time. We're done," Sean said. "I'll go in and clean up."

Dita sat down on the front steps and motioned to Karl to join her. "Can I talk to you about Sonny?" she asked.

Karl wiped his hands on a rag. "You can, but I don't know any more than you or Sean. He didn't seem like a user; you know what I mean."

"Who do you think supplied him?" Dita asked.

"I wish we knew," Karl replied. "We're investigating, but I've never known anything on this island to be as well-kept a secret as this. No one is saying anything. I might as well be listening to the wind. I've known for months that stuff was coming in, but not who or how. There are a couple of people I suspect, but I'm not sure."

"The way things get around here it's hard to believe that no one knows anything. The other morning at the news office, Jane knew I'd been to the Washashore with Addie the night before, and that Addie went into the kitchen with Harry. Neither of us told anyone."

Karl shrugged.

"What about Harry?" she asked.

"He's not talking about it to me," Karl said. "George is worried we'll have more OD's. He's on my butt to pick up something about this. If you hear anything, Dita, let me know right away. Whoever is selling could be dangerous."

As she'd expected, he was totally different when he wasn't out drinking at the Washashore. If she respected him more, she'd have thought that the drunken lout persona was an act, one he used to make people think he wasn't noticing what they were doing. But she didn't really believe this. He just drank too much.

Dita went into the house. If Karl knew anything, he wasn't about to tell her. Maybe she'd try Harry again. Mid-afternoon when business was slow was a good time to catch a conversation with him at the pub, and she knew Karl was hanging out with Sean so he wouldn't be there to butt in. She yelled out to Sean that she'd be back soon, and headed over to the Washashore. Harry was sitting on a stool at the bar reading a magazine on cars. He looked up when he heard her come in.

"Hey, Dita, what's up?" he asked, without standing.

She pulled a stool close to him. "I wanted to talk to you, Harry. Everyone is so shaken up about Sonny. I decided to do a little more on it for the paper. No one seems to have had any idea he was using. I know I asked you before; but Harry, did you have any suspicions that Sonny was on drugs?"

"I wish I had," he said, looking straight into Dita's eyes. "All the time he spent here, you'd think I'd know."

Indeed, Dita thought. Without mentioning Loretta's slip, she confronted Harry. "I heard a rumor that you know more about the people who use, and that maybe even you're dabbling in drugs."

She waited a moment. He did not respond. "I won't use your name, but is there any truth to that?"

Brenda suddenly appeared on the other side of the bar, and she leaned over between them. She was, unfortunately, back.

"Of course not," she bellowed in her raspy voice. "Dita, what the hell is wrong with you?"

"I was actually talking to Harry," Dita said, struggling not to sound angry.

"Well I'm here, too and you need to stop bugging Harry. He's sad enough," Brenda retorted, not trying to disguise her anger at all.

"I wasn't bugging him, just asking."

Brenda glared at her. "You can really be overbearing, you know, and I'm not the only one who says that. Keep it up and you won't have many friends."

Harry got up. "I need to get back to work in the kitchen," he said. Dita couldn't believe he was knuckling under to Brenda. "I don't know anyone who's using, Dita. And I certainly didn't know about Sonny. His bar bill was pretty hefty. I don't think he could have paid for drugs."

"How would Harry know?" Brenda asked.

Dita pushed back. "What about you? Did you know, Brenda? You saw him here all the time."

Brenda narrowed her eyes, turned her mouth down, and stomped away. She made herself busy polishing tables on the other side of the room and ignored Dita. Dita watched her, feeling uneasy. What did the woman know? Maybe Brenda was involved with Harry now. She'd ask Jane over at the paper. That was her bailiwick.

Harry returned just as Dita was about to leave. He motioned to her to wait. She sensed Brenda's eyes on her back, watching.

"You know our annual end-of-the-season bash got cancelled because Sonny died and then we had the memorial service and all. I was wondering what you'd think about my having it at Halloween instead. We need some cheering up around here, and I could use the cash."

Dita was surprised he'd asked her. She smiled at the thought of a party. "I think it would be fun."

"One reason I'm asking you is, is it too late to get something into the paper Friday?"

"I'll call Jane right now. You can talk to her."

"Thanks," he said.

While he used her phone, Dita walked over to Brenda. "Are you angry at me for something else, Brenda?" she asked.

Brenda shrugged. "Just didn't want you sticking your nose somewhere it didn't belong," she said. "Harry's plenty upset already. He put out a lot of money for Sonny's funeral, at your request, and he's pinched now."

"He's planning the Halloween thing. That should help," Dita said.

Brenda waved her polishing cloth. "Guess so."

So far, Dita's poking around was yielding nothing, except for anger. Maybe that's why she was assigned mundane meetings for articles. Her investigatory skills were not so sharp as she'd imagined.

Harry came over and handed her back her phone. "All set," he said. "Hope you guys come."

"But of course," she replied, and walked out the door and went home. In the next few days, she asked around the island and contacted Sonny's pals again, but no one would admit to any knowledge of local heroin use. It was only Loretta who'd let out a smidgeon about Harry, and that was before Sonny died. Now Loretta would only say she couldn't recall where she heard it. If she didn't know Loretta so well – they'd been friends since Dita and Sean came to work on the island – she'd think Loretta knew something about Sonny.

Addie would reveal nothing about anyone coming to the health center with problems. Confidential info, she'd say, so Dita knew it was fruitless to spend time asking her. Besides, Addie still wouldn't talk to her. And while attending an island support meeting for families of alcoholics and addicts might yield some information, Dita would be voted off the island if she reported on anything said there. In fact, if she went, everyone would clam up tighter than the quahogs in the Pond.

No, she was stymied for now. She'd write an article about the mystery of Sonny's drug use, and she'd just keep listening for a while, in case someone slipped around her, or came to her on their own. She'd almost forgotten, though, that her appointment with Trent was tomorrow.

As she left, she came face to face with Addie in the doorway. She tried to get around her, but Addie reached out and held her arms with both hands.

"I'm sorry Dita. I let my anger about Joel spill onto you. I don't want you investigating Joel's death, but I'm not going to stop you. And, I don't want to lose your friendship."

Dita squeezed back some tears. "Nor do I want to lose yours," she said.

Addie let go of Dita's arms, and the two hugged.

"I'm sorry too," Dita said. "You're my closest friend. I'll be careful not to upset Rachel."

"Please, do that. Forgive me for ranting at you."

"All right. Now tell me what you're doing here," Dita said.

"Meeting Mel soon."

"Talk to you?"

"Of course. Later."

Chapter Twelve

The breakfast crowd at the Books and Bakes Café emptied out around 10:30, and until the lunch crowd arrived around noon, there was a lull. Dita's interview with Trent was set for 10:45, during that lull.

Before she left the house, Sean cautioned her to tread lightly with Trent. "I know I can't stop you, but be careful. You don't want everyone on the island mad at you. He's already told you they didn't leave the Washashore together," he said.

She gave him a high five and drove off. It was an overcast day, not one on which she felt like walking the two miles to town. Only one car passed her going the other way on Founders Road. It was someone she'd never seen before, so she didn't give him the customary island wave.

Trent was waiting for her when she got to the cafe, sitting in a straight-backed chair at a square butcherblock table for four. All the tables in the Books and Bakes were salvaged from summer cottages when they changed owners, which created a variety of styles. She wouldn't have thought someone like Trent, in the arts world, would've chosen such a plain, modern style when there were polished Queen Annes and Biedermeiers available as well. And some with padded, comfortable chairs. Apparently, he wanted to make this a short, to the point, talk.

He was pouring himself a cup of tea from the painted ceramic teapot that Ellie had brought him as Dita crossed the café doorway. Steam rose from his china cup. The tea was too hot to drink, so he had begun to munch on a Books and Bakes homemade jelly doughnut. Dita thought the sugar mustache forming above his upper lip helped his looks. He was a lean man with stringy brown hair and a few notable pits in his cheeks, remnants of adolescent volcanic eruptions. But his clothes were impeccable, an oddity on Nor'easter Island, even for the upperclass summer cocktail crowd. A moss green suede shirt with a cravat, pressed khakis, real leather shoes. She wondered if he'd brought his own valet from New York. Surely, he didn't polish those loafers and iron those pants himself. She realized she was looking him up and down, giving him the once over quite openly, you might even say gawking, so she made an impromptu remark about his appearance as she greeted him.

"You are still quite New York, not into island mode yet Trent. I'm impressed," she said.

He smiled. "I'm leaving right from our interview today to catch the noon boat to the mainland. I need to spend a few days in New York. You're looking good today yourself."

"Really?" she asked, because she was wearing the same jeans and sweater she'd worn for the past two days.

"I find your name fascinating. Is it short for Edith? That's a very old -fashioned name, not common anymore," he said.

Dita realized he was interviewing her, maybe to get her side-tracked.

"It is an old family name. My favorite aunt was an Edith, and everyone called her Dita. She was a wonderful person, hard to live up to," she explained.

She needed to take control of the conversation to get on with her interview. "Can I snap some shots of you to go with the piece? Your clothes will look good in the newspaper. But maybe you ought to wipe the donut sugar off your lip first. Here," she said, reaching out with a napkin.

He leaned backwards to avoid her hand, but he took the napkin and wiped off the mustache. "Better?" He stood up.

She nodded and took a few shots of him in his finery. Then they both sat down again. Ellie brought Dita a cup of coffee, unrequested but welcome, and Dita thanked her. She didn't bring a doughnut though.

"So, Trent, where in New York is your shop?" she asked.

"Soho. And, it's not a shop. I sell fine art and upscale crafts. It's a gallery."

The man rubbed her the wrong way. The difference between an arts and crafts shop and a gallery was probably the amount of the rent. She checked her sarcasm and waited for him to continue.

"I sell selected artists' work as well as crafts that approach art, special pottery, jewelry, furniture. In fact, one of the artists on the Lorelei's wall has contracted with me to take some of her work to show. I like the rings Rachel carries in The Lorelei also, and next year when she has more made in India, I told her I'd buy some of those to sell in the gallery."

Hmmm, Dita thought. He considers Rachel's rings valuable.

"How did you start dealing in the arts?"

"I have an arts management degree. When I finished college there were few positions open in museums so I started working in one of the auction houses. That led to relationships with some of the artists and dealers in New York, and after several years I struck out on my own. I like to show unknown artists of promise."

He pulled his cell phone out and motioned for her to come around next to him so she could see the screen. She did, and he surfed through pictures of objects d'art in his shop. She didn't recognize any of the artists.

"Might we feature one or two along with the interview?" she asked.

"I'll text a couple to you if the artists agree."

"What brought you to Nor'easter Island in the fall season instead of the summer?" she asked. It was something they all, meaning her and her friends, had been wondering.

"As I said at the Lorelei when we met there, I am always searching for new artists. I wanted to come after the tourists left because everyone is too busy here to spend time with me in the summer. I've been talking with the painters and craftsmen, looking at their work, and I might choose a few more to show in my gallery. I even found a sculptor.

"Also, it's a nice time of year to relax and slow down, don't you think? I'm enjoying hanging around town and spending time in the house I rented. It overlooks the water and the west side."

He sipped his tea and pushed his plate away, then got personal. "It was quite a sad funeral yesterday, wasn't it?"

Dita was surprised. "Yes, but I didn't notice you there."

"I was in the back of the gathering at the cemetery. I saw you up front with the family. I only know Rachel through our business dealings, but she's a lovely person."

"She is," Dita agreed. "They all are. We're close friends."

"I didn't go to the reception. It was crowded when I got down the hill to the Beach Dune, so I went home instead. He was Rachel's only son, wasn't he?"

"Yes," Dita said. She was glad he had brought Joel into the conversation.

"I don't boat, so I can't imagine what happened out there on the water," he wrapped his hands around his cup.

Ooo-la-la, this was turning out to be better than she'd expected. Talking about Joel's death would have been awkward if she'd brought it up.

"You have a view of the ocean from the Bradley house, don't you?" she asked. The Bradley house was farther along the same street Carol lived on, right atop the cliff. "Can you see the fishing boats out near the wind turbines?"

"I have a beautiful view, and I often watch the boats from the kitchen window," he said. "I heard that Joel's was small? A blue outboard?"

"It was," she said. "Have you ever seen it?"

"I don't know. Perhaps, but I don't recall it from any other boat out there. They're too distant to tell one from the other, especially such a small one. What do you think happened to him?"

Dita realized she was the one being interviewed now. Trent had tried to turn their meeting around again. She thought that was odd and remembered Sean's warning.

"I don't know. He might have fallen overboard pulling in a line. There's a small chance it was suicide. And, he could have been pushed. It happens." She tried to be calm.

"Murder?" Trent asked, unwrapping his hands and raising his teacup for another sip.

She shrugged and said, "But that's been ruled out by the police, so..."

He lowered his voice to an almost confessional tone and reached out, covering her hand with his, which was cold despite his hot tea. "You still think so, I can tell."

Dita's pulse quickened. She pulled her hand from under his. "Not really. It's just one of the possibilities, but I think improbable. What do you think?"

"I take a darker view of the world, so I think it could have been," he said. He poured more tea into his cup from the pot.

"Maybe you saw or heard someone else when you left the Washashore the same time as Joel?" Dita asked. "Was someone waiting out there for him? Did he get into a car?"

"I'm afraid I don't know. We went different ways in the parking lot. I got into my car and didn't notice him again. Like I said before, I didn't even know who he was."

"Then you didn't pass him as you drove out."

"Perhaps, but I don't recall." He lifted his cup once more.

"Trent, you were the last known person to see him alive," Dita said, leaning toward him.

"And, so? We went out the door at the same time, but it was a coincidence. I'd never seen him before."

"I saw Joel fighting with someone out on the street near my house on his way to the Washashore. Did you see a fight in there that day?"

"The afternoon you say Joel was at the Pub, I was waiting for someone who never showed up, and it was quiet. I didn't speak with anyone, just the barmaid, what's her name, Barbara?"

"Brenda," she said. She wondered who he was waiting for, and was about to ask, but he pushed his chair back, and left a tip on the table.

"I enjoyed our talk, but I see the ferry coming in. It's time to go." He stood up and slid into his winter coat. As he did, his shirt pulled up at his wrists and Dita saw bands on both arms. She recognized them.

"Seasick remedies?"

"Yes, I find the ride nauseating," he replied. "I like the island enough that I might open a branch of my gallery here. If I do, I'll fly over. I could never get used to the boat ride."

"Try ginger beer. There's some for sale here and on the boat. It settles your stomach. Anyway, thanks for the interview. Have a good trip to New York."

She watched him leave and disappear down the side stairs to the harbor. Their conversation had unsettled her. Often after an interview she felt she knew something about the person, something was revealed. But with Trent, she felt held at a distance. He'd never said what he loved about the art he sold, what moved him in a painting. She hadn't asked directly, but usually that kind of information would be volunteered. It should have bubbled up when Trent spoke about the kind of art he carried, or when talking about how he got involved in his field. Or at least when he was showing her his slides of the artwork. That would have been the meat of the story, yet he hadn't offered it. Maybe she would get another chance to ask more, but she doubted she would get what she was looking for.

Since it was bordering on lunchtime, she lingered on in the café. She ordered food and browsed in the book corner, skipping the paperback classics and the more or less classic mysteries, moving to the new publications. She brought one to the table, an author she'd never read before, and thumbed through it while waiting for her quiche of the day and side salad. Suddenly Loretta was standing over her, peering over her shoulder.

"That looks good," Loretta said.

"Hello to you, too," Dita replied.

Loretta flopped into the chair Trent had vacated. She looked jaunty today, with a red silk scarf that covered half her face and a red beret. Perhaps this was island dress up day, but whoever declared it had forgotten to tell Dita.

"I just got in from the mainland on the ferry, in case you're wondering," Loretta said.

"That would explain your Sunday best scarf and hat."

"Talking about best clothes, I bumped into that Trent guy going to the boat when I was walking up here. Mr. Dapper himself."

"Right. Trent guy, really? Didn't he say you work for him? Remember that day at the Lorelei?"

Loretta shook her head no. "The Bradleys hired me to clean

while he stays there. They're worried he's a slob, and he is. They know him in New York. The Bradleys pay me, not him."

"Oh. What do you think of him?"

"Meh."

"Me too. Do you iron his clothes when you clean?"

"Of course not. That looks good," Loretta said, pointing to Dita's quiche. "I think I'll get one. You'll stay, won't you?"

"Of course. I want to know if you managed to catch up with Mankawicz yet. He seemed preoccupied at the gathering for Joel. Seen him since?"

Loretta shined a smile at Dita. "Oui, oui."

"Am I reading a French romance novel?" Dita asked.

Loretta laughed, "I was a big fan of those and that's why I can tell you I won't see him again. Bad girls never win. Now you have to tell me why Addie was so mad at you."

"Old news. She's forgiven me. Go order your food."

Loretta waited for counter service, which was slower than usual, as Ellie had gone out the back door for a smoke.

"Speaking of Addie," Loretta started to say, when she returned to the table.

"Were we?"

Loretta gave Dita a hard stare with her cocoa browns. "As I was saying, Addie seemed to be doing as well as could be expected with Joel's death."

"And you think expelling her fury on me was part of doing well?"

"Okay, maybe not so well. But I thought we could bring some meals up to Rachel for a few days. We should make sure she eats and it doesn't all fall on Addie."

"I have a meeting to cover later this evening, but I could cook up something when I go home now. Or even better, if Sean goes clamming and makes stuffies, we could bring some of those over."

"Stuffies? I'm coming. What time?"

"You'd better ask Sean."

"I will. By the way, what meeting are you covering?"

"The exhilarating, scintillating, planning and zoning commission."

Loretta rolled her eyes. "Maybe working shifts in the bar and housecleaning aren't such bad jobs after all. How do you stay awake?"

Dita was reluctant to tell the truth, that even some of the board members were unable to stay awake. There was one who rarely spoke. In fact, his eyes were often closed. But whenever something important came up, his eyes snapped open and he led the others to a decision. Dita didn't think he was the kind to use meditation techniques, at least not knowingly. She thought he fell into a semi-trance naturally. But she kept her eye on him so as not to miss important moments.

She did have her own secret for staying awake. She took a lot of notes. She wrote everything down and wrote constantly. Sometimes she couldn't even read her own script. But the act of recording it all on paper kept her half-awake and helped her remember what had transpired. She didn't want to tell Loretta the truth because everyone thought she was super attentive.

"Oh, Loretta, it's really tough sometimes, but I can always get more information with a phone call afterward," she said.

"I suppose," Loretta answered, between bites. "I left my car on the mainland for repairs. Can you drop me home?"

"Of course. And Mankawicz?"

"Just a couple drinks at the bar. He has other plans besides me, I guess," Loretta said.

They finished their lunches, paid up and left. Dita decided to take the book and added it to her bill.

"Can't wait 'til you're done with it," Loretta said. I'm next."

"Maybe you want it first," Dita said, handing it over to her. "I'm reading something else right now anyway."

They swooped across the empty town, past the white Victorian hotels with their inviting porches, past Bridgegate Square and the Washashore Pub.

"I was talking to Maria yesterday," Loretta said. Maria, Dita knew, was the owner of the Beach Dune. "She realized how nice it was to be in the Dune again on a fall day, even though it was for a funeral, and she's considering opening for a few days a week this winter, maybe Thursday through Sunday. She wants to have Thanksgiving dinner, you know, do a turkey dinner like the old owners did years ago."

"How nice that would be," Dita said. "Remember when we all went for that? Mashed potatoes with gravy, homemade cranberry sauce."

Loretta interrupted her, "Juicy turkey with the skin."

"What about the vegetarians? There's a lot of them here."

"She has dishes on the menu in summer, so I'm sure she'd have something," Loretta said. "I hope she decides to do it. I could use some more money waitressing. You could come on shifts with me, like the old days."

"I could. Should I call her?"

"Yes. She would have to order the food pronto. Thanksgiving's coming up."

By now they were almost in New Harbor, close to Loretta's apartment. She lived in a six-unit complex that had been designated affordable for islanders like her in low-paying jobs.

"Want to come in?" Loretta asked.

"Thanks, but I need to get home and cook something for Rachel. I haven't heard from Sean so I doubt he's doing the stuffies today."

"I just realized something. We don't have to bring anything over to Rachel today because she has all the leftovers from the funeral," Loretta said. "So don't go home and cook for her."

"In that case, I'll go home and take a nap," Dita said. "See you." And she drove off.

Chapter Thirteen

The Halloween bash at the Washashore pub was the party everyone thought they needed to get over the sudden loss of Sonny. Word had gotten out on social media. That, along with a harvest moon and sweater weather, drew a swarm of people over from the mainland making the island streets feel summerish. When Dita arrived at the pub with Sean at 9 the party was pulsing. She figured Harry was racking up the profits that would help get him through the winter. Brenda was at the door collecting the $10 cover charge. Chummy for a change, she told Dita there were few complaints about the price. Dita could see people clustered at the bar ordering drinks, others at the tables eating dinners. The place was Halloween festive.

"You guys went all out with the decorations," she deadpanned to Brenda, glancing around at the spider webs and corn cob clusters hanging on the walls, a perfect addition to the usual decrepit look of the place.

"My idea," Brenda replied.

She seemed too excited about the turnout to catch Dita's sarcasm. Dita paid the cover charges for herself and Sean, who had already disappeared into the crowd, and went in. She was wondering where Addie and Loretta were when Addie found her.

"We tried to call you to give you a ride, but you didn't answer," Addie said.

"We took a nap after work," Dita said. "Besides, it's so nice tonight, we walked here. What did you do with Danny?"

"He's trick or treating with his friends over on the west side. They go in packs there, and everyone sleeps over with friends. We'll get him in the morning."

"I like your costume," Dita said. Addie wore a fringed flapper dress she'd borrowed from the historical society.

"And I, yours," Addie said.

Dita laughed. She wore a boxy, white lab coat Addie dug up at the medical center, not a princess gown like many of the ladies. "Our husbands were even less creative."

Sean and Mel, not keen on dress-up, went as bikers, barely out of their everyday clothing in leather jackets, jeans, and boots with do-rags added to their heads. They were on the other side of the bar hanging around the pool table with a bunch of guys. There were a lot of faces Dita didn't recognize, and that didn't even include those covered by masks. She and Addie spent a few minutes trying to identify people. *The Island Gale* had sent Patty, their photographer, who was working her way around the room snapping photos. Trent was there in his moss green jacket. He'd come as a New Yorker, Dita quipped. Even Rachel was there, costumed in a South American embroidered dress she'd brought home from a buying trip. Harry and Brenda were working in skeleton tee-shirts. Loretta was working too, but in a witch's hat with a crocheted black scarf and pointy black boots, cracked and weathered, of course. A couple of the monied summer people had shown up, one of the doctors from New York and a woman who'd made it big in a television series. They huddled in a corner, both with coifed do's, their faces nipped and tucked, as tight as drumskins. Dita caught them surveying the scene, looking everyone over. They must not have found anyone to their liking as they disappeared shortly afterward.

Addie wandered off to join Mel, leaving Dita alone to wonder who among them was using or selling. This had become a habitual game with her, looking at someone and deciding which category they belonged to. But in reality, she had no way of knowing. *"And drats,"* she said to herself, *"no one came outfitted as a drug dealer,"* though she was pretty sure there were a couple of them there. Her investigation was stalled. She was about to drop into self-pity when she was interrupted by a pirate in a striped tee-shirt. By his round belly and deep voice, she recognized their friend Teddy, whom she thought had been wintering in Massachusetts.

"Ho, ho, ho, I'm here," he said, planting himself in front of her.

"Are you a pirate or Santa Claus?" she asked.

"Aargh. A pirate and I'm here to stay. Where's that husband of yours?"

"Somewhere," she said, waving her arm. "Pool table, maybe? And what do you mean, you're here to stay? Did you find buried treasure?"

"Of sorts. Someone bought my business. I'm leaving Massachusetts."

Dita must have shown her surprise because Teddy looked up at her and reached out to hug her with a smile on his face.

"I was approached by a large company that wanted my particular software, and they made an offer no one in their right mind would refuse," Teddy said. "Being in my right mind, I took it. So, I'm celebrating."

"Awesome!" Dita said.

He pointed to some summer people in the corner. "But don't treat me like I'm one of them," he said with a smile.

"I hope you never act like them."

He waggled his eyebrows. "Don't even think it," he protested. "I need to find Sean. Oh, I see him. I'll talk to you later, dear wench," and he made his way to Sean, across the room.

Dita knew their friend was a computer nerd genius, but still, she was surprised he would give up the company he'd built himself. And moreover, move over to the island. Maybe he hadn't been happy in his life on the mainland. His live-in girlfriend left a year ago, and he hadn't mentioned anyone new the last time they'd seen him. Teddy wasn't the most attractive of men, with his round belly and the mess of hair he couldn't be bothered to cut or comb, but he did have an engaging smile and a convincing line of malarky. Sean would be happy to have his buddy around more. They'd met at the town dump one summer day, and despite a fifteen-year age difference, built a friendship around their mutual love of motorcycles. Teddy's house here was one Sean checked in winter, but for free.

Mel popped out of the crowd and pulled Dita onto the dance floor. "Someone needs to start it off," he said, "and Addie's disappeared."

Dita hoped her friend wasn't in the kitchen with Harry again. This time Dita wouldn't believe Addie's excuses.

Several other couples joined in once they knew they wouldn't be out there alone with spectators judging their incompetent dancing. Then Sean stepped up with Addie. Dita felt her husband take her hand, and they switched partners with their friends. For a few moments, she and Sean moved as one. She surrendered to the music and let the moments with him draw her into a reverie. *Dancing makes one mindful*, she thought. Who needs Yoga?

"Did you see Teddy?" Sean asked, bringing her back into the room.

"I did."

They clutched and separated and twirled and dipped. As they heated up, she unbuttoned and opened her lab coat, which flapped to the rhythm like an unhinged window shade. She felt her heart beat against his when they clinched, and then, as though their unity offended the gods, her right foot landed smack on top of Sean's left toes.

"Ouch," he yelped, hopping on his good foot. "Time to take a break."

"I'm so sorry," Dita whispered, bemoaning the fact this always happened when they danced. Was it her clumsiness or Sean's?

"I'm boiling anyway," he said. "I need another beer."

He limped toward the bar favoring the right foot. The guys were stacked three deep there in animated conversation about last night's sports.

"I'm going to sit for a few minutes. I'm sweating," Dita said, even though he had already gone and couldn't hear her over the music and the shouting of the crowd. She looked around for an empty seat; there were none. The odor of beer and smell of sweat overlay the usual stale stench. She began to retch, and pushed her way through the crowded floor to get closer to the open, front door. While she caught her breath there, Loretta swept by. Dita grabbed her by her witch's scarf.

"Stop! Moment, please," she said.

"Okay, but I'm busy taking orders," Loretta said. "And don't strangle me. Did you notice Rachel flirting with your friend what's his name?"

"Teddy?"

"Yeah, him. Over there," she said, pointing. "Gotta' go." She slipped away to a customer gesturing to her.

Dita looked and indeed, Rachael was smiling at Teddy. Well, Dita thought, that was a good thing, Rachel cheering up a little. Addie gave Dita a nod from across the room and looked over at her mother. Dita nodded back.

Then the fight started. At least, she thought that's when it started. She didn't see what set it off. What she saw was a guy with a fright mask and a scarecrow with a straw hat arguing, pushing each other.

"*Just what we need*," Dita muttered to no one in particular. It reminded her of the last time she saw Joel, in the storm, passing on her street.

It was the fright guy who threw the first punch. It landed on the scarecrow's ear and the straw hat went flying. The fight went into overdrive, the two men grabbing and kicking and shouting, a violent version of the dancing she'd just done in that same spot.

"*Uh, oh,*" she thought, "*so much for the dance floor. Now it's a boxing ring.*" Though repulsed, she couldn't take her eyes off them. The fright guy was stockier and taller, yet the scarecrow stayed on his feet. Two more guys joined the fray, another tried to break it up, and then, as men seem to do, they came from everywhere; more piled on, arms and legs akimbo, total chaos. The scarecrow was knocked across the pool table scattering the balls; a group of ghouls upended chairs and cocktail tables.

"*Who thought this joint could look even worse?*" she asked herself.

Suddenly Loretta was standing next to her again. "Will you look at that?" she asked, clapping her hands and jumping up and down. "The guys can't resist jumping in."

"It's like a testosterone magnet," Dita said, looking around. "If I could spot Sean, I'd drag him home before he gets drawn in."

"I don't see him but this is getting really good. The scarecrow is out of his mind," Loretta said pointing to the man, who had leapt up from the pool table to rip a cluster of corn cobs from the wall.

"Who is he anyway? And the fright mask?" Dita asked. "I can't place either of them."

"I think they are the sailors who moor across the street from you in the Salt Pond," Loretta said.

"Oh, great. Neighbors," Dita said. "Or should I say it this way, great neighbors."

They watched as the scarecrow charged into his enemies, parrying with a cluster of cobs. Loretta cheered along with everyone watching.

"Do I have to hold you back?" Dita asked. As repulsed as she herself felt, Loretta was turned on.

"No, you don't. I have no testosterone."

Harry ran out of the kitchen carrying an air horn he sometimes sounded when customers left big tips. He galloped toward the fight, pushed at the knot of men while sounding the horn, herding them toward the back door and the parking lot. As they tumbled out, some on their kiesters, Karl appeared, in uniform. Dita could hear him groan.

"How that man hates to do his job," Dita said to Loretta.

"Yeah, he's looking around to see if any other police came so he can back off and watch," Loretta said. "No wonder he can't get a bead on your drug dealers."

"My drug dealers?" Dita asked, but Loretta's attention was on the melee again.

The off-islanders in the knot of opponents thought Karl was in costume and ignored his orders to disperse so he discharged his gun into the air to get their attention, then got caught up in the fracas, as often happens when someone tries to intervene in a fight. By the time the men exhausted themselves, slowed down by the wail of Chief Gomez's police siren, Karl had a black eye. The corn cob scarecrow was placed in the Chief's police car in handcuffs, and the bandit in the fright mask who'd begun the fight was being held by Dave, the new guy on the force. Dita couldn't find Sean. As the pile of drunken guys untangled more, to her dismay he crawled out of the pretzel along with Teddy and Mel.

"*Go figure,*" Dita said to herself, and she gave them all a look that said, You, too?

She thought she knew Sean, but maybe not so much. She was so angry she stomped away to the Ladies Room where Sean couldn't follow her; and where, she thought, better behavior prevailed. So it might seem, but when she entered a stall, lying on the floor in front of her was a bloody syringe, the first evidence she'd actually seen of drug use on the island. One part of her wanted to scream while the other, the reporter, thrilled to the fact that she'd finally found some evidence of opioid drug use to put in the paper.

With at least 60 women at the party, she had no way of knowing who dropped it there. An island woman or one of those visiting? She snapped a picture with her phone. She'd call Patty in if she was still out there for a better one.

Patty was gone, but she bumped into Addie. Dita could hardly get the words out to tell her, she was so excited. Addie was standing with her hands on her hips looking miffed about the fighting.

"Mmmhmm," she said, with a grimace when Dita told her. "Could've been someone from over there. Do you believe those guys? Where is Mel?" She scanned the room, her hand like a brim over her eyes.

Dita knew "over there" stood for mainland, someone who didn't live here, because Addie was more concerned with finding Mel right now. She could have told Addie there was a bomb in the bathroom and gotten the same response.

Dita was not going to be the messenger who told Addie that Mel had been in the fight and was brushing himself off. She let Harry know about the syringe instead. He threw up his hands. She also should have avoided being that messenger. Brenda was standing next to Harry. She mumbled, "I'll go," and rushed off toward the Ladies Room to clean up.

Dita waded through the crowd to Sean.

"Party's over," she said, straightening his torn shirt and hustling him to the doorway. "You know, just because you dressed up as a biker doesn't mean you have to act like one."

Addie was standing outside. "Coming with us?" she asked. "I have to get this one home to bandage him."

Mel stood next to her, a bloody gash on his cheek, tearing through his dimple. Was it Dita's imagination or was Addie's face as red as her hair? It was not her imagination. She thought the atmosphere in the car might be as fraught as the fight in the Washashore.

"Thanks, but we'll walk," she answered, linking her arm into Sean's and pulling him forward with her. They were on the street just in time to see Teddy start up his Kawasaki and zoom off.

"It'll be nice to have him around," Sean said.

"Yeah, maybe you guys can find more fights for entertainment."

"I was trying to break it up."

"Mmmhmmm."

"Anyway, those two guys were from somewhere over on the mainland," Sean declared. "That's how the trouble always starts. A bunch of guys come over to drink themselves into a decorticate state and then get into it. " He ran his hand through his hair, brushing it off his forehead, as though straightening it would neaten up his conversation with Dita.

Dita sighed. "Decorticate or deliriously drunk? And it's always the fault of those guys from somewhere else. Loretta thinks they're the sailors who moor out in the pond. That makes them our neighbors. Anyway, I hope Harry's take was good so he'll have some money left once he repairs the damage."

The moon had not yet set. Their bodies made giant shadows on the pavement as they walked. She was still as wound up as a Nor'easter, undecided as to whether to tear Sean apart or just rough him up.

"Let's go over to the beach," she said.

The moonlight beamed onto the water, forming a white lane that might have stretched all the way to Portugal. The sea shushed ashore in ripples. Dita tried to stop thinking about the fight. She was not as angry as Addie. No one had been seriously hurt. But that Sean had jumped in added to her doubts about his readiness to parent. Could he step up to be a competent father? Better not to bring it up with him right now. Move on.

"With the island's dinosaur Internet, I can't imagine Teddy'll bunk here permanently," she said.

"We'll see. You have to admit, Dita, though you're a little worked up about the fight, it was a great party, wasn't it? Exactly what the island needed."

And, just when she had forced herself to stop thinking about it, he'd reinforced her doubts about him.

She drew him close to her. "Really?"

She waited, letting her intent sink in. Then she asked, "And the bloody syringe I found on the floor of the ladies' room. Would you say that belonged to someone from over there, too or might we have a bit of a problem here?"

Chapter Fourteen

Dita's article on the Halloween party ran in the *Island Gale*, but it was Patty's photos of the brawlers that made the front page. What made her think it would be her picture of a bloody syringe that would get priority? Mary laughed when she suggested they run it there. She asked Dita how many papers she thought that would sell. Instead, Mary chose a photo of the knot of brawlers, and one of the sailors, hats and masks askew, being escorted into the police cruiser. They were blown up across the top fold, covering an entire half-page. Everyone would want to read about that. A crazy bar fight, oh yeah.

The two fighters turned out to be the sailors, as Loretta had said. When she brought a copy of the paper home, Dita looked out the window at their boat. She grimaced as she lay the newspaper out on the kitchen table in front of her to get a better look at their faces. She didn't think she recognized them from around the island. But she thought she recognized Sean's feet sticking out from the middle of the brawlers' pack in the photo. She tsked her tongue in disgust, scrunched the paper up into a tight-as-she-could-make ball and tossed it into the recycling bin. Not a Halloween she would want to remember. And, although the brawl would sell more papers, she thought the public emergence of drug problems among the winter community was more important, wasn't it? Maybe only to her. She started to text Mary with just that thought when an incoming text interrupted her.

It was from Addie, asking her to come right over to the house, ASAP. BRT, she replied, and she grabbed a jacket and sprinted out the door and down the street. She was there in minutes and let herself in. She found her friend in the living room.

Addie looks worn, Dita thought, noticing that her friend's eyes were puffy and her curls coiled out in random directions. She was leaning against an embroidered pillow on the couch with her feet up on the coffee table. If she was a smoker, Dita thought, she would have stretched an arm across the top of the couch, propped her wrist on it and dangled a lit cigarette between her fingers. There were times, like today, when Dita wished everyone still smoked, and she and Addie could send puffs of sadness into the air, together, as they talked. But they did not, and had no prop to keep their tears in check. Dita sank into a chair directly across from her.

"I asked you over because I need a favor," Addie said. "But, you can't tell anyone, not even Sean."

Dita imagined Addie exhaling another stream of smoke. The last time Addie asked her a favor was after Joel's funeral; and she wasn't asking then, she was demanding. She hoped this did not involve Harry.

"And Mel and Danny? Rachel? Are they in on the secret?"

"No. Definitely not. Don't tell them."

What was Addie about to say? Dita came prepared to listen to Addie grieve more about Joel. Now she wasn't sure what she'd been called to hear. Please, she wished silently, not Harry.

"This whole thing with Joel going missing, and then, you know...I must have missed some birth control pills," Addie's voice was flat, matter of fact, as though she was speaking about someone else's problem. She removed her feet from the coffee table and rested her elbows on her knees, clasped her hand around her face and stared into the room. Dita waited.

Then Addie looked right at her. "I'm pregnant. It's not a good time for it. Maybe six months ago it would have been, but not now."

Dita was surprised, but why the big secret?

"Okay, that's great, I think. Addie, you wanted another one," Dita said.

"Yes, I did, but Mel and I, we're not getting along. Halloween night clinched it for me, seeing him in that fight. I think I already mentioned to you that he might have someone on the mainland. It's not a good time."

Dita started to disagree and Addie cut her off, clenched her teeth, and said slowly with emphasis, "I-do-not-want-a-child-right-now."

She paused and reached out to clasp Dita's arm. "I'm not happy in my marriage, and a baby would complicate things even more. Dita, listen to me. Mel and I have grown apart. We lead separate lives when he is away, and that's starting to overlap into our time together."

There was a bag of potato chips on the kitchen counter. Dita could almost hear them calling her name. She got up and grabbed them and a bowl, and put them on the coffee table. When anxious, eat.

"Get the dip out of the fridge too, why don't you, and bring us each a bottle of beer," Addie said.

"So, what are you going to do?" Dita asked, once the beer tops were popped and they were crunching chips and dip. She had a feeling she knew what Addie would do, especially since she'd told Dita to pop some beers. She would do what countless other women do, what many of Dita's friends did when they messed up. She asked anyway. "Well?"

"I made an appointment at a Women's Center in Connecticut. I'm going to have an abortion. I want you to take me."

"What about the morning after pill? Did you try that?" Dita asked.

"Have you ever seen those in any store here? We have headache remedies and skin creams and sun block. And the health center has antibiotics. We don't carry the morning after pill because no one here would want anyone to see them buying it. There are no secrets here."

Almost no secrets, Dita thought. Except who's using lethal drugs and might be next to die.

"And," Addie said, "I couldn't get to the mainland to buy any."

"But Mel could have picked it up."

"Oh, right." She raised her voice into a falsetto. "'Mel, dear, would you pick me up some Plan B when you take the ferry home later?' I don't think so, Dita. We haven't talked about our problems yet, let alone separating. Besides, the pills to end a pregnancy are not exactly the same as the Plan B ones."

Dita felt sad. She didn't want Addie to terminate her pregnancy or her marriage.

"I have to ask. Are you sure?"

"I am, Dita. You probably think I should have the baby anyway. Lots of people are single parents these days; and, yes, I could probably manage two as I already have Danny, but that wouldn't be fair to Mel either. If I have this child, Mel will stay with us, but not because he wants to. We need to work through our problems. I don't want a loveless and resentful marriage partner."

"Okay, I get it. Of course, I will take you. It's your choice. But that doesn't mean I'm happy you feel you have to."

Dita went over to the couch and sat next to Addie. She put her arm around her. "We're in this together."

"Thank you. It's next week on Thursday and we have to stay overnight on Wednesday. I need an ultrasound the day before if they recommend a surgical procedure. We'll take the plane. Don't worry about the money. I'll pay your way. I left my car at the airport on the mainland last week."

"But wait. Couldn't you just get the abortion pill prescription from Dr. Bennett?"

"I could, but like I said, I don't want anyone to know. Yes, he would keep my privacy, but any of the staff could be around the corner when we talked, or could see my chart. It's too risky."

"That doesn't boost my confidence in the health center."

Addie shook her head; her curls bounced. "I'm not saying people break confidence there. But it does happen once in a while. And I don't want them knowing my business. I might get the pills at the clinic in Connecticut. I'll do whatever they advise. And if it's the pills, you'll be with me to help."

"What are we telling our families?" Dita asked. She knew they all would want to know why they were flying off and where they were headed.

"We'll tell them we're going to a boutique on the Connecticut shoreline. I have to find something to wear for the nursing convention this fall. I'm giving a talk on rural health care, so I want to look good. And we'll say we're having a girls' night out there, because we will."

"Okay, I guess."

"And, my dear Dita, we have time to browse the shops on Wednesday. I really do need something to wear. My island rags won't do."

Addie's phone buzzed. "Danny's on his way home."

Dita gave Addie an extra good bye squeeze. "If you're sure, I'm in. But let me know if you want to talk more about this."

With that, she was out the door. She knew she couldn't question Addie's decision more. After all, she herself was totally ambivalent about having a child. When she was honest with herself, she acknowledged that poverty with Sean wasn't the only thing holding her back. She didn't feel that abortion was wrong. Is it better to have a child who is resented through no fault of its own? Still, she felt so sad.

Addie and Mel were their closest friends. She hoped they didn't separate. It wasn't only their lives and Danny's that would change. It was Sean and Dita's, too. They spent so much weekend time together as couples. She'd noticed that when people separated, their friends' marriages grew shaky. It forced their own introspection. Would the cracks in her marriage emerge as they were faced with those of their friends? Would she decide Sean would never be adult enough to have children? Would he find her need to move forward and be settled unappealing?

Dita felt that her life was changing too fast. Joel's death and Sonny's, Sean's difficulty finding a real job, and now, Addie's marriage.

Addie was offered the pills. When it was over and they were in the airport waiting for their flight home, Addie asked Dita why she was so quiet. Dita admitted she was upset that Addie and Mel might separate and divorce. It was difficult for her.

"Will you ever tell Mel about the pregnancy?" she asked.

"Maybe," Addie said. "It depends on what happens. Maybe things will straighten out, and then I'll need to. Otherwise, no. And I know you want to tell Sean, but you cannot, ever. Please?"

"I won't," Dita said. "I just wish you two would figure out a way to stay together."

"So do I, but, come on, Dita, if Mel is in love with someone else, there's no path for us to take together. I can't live like that, with a man whose heart is yearning for another woman. I would lose my sense of self."

"I know. I just hope that's not real, this other love of Mel's."

"Me too."

Once they boarded the prop plane, there was too much noise for conversation. They both looked out the small side windows, and watched the water below them become an impressionist painting until the plane descended and houses on their island appeared.

Chapter Fifteen

Dita needed to concentrate on work. Her investigation into island narcotics would continue, but she only got paid when she wrote something that made it into print. Since money was tight she took some bread-and-butter assignments like covering board meetings. Sometimes important decisions were hammered out at them, especially during the planning and zoning meetings. At other times, not. Either way, Dita always needed to dredge up a story, preferably a long article one to give her a decent paycheck.

The last time that body met, she sat at her keyboard afterward thinking if only she could describe it from the curmudgeon within her. She could open her article with: *The meeting was interminably boring and almost put this reporter to sleep.*

The people talked on and on and on.... like Mr. C, who liked to hear himself pontificate. Members of the commission tapped their feet or their pencil erasers, or drooped their heads toward their papers and made believe they were writing something important. She could follow that up by describing her favorite presenter to the commission, Mrs. Z. *She thought she owned the whole island and didn't like to agree with anything anyone else did. She ranted about her poor, unsuspecting neighbors, whose new garage may or may not have been built one meter over the allowed footage.* Dita, who actually liked Mrs. Z when she bumped into her at the grocery store or on the street, thought maybe she just didn't have enough other things to do. Her life had dwindled down to the minutia around her, and if someone had explained to her how miserable she was making her neighbors feel, she might actually back off.

The craziest thing about it was, to Dita, the building rules were spelled out in simple English that anyone who graduated from grammar school could understand. There was even a checklist. Yet everyone seemed to want an exception to the rules. If Dita ran the town, she would either not allow exceptions, or she would do away with the rules completely. Then everyone could stay at home and watch their favorite TV show, or go down to the Washashore and have a few drinks. Because, Dita thought, these meetings were driving her to drink. But they were paying her gas bill.

And so tonight a grumbly Dita covered the evening planning and zoning meeting at the town hall: a typical village municipal building, a grey, wooden rectangle with a cupola-covered, white front door. Unlike the fire department and police station, the town hall strutted one architectural flourish, a large glass atrium. Since no one had figured out how to use the area under it, other than for its extra light, it became an empty expanse to walk through to get to doors and hallways that led to offices. It was like a roadway roundabout.

When Dita arrived, there were few cars parked in the lot. That meant it would be a short meeting. Good for going home, not so great for lots of words in the write-up. She went in and picked up an agenda. It had but two items. Tonight there would be no battles for control of the limited island land, just a couple of small matters. The Wisherts wanted to extend their deck; the Streights wanted to replace a porch and take another foot of land that, unfortunately for them, was in the wetland buffer. No decisions were reached. Both parties made their cases, which were weak on principle, but highly desired by them.

When they finished, Dita left the town hall and made her way to the parking lot. She stopped to take a deep breath of air. It was heavy with humidity. The sky was covered with thick clouds. The moon and the Milky Way were both obscured. Dita could barely locate her car in the fog, a dark gray cloud that had dropped down low and settled over the island.

She detoured to the Washashore on the way home for one drink to shake off the gloom from the interminable sparring of the meeting's litigants. There was no need to vent her dismay to Sean.

Harry was tending. It was a slow night and the pub was almost empty. He was already pushing a mop behind the bar and didn't seem to be in a chatty mood. She had the feeling he would close right after she walked out and maybe wished he had before she walked in. Still, she might be able to draw him out about Sonny. She sat on a stool and after he finished his corner, he called over, asking what she wanted. She ordered a Tia Maria, a favorite, as it tasted like the best and richest coffee in the world, only with alcohol. The liquor came in a pretty shot-sized glass, since the alcohol content was high. Was she drinking too much? Were all the issues on her mind causing her to need a quick drink to quiet her anxieties? She hadn't lied to herself that she stopped in to talk to Harry about her drug investigation. She knew tonight she wanted a drink.

Harry lingered a moment to ask if she'd seen Addie lately, and she shook her head no. In fact, Addie hadn't yet texted her back today. She wondered if he had heard from her. He was a nice enough looking guy, some would say handsome, with blondish hair, gray eyes, and a good chin. His arms were sleeved with tats, which bothered Dita. They melted into each other, creating the equivalent of a four-year old's scribbled drawings. Why have tats if no one could read them? But he had an easy demeanor and was usually ready to make small talk, if you wanted to, except tonight. She tried anyway.

"Harry, you saw Sonny more than most of us. Would you have thought he was doing heroin?"

Harry stared into her eyes with his grays. Well, they were red-rimmed grays, and she wondered briefly about that.

"I can't imagine him having the money for a habit. He did small jobs for me to work off his bar bill. Unless he was selling on the island, which I highly doubt, no, I wouldn't have thought he would die of an O.D. Maybe it was his first time shooting up. A lot of people snort now and then."

This was Dita's chance. "Anyone in particular?"

"Not really," he said as he started to back away, too quickly she thought.

She knew then that he did know. She wondered again about him asking for Addie. Was her friend really having a clandestine affair with him? She didn't think carrying on with him would be worth Addie ruining her already shaky relationship with Mel, however she knew well that these attractions had nothing to do with logical thinking.

She tried to draw him back, turning his question around. "Have you seen Addie?"

"Only for a minute. She stopped in to look for Mel. Boy, is she angry at you. I'd say you ought to give up on the murder angle." He raised one eyebrow, gave her a smile, and moved on with his mopping.

Dita was flummoxed. Addie had even spouted off to him. Anyway, he was wrong. They'd made up ages ago. That told her he hadn't seen Addie lately, or if he had, it was only for a minute. She drank her Tia quicker than she'd planned, and texted Sean that she was on her way. He texted her back to be wary of the deer on Founders Rd. Rutting season had begun. The males went crazy chasing does in heat, as brain dead as summer vacationers. Caught up in their mating frenzy, they bounded out from bushes and dunes, taking no heed of traffic.

Far from being woozy from the strong liquor, Dita was hyper-alert from its caffeine. She hopped into her Toy and turned it on, backed out of her space and off she went at a crawl, although she was looking forward to getting home to Sean. She wondered how he thought she could avoid hitting deer when she couldn't even see the road right in front of her in the fog. Still, she made sure to slow down even more when she heard the crunch of shells as she drove over the Gull's dining room, heeding Sean's caution. This was where the deer frolics often began.

She tried to keep watch on the sides of the road; and then, bin-go, she spotted a pair of eyes staring back at her. She could barely discern the shadowy outline of a deer poised to leap. It froze for a moment at the sound of her motor, as deer do when they are startled. Dita slammed on the brakes, and lurched to a stop. The animal could run past or turn around and retrace its path back up the dunes.

But her reaction was dead wrong, as Sean would later tell her, "You should have hit the gas to get past it." Nice to know. She sat there, waiting for the deer to make a decision, assuming there was more than one as there often was.

Great, she thought. *I'm in a stand-off with a deer. A horny deer.*
It decided on a direction, and leapt out, slamming into her front fender with a dull thud. So much for waiting. The karma of the universe was not in sync with Dita's wishes.

"Noooo!" she shouted. "I stopped to save you."
Now it was Dita who was frozen in place. The deer dislodged

itself and disappeared into the darkness, not unlike the birds that flew head first into the window glass in the fall, crashing and reeling, then disappearing. She always felt guilty about the birds, and now, the deer. It seemed to her that humans hurt other beings just by engaging in their daily acts of living. Much as she yearned to continue on home, she knew she needed to try to find out what had happened to the creature.

She pulled the car over to the side of the road, facing it inward so she could see the shapes of the dunes, and jumped out, leaving the motor running with the lights on. There were dents and blood and tufts of fur in her fender, but no deer within sight of the beam from the headlamps. She wondered whether it was badly injured. If it was bleeding profusely, she needed to call the police station. Whoever was on duty would come and put it out of its misery. If it was mostly stunned though would she be able to locate it in the dark?

With shaking hands, she turned on her phone light and pointed it down toward the sandy verge to search for the small indents from its hooves. She found them. A badly hurt animal would not get very far. The trail led up into the dunes. She followed the trail, thought about calling for help, and decided it was better not to wake anyone else up unless she could locate the animal. That probably wouldn't happen, what with such poor visibility in the night fog.

At the top of the dune, not seeing a carcass or a wounded animal within her cellphone beam, she decided to turn back. It probably was just stunned and scraped, like her car. She wouldn't find it in the dark. She could call it in in the morning.

Suddenly she heard something that sounded like a gun going off not far from her. There was no hunting at night; she knew that. Was someone jack-lighting? It could be why that deer was fleeing toward the road in the first place. Perhaps she'd been hasty judging their mating instincts. Then there was another shot, and a buzz right by her ear. She broke into a cold sweat. She'd never been so frightened in her life. She had almost gotten hit. Was someone mistaking her for a deer? Surely no one would be aiming at her. How could anyone even see her?

"Stop, I'm not a deer!" she shouted, as loud as she could; and then the sand in front of her sprayed up. Another shot. Someone was shooting at her. Her chest contracted. She thought she might be having a heart attack. She felt faint, light-headed and unsteady. She clenched her fists and willed herself not to fall; if someone was after her, they would get her then for sure. This was not jack-lighting for deer. She turned off the light in her phone.

"Think fast. They know you want to get back to the car. Keep going through the dunes, leave the car where it is, run home, run home, run home." By the second time she'd thought 'run home', she was running, heading down into the valley between the lines of tall dunes. The soft sand slowed her escape, and she twisted her ankles more than once. *"Better without shoes,"* she thought, as she pulled one off with the toe of the other, then bent to free the second one.

She sped up, leaving the sneakers behind. She ran toward her house in the low dips where she often sheltered from the wind on long walks and, where the herds of deer sometimes slept. Another shot rang out, but towards the path to the car, not where she'd gone. Now she knew they couldn't see her in the fog.

"They're just guessing," she thought with a momentary drop in anxiety. *"They're going the other way, but, that could change."*

She pushed harder, faster. She was glad she'd had the caffeinated liquor. It was giving her energy she wouldn't have had. There was no need for a light to find her way through the dunes. She lived straight through, now less than a five-minute run if she could maintain her pace. She'd never been one of those exercisers who pushed and pushed to stretch her limits. She'd always been satisfied to pace herself to get exercise but not win races. She just hoped she didn't run right into a rock, twist her ankle and fall.

She didn't think there was anything but small ones out there, only large enough for a bit of a stumble. Though she'd never cultivated her speed, her long legs and fitness helped her. She knew she could outlast most of the out-of-shape men on the island. Dita hoped her pursuer was one of them, not one of those local tri-athletes.

She chanted a mantra under her breath to keep herself going. "I don't want to die, I don't want to die, ommm, I don't want to die." More bullets, but toward the car again, not her. The hunter still thought she was trying to reach the road. Should she go down one of the trails to the beach where the sand was harder and she could go faster? Her feet were cold, going barefoot at night in November was not a delight. And, then she stubbed her toe and tripped, turning her ankle as she fell. This time her stumble was not due to her deep thoughts, but to the zero visibility and the unexpected charred remains of a party campfire.

"Ouch!" she forgot not to make a sound. It just bellowed out on its own. Now whoever was following would know she was still in the dunes. A shot rang out toward her. It let her know someone was coming. She didn't know what to do, which way to go, toward the beach, toward the road or straight? But she wasn't going anywhere lying on the ground. She put her arm out to push herself up and felt something soft and wet. She ran her hand over it and realized it was a deer, maybe even her deer. No time for grief. She needed to get out of here.

Run, she ordered herself, and she did, straight ahead again, the shortest route home. The pause had helped her regain more wind and she used it, speeding faster than before, even with a lame ankle. Her feet touched down silently. There was no sound now, except for the soft shuss of the low tide sweeping onto the beach below.

She'd never been shot at before, hunted like the deer. She realized how frightened they must be while they were chased. Did their hearts pound through their chests like hers? Islanders used to wonder aloud how the deer knew during hunting season to gather in conservation grounds, where there was no hunting allowed. Now Dita knew. Those deer sensed what was at stake. She wished she had a safe conservation area like they did.

Could she call Sean? Reach him without being heard? She couldn't risk it. Her path ended near the house, but she'd head straight through without hitting the beach and come out just below the parking lot. She hoped whoever was chasing would not go along the beach and beat her. Or worse yet, drive the car, her car, to her house to kill her. She was thoroughly winded now. She had to stop a second to take a deep breath and hope for a third wind. She ran again. Suddenly there it was, the beach path with her backyard path beyond it, and the lights of the house. Rosa rugosa prickers tore at her clothes. She didn't hear any more shots. She zoomed up the three back deck steps to slide into her house, and locked the door, shouting for Sean.

"Wake up! Someone is trying to kill me."

She found him and shook him awake. He'd fallen asleep in his chair watching the Thursday night football game, as usual. Sports, the male sleeping pill.

"Wake up! Get up! Get your gun. They're chasing me. They may come here!"

Dita was shaking. Now that she was home and not running, her fear overcame her. Maybe this was the first time she'd ever been glad Sean kept a gun. She knew it was just a guy thing to do with him, part of the veneer of machismo even nice guys wore. But now she needed him to get it.

"Okay, I'm up," Sean said, slowly unfolding to a standing position. "What are you talking about? Calm down." He reached out to hug her, but she jumped back.

"We don't have time. Someone shot at me. Get your gun."

He hadn't noticed her hand, covered with blood from the deer. Now he did.

"Did they hit you?"

"No," she said, looking down, "this is from a deer. Sean, hurry."

She stepped to the kitchen sink and washed her hands as he headed through the living room to the basement door and disappeared down the stairs, shouting to her to call the police. The gun case was installed in a hidden corner of the cellar, behind the hot water heater. Dita's heart was beating at a furious pace, like a metronome gone mad, as she heard him moving around downstairs. She breathed again when she heard him return up the staircase, his pace seeming like a shuffle to her.

"Did you make the call?" he asked.

She shook her head. He picked up the phone and dialed 911. Then he drew her to him.

"You're shaking," he said, rubbing the sleep out of his eyes. "Let's have coffee so I can see straight if I have to shoot someone. There's some leftover in the pot. And tell me what happened after that meeting."

He sounded calm. How could he be? Did he realize someone tried to kill her? He sounded like he was speaking and moving in slow motion. Maybe that was her fear doing that. She started to tell him her story, but around the part where the second shot was fired, she was interrupted by knocking on the front door. Sean went to open it.

"Don't go!" she shouted. Her hands shook harder, her coffee lapped over the edge of her cup.

"Relax, I've got this," Sean said.

She looked at him and thought, *"Really? Apparently, he thinks I am delusional."*

Dita turned away from him. The knocking began again, this time on the slider. "Sean! They're out here now."

He turned around, gun aimed and cocked, and flipped on the light. Then, he pointed the weapon toward the floor. "Dita, relax. It's just Karl. He sure got here fast."

"*Quite a feat for Karl,*" Dita thought.

Karl was in uniform. Sean slipped the slider open for him. He wasted no time letting them know why he was there.

"Evening. I see you're both here. Dita, that's good. I was concerned because I saw your car down Founders toward town." Apparently he hadn't received the dispatch from the police station yet. "It was still running and no one was in it. Everything okay?"

He looked at Dita. "Whoa, what's on the back of your hand?"

Dita hobbled as quick as she could to the sink and flipped on the faucet again. She'd missed a spot.

"Deer blood!" she shouted.

She grabbed the soap dispenser and foamed her hand under the running water.

"Everything's not okay. If it was, my car wouldn't have been there running without me, right?" Dita replied answering his question.

"I feel like Lady Macbeth right now," she said, still scrubbing, though this time the blood was gone.

"What happened out there?" Karl asked.

Dita went through a short version of her story again, but Sean cut her off.

"Before we get into this, I think we ought to pick the car up, Karl. It might run out of gas," Sean said.

"No need," he said. "I called it in and picked up Dave at his house. He lives around the corner from there. He was due on shift anyway. I drove the car here for you and he got the patrol car." Karl sat down on one of the wooden kitchen chairs. He took off his jacket and hung it over the back. Dita dedueced he had decided to stay a while.

He refused the coffee Sean tried to hand him. "No thanks, I'm off duty now. Do you have a beer?"

Off-duty? What about searching for her hunter?

Sean got one for him, but stuck with coffee himself. Dita gestured no to both with her wet hand. She repeated her story from the beginning when she left the meeting. She felt like she was floating above herself as she repeated the sequence of events.

"What kind of gun was it?" Karl wanted to know.

Dita was getting tired. "What kind? The kind that kills you, I guess. I don't know, I didn't see it."

To her, the sound of a gun was a gun, not a rifle or a shotgun or a pistol or an Uzzi. She didn't identify cars on the road either. They were silver or black, big or small, sports cars, sedans or trucks or SUV's. She didn't care beyond that. Ask her what kind of bag someone had, she'd take a guess. Ask her if a painting was a Picasso or a Monet, if a dancer was Baryshnikov or Nureyev, that she knew. And she knew a Hemingway, or an Isabel Allende. But no, the sounds of guns were just, gunshots. In that respect, she was a poor reporter. On this island, she hadn't needed to identify guns. Until now.

Finally she answered. "Maybe a rifle? Karl shouldn't you be out there finding whoever it was that shot at me?"

Karl leaned back in his chair and asked, "You sure it wasn't someone setting off fireworks down on the beach?"

"If it was, why'd they aim them at me? And who sets off fireworks in a damp fog? They don't ignite."

"Or maybe a car backfiring?" Karl added.

"There were no other cars," Dita said, her voice lowering with irritation.

"Did you see anyone?" Karl asked. "Recognize anyone?" He tapped the toe of his boot on the floor as he questioned her.

She realized she'd seen him do this before, maybe when he was talking to Sean at the pub, or at a town meeting. Was he afraid to go out and look for the killer? Because she would have died out there if she'd been hit. Or was that how he thought things through, with his toe in motion? Dita pasted a smile on her face. She had to be civil, and she pulled herself together to ask him her most important question.

"Did you see anyone out there, Karl? Anyone driving away?"

"No. Yours was the only car on the road. You said that too."

Just then, they heard a truck drive up from the beach through the parking lot. Dita jumped.

"Someone left the beach," she almost shouted.

"Let's go after them, Karl. I've got my gun. C'mon, we'll use my truck." Sean was halfway out the door.

"Sean, wait, there are always people parked on the beach. That doesn't mean they shot at Dita." Karl stayed in his chair. "Dave's out there, near the pavilion anyway. We don't need to go. He'll stop them."

Dita looked out at the street. The truck had turned away from town.

"It went the other way, Karl."

"I'll call Dave."

"I'll go after them," Sean said, while Karl was talking into his phone.

Dita knew by the time Dave drove up that way, they would be long gone, turned down a driveway or a side road. She was glad Sean was going to follow them. Sometimes Dita thought Karl got paid for nothing. She heard Sean gun his engine and take off down the road.

Karl must have felt embarassed, because now he tried to turn detective in his own plodding, defensive way. "Are you working on a new story, Dita getting some other people angry?"

But who had she gotten angry about Joel besides Addie? "I wasn't aware I made anyone angry. I wrapped up interviews with people who might have seen Joel in the days before his body was found. I don't know why any of them would be mad. Although, by the way, I still don't believe he killed himself. I knew Joel pretty well and he was not unhappy."

They ran out of things to talk about. Dita sulked in silence, Karl asked for another beer while they waited for Sean to return. When he did, Dita was disappointed. He'd followed the truck to a development with a warren of small roads and lost it.

"Probably pulled into one of the cottage driveways, Sean," Karl said. He tilted his chair back toward the wall and looked at Sean. "She does realize Joel was a mental patient, doesn't she? Suicide is not out of the question."

Sean didn't respond. He looked at Dita instead.

"What is that supposed to mean?" Dita asked. "Yes, he had a few psychotic episodes. But it was a long time ago. He's been better than some of the so-called normal people on this island who drink themselves to death every day. I'm sure you know a few of them." Now Dita was angrier.

Again, Karl looked at Sean instead of her.

"I wonder who she might mean?" Karl asked.

Sean shrugged. He was peeved at Karl for not going after the truck with him.

Karl took a swig of his beer and set it down on the table. "All right then. Just sayin'. The voices could've kicked in again. Maybe he stopped taking his meds. Stop digging at it Dita. You'll get yourself killed. Anyway, I've got to get on home. We'll search for the shells tomorrow," and after taking a last swig on his beer bottle, he put it back down on the table and stood.

"Make sure you loop us in if you think you have something," Karl said. "What happened tonight might be just a warning."

Dita felt prickles rise on her arms and legs.

"All the more reason for you to have chased that vehicle down. By the way, you'll find a dead deer out there in the dunes," she said. "And my shoes are out there too. Would you bring them back when you do your search tomorrow?"

"I'll get those," Sean said. "In fact, I'll meet you in the morning for the search, Karl."

Karl headed for the door. "Dave will be patrolling around your house until dawn," he said. "We'll go early, Sean, but we'll probably be out there for hours. Catch up with us when you're ready."

Dita took the empty beer bottle and threw it into the recycling can.

"Oops, we let him walk home. Hope no one shoots at him; or do I?" she muttered. She sighed and looked at Sean. "I find it odd that he wouldn't go after the truck that pulled up from the beach. I would think he'd have wanted to at least question them, look inside and see if they had a rifle in there. I know he's lazy, but come on."

She continued to grumble, "Joel was a good guy, a real human being. I'm going to miss him. I hate hearing people reduce him to something he had no wish to have. I'm tired of needing to defend him. It's like blaming someone for having arthritis or kidney disease."

"I know. I liked Joel too, and I'm not as big a fan of Karl. He can be pig headed sometimes."

"Sean, he didn't seem overly concerned about someone shooting at me."

"Well, I'm concerned. Who knew you were on your way home? Who was at the meeting and the pub?"

"Almost no one. The five commission members were at the meeting, the two presenters and their lawyers. Even Mrs. Z and the commission's lawyer were missing. And only Harry was in the bar. At least, I didn't see anyone else. Come to think of it, I did hear someone, maybe Brenda, rattling dishes in the kitchen."

"It also could have been someone else who knew you were covering the meeting and was out there waiting for you to go home. A lot of the hunters especially know where the deer bed down for the night. Stir them up, and then odds are you have a crash in the fog."

The small herd that lived in the dunes roamed from the beach pavilion to the yard behind Dita and Sean's, like they did before that house was built. Sometimes they continued through to Karl's house to get a drink from the frog pond in his yard. Occasionally they slept under the neighbor's satellite dish out back, but their usual bedding spot was in the dunes near the pavilion.

"It wouldn't be too hard to rustle them up if you wanted to stampede them," Sean said. "When Karl finds the shells, we'll know what they used to shoot at you. That should help ID them. Most of us know what guns people have here."

Dita's eyes were closing as Sean spoke. He placed his hand on her shoulder.

"We're both tired. Let's go to bed," he said, and he picked up his gun and took it with him.

"My ankle is sore," Dita said, as she hobbled through the house. "And by the way, don't shoot me by mistake."

"Don't worry. Sometimes I am an asshole, but not that big an asshole," he said, laughing. Then he added, "If I shoot you, it will be on purpose," and he grabbed her with his free arm, pulling her to him for a kiss.

"Don't even joke about that."

Chapter Sixteen

By morning, Dita's ankle was swollen and throbbing. Sean looked at the size of it and declared it needed immediate medical attention. They skipped breakfast and drove to the island's small health center, another gray, wooden New England style cottage with two examining rooms, adequate enough to serve the year-round population, but overwhelmed by tourists during the high season.

Dita leaned on Sean and hopped from the car to the waiting room, where she sat on one of the worn, slipcovered chairs while he went to the desk. It was Addie who came to greet them, as the assistant was not yet due in. Dita thought her friend looked quite professional in her flowered smock and white pants and shoes. Even her usually unruly hair was tamed under an old-fashioned white nurse's cap, one of those that looked like an upsidedown paper cupcake container. Hardly any nurses wore them anymore, but Addie felt it helped her maintain her role with her friends and neighbors.

She motioned to Sean to help Dita into an examining room and up onto the table.

"How did that happen?" Addie asked.

"Long story. I'll tell you later."

"Let's take a look at it," Addie said, running her hands over Dita's leg. "I don't think anything is broken, but Dr. Bennet will probably want an x-ray. I'll be right back."

Addie stuck her head in the doc's office and returned. "X-ray it is." She helped Dita off the table, and hobbled her to the machine. The Center had just purchased a digital one, which made everything faster and easier.

"The doctor will be with you in a minute," she said, bringing Dita back into the exam room, this time seating her in a chair. She took the seat next to her.

"How are you?" Dita asked her friend.

"I'm fine, Dita. Moving on. Here's Dr. Bennet."

He didn't look like mainland doctors. His white doctor's coat hung open over a gray tee shirt and stone-washed blue jeans. A wide black belt with a brass buckle secured them around his trim waist. A thick shock of salt and pepper hair fell rakishly over his forehead, and a bushy mustache grew above his cupid's bow. He could have been a model for aftershave ads. His demeanor had none of the formalities of doctoring.

Dr. Bennet acted like an old friend, though he and Dita had hardly ever met. When he examined her, he ran his hands over her lower leg, just as Addie had. This time, though, Dita enjoyed it. "Not broken, Dita. Addie's right. It's just a minor sprain. Keep it up and iced, and it will be fine in a few days."

He made his pronouncement and was gone. Dita wondered if the rumors about him and the young island mothers were true. If so, Addie wasn't spilling. Addie called Sean in, he took Dita's arm and guided her back to the car.

"Let's get you home," he said. "I want to get to the dunes before Karl finishes the search without me. He said he'd be there early and it's nearly nine now. I should be with him when he finds the shells or the deer."

Dita was glad he was going. She told him not to forget to find her sneakers. He said he wouldn't, then he got more serious.

"You're going to have to be more careful. I know you think you haven't gotten any useful information, but maybe you ought to go through your notes again, think about who you've questioned. You got under someone's skin. Someone thinks you know something or they wouldn't have gone after you. You're lucky it was so foggy last night or you might be lying out there in the dunes instead of nursing a sprained ankle."

When they got home, he brewed a second pot of coffee and left her stretched out on the couch with a pillow under her ankle and an ice pack on top of it. He even brought her cell to her when it binged with a text.

"It's Addie," he said, handing it over.

Dita read the message. "She's on her way here. It's a slow morning at the medical center."

"Good. You'll have company while I'm out. I'll be back when we're done. By the way, this afternoon I'm meeting with Mankawicz to ask for financial backing. I called him yesterday."

She gave him a thumbs up and he left. She was glad there might be good news, because otherwise, she might just lie there on the couch feeling sorry for herself.

Addie arrived within minutes with a bag of pastries from Books and Bakes.

"Yoohoo," she called, letting herself in.

"Yoohoo, too. I'm right here."

"I brought croissants. Is there any coffee in the pot?"

"Yes."

Addie poured coffee for both of them, and set Dita's on the side table next to the couch. She pulled up a chair and set her coffee and pastry on the table with Dita's. She took off her cap and carefully placed it on the coffee table in front of the couch.

"Make yourself at home," Dita said.

"Okay, already did. Let's talk."

"Let's eat instead."

"Very funny. And by the way, your leg isn't raised enough," Addie said, positioning another pillow under Dita's ankle.

"You promised the long story; so, how did that happen?" Addie asked, pointing at Dita's swollen ankle when she was finished arranging it properly.

Dita told her, from the Washashore Pub to the dunes and home. Addie listened without interrupting, most unusual for her.

"Sean is out there now with Karl searching for bullet casings or shells or whatever they leave behind, my shoes, and the dead deer," Dita said.

"Oh, how horrible," Addie said. "You are so lucky it was a foggy night, or you might have been hit."

"Right. Sean already told me that. I don't need to hear it again. Tell me, why was I hunted like an animal?" Dita asked.

"Are you working on an article about crimes?"

Dita cleared her throat. "I was, but peer pressure forced me to stop."

At first, Addie looked confused, but then Dita saw her friend's eyes spark and she knew Addie'd gotten it.

"Ohhh," Addie said lengthening the word. "You think this is about Joel."

Dita nodded.

"But...." Addie said. "But it can't be, can it? I thought you were looking into the drug trafficking."

Again, Dita nodded. "Both."

"No, this has to be some mistake. Joel had nothing to do with that."

Dita told Addie why she suspected foul play in the first place. "The day I saw Joel walking to the Washashore Pub in the gale, he wouldn't have gone fishing in his outboard. And he was fighting with someone. Since seeing the fight on Halloween, I'm thinking it may have been that scarecrow. I caught a glimpse when his mask was down.

"Addie, if Joel did suicide, he'd have washed up sooner. If the storm got him, he probably would have lost control of his boat closer to shore. You see why I say murder?"

Addie stood up and began to pace. She was silent, though, listening.

"Then there's Sonny's overdose. The man who hardly had a nickel in his pocket supporting a habit? By the way, while you're pacing around, let Tuffy in, would you?"

Addie went to the door and called him. He bounded over to Dita and tried to jump onto the couch with her. The pillows went flopping to the floor. Addie shooed him away and restacked them.

"What do the police say about last night?" she asked.

Dita frowned. "So far nothing. I'm waiting for them to finish searching the scene. Then I hope to talk with George. I'm tired of Karl. He thinks I made someone angry. Duh. He has a bias against Joel having done anything but jumping off his boat in a state of deep despair. No one will even talk about Sonny, except to say he didn't have money to support a heroin habit. Well then, why did he die as though he had a heroin habit?"

"Please leave the investigating to the police, Dita. If what you think is true, that someone is responsible for Joel's death, and Sonny's, you'll be in more danger if you keep pursuing this."

Addie took a sip of her coffee. "You could have died last night."

"Yes," Dita agreed.

"I was so mad at you after Joel's funeral, I almost could have done it myself. I still want you to stop looking into these deaths, but not because of my mother or me. It's because I care about you and don't want you to get hurt."

"I appreciate your concern. I also have concerns. How are you feeling? No after effects from those pills?"

Addie flushed. Redheads couldn't hide their feelings.

"I'm fine. No physical problems. A bit wistful, you know, thinking what could have been, but I still feel it was the right decision. Mel and I, we're kind of bumping hips when we pass each other, know what I mean? We're not in sync, and our efforts to connect just don't work. it's kind of a relief for me when he leaves now. Honestly, Dita, I can't see my way through this. I just have to hang in and wait for him to decide what he wants to do,"

To Dita, it sounded as though Mel and Addie had talked about their problems. "So, you've discussed this."

Addie shook her head. Dita rolled her eyes. "No? Maybe you're imagining all of this, a girlfriend, Mel wanting out...maybe it's you, now don't get mad, feeling attracted to Harry and denying it to yourself."

"I wish," Addie said. "And I'm not that attracted to Harry."

Dita smiled at her. "Are you sure?"

"I am. Now let's just drop the subject. Getting back to your problems, don't get mad, Dita, but I really don't know why anyone would want to kill either Joel or Sonny. They didn't bother anybody, or pry. I know more about the people on this island than either of them, or for that matter, than you."

"Right. Addie, who do you think might have done it?"

"You are kidding, aren't you?"

"Nope."

Dita brushed the croissant crumbs off her sweater and Tuffy ran over to eat them. She was glad she had him to distract her. She couldn't imagine who had shot at her, or killed Joel or Sonny, and she was serious when she asked Addie to think of someone.

"Offhand, no one comes to mind." Addie reached out and put her hand on Dita's. "You need to be careful. Why wasn't your door locked when I arrived?"

She went to the front door, then to the slider, and locked them both. Odd as it seems, it hadn't occurred to Dita to ask Sean to lock the door when he left, they were both so used to living without fear on Nor'easter Island. The only time recently she had locked the door was when they'd left Danny alone in the house.

Addie had more to say. "I know you can't stop yourself from snooping around about this, even though you almost got killed. Please, don't let my mother know, and whatever you do, don't let Danny find out you've been shot at. He's distressed enough about Joel."

Dita would never do anything to hurt Danny. She loved him like family.

"Of course not," she said. "But you know this island. Even the kids will be talking about it. We might have to tell him."

"I hope not."

Addie thought she should get back to work, but Dita wanted her to stay until Sean returned from the search through the dunes, so they played a friendly game of Scrabble while they waited. They were often an even match, but today Dita was distracted, and Addie beat her with a seven-letter word at the end of the game. "Drats!" Dita said. "How do you do that?"

Addie grinned.

Soon they heard Sean tromp up the deck steps and take off his boots, shaking the sand off against the railing. Then he tried to get into the house. He banged on the slider.

"I'm locked out!"

Addie let him in. "I told your wife the door should be locked since someone tried to shoot her last night."

"I guess I should have thought of that," Sean said. "Dita, you'll never guess what killed your deer."

169

"My deer? Just a few weeks ago, Loretta referred to the drug ring as mine. I refused to take ownership. But if I guess in this case, given that the deer died, that would be on me. My deer."

"No, you didn't kill him. He bled a bit on his shoulder where he bashed into your car, but there was a bullet in him. We, Karl and I, think he was hit by one of the shots fired at you. Or, maybe someone really was out hunting, although they couldn't have picked a worse night." He dangled her sneakers in front of her. "Found them."

Dita was relieved she hadn't been responsible for killing the deer, but she was not reassured about her safety.

"Did you find any shell casings?"

"Mmmhmm. They used a 30-gauge caliber rifle. Karl dug the bullet out of the deer and took all the other casings we found up there to the station. He's going to check to see who owns one of those, though he's pretty sure from hunting with the guys that there are a bunch of them around the island. Even I have one. There's a gun dealer on the island who probably has a few of them. It has about a 150-foot range, but you can use a scope with it."

"A gun dealer?" Addie asked."

"Yeah."

"Just what the island needs," Addie replied. "I don't trust Karl. Maybe you should call George and tell him what you found."

"Don't have to. He was out there searching with us. It's not easy to find shell casings in the sand unless they come from a shotgun. While we were there, I told him your story, Dita," Sean said. "Now he has to figure out who did the shooting."

He began to pace, hands in his front pockets, elbows sticking out.

"Sean, sit down," Dita said.

But he continued, back and forth, from the back of the kitchen to the end of the living room, and over again.

"You're making me nervous, Sean," Addie said. "Sit down please."

"I can't. Now that I've seen the bullet casings, and the hole in the deer, I'm really frightened for Dita."

Addie folded him into her arms. "I don't hug you much, but you know Mel and I are there for you both. We'll keep pushing the police to figure this out."

"I'm home now and I'm safe, and I'm ready for a nap," Dita said. "Addie, you beat me up in that game, and now Sean's wearing me out with his worrying. Why don't you go clamming or something, dear? Have you looked out the window? It's sunny, the wind isn't blowing and the tide is almost low. Do you hear the clams? I do. They're calling Sean, Sean, come dig us, we're waiting for you. Except, what about Mankawicz? Weren't you meeting with him?"

"I think I hear them, too," Sean said. "He cancelled."

"Oh," she said, almost in a sigh.

"He has to think about it. That's code for screw you, you're not getting my money, island trash." He shrugged. "Maybe I will go if you're taking a nap, Dita. Clamming helps me think. I need to dig deep into who could have shot at you last night. I know all the guys here in the winter, even on construction crews. And, I know who has guns, and what kinds of guns. Some quiet out in the water might help me raise up a name for you. And, also to figure out another possible funder for me. If I get enough clams, I'll make stuffies later."

Addie opened the door, took a breath of air and turned around. "You're right. The clams are shouting. I hear them too. I need to get back to work. We'll come round later, me and Danny and Mel to keep you company with your clams." With that, she left.

"I guess I'd better get a full bucket," he said.

"Sean, get me a glass of wine before you leave," Dita said.

"Already? I'll only be a little while, and we can have some drinks when I get back," he gestured toward the window. "Look, Karl just went by. You have his cell number if you need him."

"That doesn't comfort me at all," she said. "Lock all the doors, even the basement. And bring me that wine."

"Okay," he agreed reluctantly, and he locked the two doors, and brought her a small glass of red wine. Then he trooped down the cellar stairs to get his wetsuit, hood, gloves and booties, because even though it was sunny, it was cold. He left from below, wearing the suit, and waved goodbye to Dita. She wished she could go too. She loved to clam, but in summer when she could go barefoot and in a bathing suit. She liked to dunk underwater to take a breather from raking, and to search for scallops. They were the undersea beauty queens, with their tiny blue-topaz eyes set like jewels at the point of each pleat on the shell. She almost couldn't bring herself to eat them. Almost.

And then there were the clams. Though not as gorgeous as the scallops, but even they were pretty when their shells were closed. There was a symmetry to the rings, and their dun color was pleasing, as was their smooth, cool feel when they lay in her palm.

She heard Sean grab his clam rake from the hook on the outdoor shower wall and then his floating pail, one he'd made by securing a flotation ring around its bottom. She watched him hop into the truck and head across the street to the beach on Sailor's Pond. Though it was a short walk from the house, in a wetsuit it was a gawky trek, so he drove. Dita kept an on eye him from the window, Tuffy stood next to the couch watching with her. She could see Sean pulling on his boots, his hood, and his gloves. Then he carried his bucket and rake to the end of the boardwalk, across the short beach and into the water. He looked like he would tip over with each step. But when he waded in, he looked more like a great blue heron. He was tall, and lean, almost willowy as he swept his feet through the water. He followed the shore as it curved and led into the pond until he reached the point. Then he turned. She could not follow him any further, but she knew exactly where he was going. He was headed to his favorite clamming beds on the other side of the point, ones that were closed all summer so the tourists wouldn't deplete them and reopened in the fall and winter for the year-rounders.

Before she turned away, she noticed the black sloop was back, moored on the other side of the pond near the public boat ramp. It was about a 40-footer, not an extravagant boat, an older wooden sailer. Sleepy as she felt, she leaned over to look through the telescope, and searched the decks. No one was about. She drank her wine, and drifted off into a nap.

It couldn't have been more than a half hour before Loretta cranked into the yard, her injured muffler announcing her arrival, waking Dita up. She had hoped Rachel might drop in on her way to or from town, but she wasn't aware Loretta would be in the neighborhood. Yet, there she was in the front yard, climbing out of her relic of a car. Dita wondered how she even got that wreck started anymore. Today it didn't shut off when she turned the key. Instead, it belted out a couple of coughs and shuddered to a stop. Hadn't Loretta told her she'd been on the mainland to get car repairs that day they had lunch at the Books and Bakes? It didn't sound like a mechanic had turned a wrench under that hood in eons.

Loretta stepped out of the relic like it was a stretch limo and she was Elizabeth Taylor going to the Oscars. She carried a bowl in front of her. She climbed Dita's steps and tried to open the door without knocking like she usually did. Dita heard her shout with surprise. She yelled back for Loretta to wait a minute and hobbled to the door to let her in.

"I'm sorry I got you up, but your door was locked!" Loretta said. Today, she looked her old island self, definitely not like Elizabeth Taylor, with a tattered sweater and her ripped leggings, and for a scarf, an old woolen one Dita thought maybe she had knitted five years ago. She made a mental note to remind herself to knit that new blue one for her friend.

"I heard Sean was going clamming so I brought you a salad from the grocery store," she said as she swooped in. She put her bowl on the coffee table and leaned in to give Dita a hug.

Dita was astonished. How Loretta had heard that? No one but Addie knew Sean was clamming.

"Loretta Crandall, how do you know that?"

"I saw Addie at the grocery store on her way back to work," Loretta explained with a crooked smile. "And I also heard you twisted your ankle."

Loretta took a breath. She moved back, away from the couch, looking at Dita. Unlike her car, she came to a full stop, cocked her head to the side, and seemed to be waiting for a signal from Dita. But Dita didn't play, so Loretta blurted out, "Addie said someone shot at you."

"Yes, ergo the door was locked."

Loretta rushed back to Dita's side and sat in the same chair Addie had. "You need to be careful. There are some bad things going on. I overhear things at the pub."

"Like what?" Dita asked.

Loretta did not answer.

"Might you have overheard someone brag that they planned to take pot shots at me?"

Loretta hung her head. "No."

"Well then. What bad things have you heard? Maybe something about heroin?"

Loretta bolted up and went to the kitchen. "Should I put the salad in the fridge? I think I should."

Dita knew Loretta and knew she was avoiding the question. Her admission that she heard things at the pub was a slip.

Loretta found a spot for the salad. "I can't say. Just, watch out. Dita, I think you should stick to writing up town meetings and doing fun interviews. Forget stalking the heroin ring and finding a murderer for Joel. Stay out of the way. I'm worried about you. This snooping can only bring trouble."

"I already know that from last night," Dita retorted. "You need to help me with this."

"I don't know enough for sure, so I can't say. I'm sorry."

Dita was exasperated with Loretta. Now she was warning Dita off. She must know more than she was letting on. Maybe she would slip again, but pushing her was not going to work.

"It might be time for Sean to wade back to shore," Dita said.

Even in his wet suit, he couldn't stay out there too long in the cold. She glanced out the window and there he was, working his way back around the point, floating his bucket in front of him. She sure hoped it was full given all the people who were coming to eat. She watched him wade back to shore and climb into his truck.

"Here comes dinner," she said.

"You're so lucky," Loretta said. "And he cooks them, too."

"Mmm, he makes the best stuffies."

"That's why I'm here," Loretta chuckled. "Well, and to see how you are of course."

"Of course," Dita agreed, but how come she didn't feel convinced?

Chapter Seventeen

After they had stuffed themselves with the stuffies and everyone had left, Sean and Dita acknowledged what they both knew, that there was no backing for their fitness center. They were commiserating, hoping Sean could work for the town, when his phone rang. It was Teddy, who said he wanted to stop by in the morning. Sean invited him for breakfast.

He arrived earlier than expected. Dita was feeding Tuffy, limping about in her favorite cotton bathrobe, pilled with age of course, and her skating penguins flannel pajamas. She heard Teddy's motorcycle engine coming up the road, a low grumble, not the ear-splitting grind of Harleys or the high whine of the small Japanese bikes.

He looked very un-Teddyish today. He was wearing a maroon hunter's jacket that one catalogue company might have labelled "weekend wear," with a Nor'easter Island brimmed cap, worn jeans and expensive sneakers. His usual island wear was a black motorcycle jacket with worn sneakers or boots and a tee shirt.

"Don't you look spiffy," Dita said, pulling out a frying pan and getting some bacon and eggs out of the fridge.

He looked her up and down, chuckled and remarked. "I guess I can't say the same for you. The ankle bandage makes the outfit, though I do like those penguins."

"We overslept," she said.

"What happened to your ankle?"

Just then, Sean came down the stairs and gave his pal a slap on the back. Dita was relieved she didn't have to explain yet again.

"You selling another company today?" Sean asked.

"Actually, I'm buying. I'm closing on the Double Ender Inn today."

Dita nearly dropped the tongs she was using to turn the bacon. Named after the type of boat islanders once built, The Double Ender Inn was the premier hotel on the island. Set on a grassy hillside, the grounds had long, breathtaking views of the ocean rivalling those of the cemetery. The buildings had 120 guest rooms, a formal restaurant, a casual breakfast bar with tables, the best porch on the island, adjacent cottages, and parking. The owners were casual acquaintances of Dita and Sean.

"I had no idea they were going to sell," she said. "Did you, Sean?"

He shook his head.

"I don't want it public yet," Teddy said. "Please don't put anything in the paper."

Dita murmured her requisite of course not. No one ever wanted her to report what they did in the paper. She continued to cook while the guys carried on their conversation.

"I'll tell you more after you tell me what happened to Dita," Teddy said.

Sean related the story, including the search for the bullets. Dita could almost feel Teddy's eyes on her back.

"Holy moly. Dita, you must have been terrified," he said. "I wouldn't step out of the house if that happened to me."

"Obviously, it would be even more difficult for me to do that without Sean to help, as I hobble around like this."

"Of course," Teddy said. "You think it's because you're looking into drugs on the island? I read your article on it and saw that picture from the Halloween Party, the hypo."

Dita shrugged. "Probably. Maybe because I still push the theory that Joel was murdered."

"But the police don't agree with Dita," Sean said.

Teddy shook his head and said, "I know. As far as the drug problem goes, I've walked in on a few people snorting, now and then in the men's room at the Washashore. No one ever seemed too concerned. In fact, they offered to share with me."

"Who was it?" Dita and Sean both asked.

"Summer workers. Doug someone, Gray Carter, Barry Dolton. They worked at the Dish-out Grille. I never saw any islanders, at least none I knew. It must have gotten way out of hand if they've resorted to shooting a reporter."

When the bacon crisped, Dita took it out and drained it on paper towels. She cleaned the grease from the pan, poured the eggs in and dropped bread into the toaster. Then she popped the question.

"How much money did you get for your company, anyway?"

"A f'n lot! I needed to invest some. I'm going to hire someone to run the place. I don't want to do it. "

Dita could read Sean's face. She could see his disappointment that he hadn't known Teddy might be a source of funding before he spent a large chunk on the hotel.

Teddy was astute. He wasted no time. "Sean, I know you want to start a fitness center. I could find space for one in the hotel."

Dita's heart sped up. She stopped buttering the toast.

"A full-service gym would be good for my hotel business. I could hire you as a manager, or you could lease from me. Both are options. Let's figure out the finances for both."

Sean brightened. He looked happier than Dita had seen in ages.

"My preference would be to lease the space," Sean said, "but I don't have the money. I would also need to lease the equipment. Greg's machines got spread around the island when he closed."

"I heard Greg's sports car was repossessed."

"The Mazarotti," Sean said.

They both laughed. Greg was not a popular person on the island. He ran the former gym like it was Russia and he was Stalin. Dita and Sean had been suspended for turning the heat up to 65 on a subzero day.

Dita put the breakfast on the table, fetched some plates for the three of them, and threw a piece of bacon to Tuffy. Then she took a seat with the two men.

"Good bacon," Teddy said. "Hard to find. Did you get this at the Moonstone Farm?"

Dita nodded. He and Sean discussed the business alternatives. Dita got up and poured orange juice into small glasses and brought them over.

Teddy set his reading glasses on the table. "I think this would work out better if I hired you to manage the fitness center with the option to buy the business and lease the space after two years. We could get it up and running, see how it works out. Once it's going for a while, you'll know what's what."

That sounded good to Sean, but Teddy had one codicil. "I know you've done exercise training. I've seen you do it at Greg's. What I don't know is whether you can manage a business. I don't want to do the day-to-day on it, or the books or repairs. I'm developing a new computer algorithm and I want to spend my time on that."

Dita hoped he wouldn't ask if Sean had an MBA.

Instead he asked, "Do you ever go to that gym near the ferry, Sean? I think I've seen you there once or twice, the one that's open all night, the 24/7 place?"

Sean nodded.

"I was in there the other day. They're looking for a part-time manager a day or two a week. Why don't you apply? Learn the ropes. It's going to take months before our space is ready. I can talk to Doug, the owner. I know him because I stop in whenever I'm coming here."

Sean rubbed his chin. Dita wondered if his next step would be to grow a beard so he had something more substantial to rub.

"I'll go over there and apply," he said. "Teddy, I'd be forever grateful if we could pull this off. I was at a standstill with it, thinking of talking to the town manager about a road crew job."

"I'll be glad to have the gym with a standup guy to bring people into my business. And I'll get to hang out with my good friend, too. This is a win-win for both of us, if you feel up to the management part."

He stood up and reached out to shake Sean's hand.

"Guys, I 've got to get over to the Double Ender. Going through with my architect and contractor to reconfigure some of the space. I'll include a gym. I was thinking about a spa too, but now I might drop that and give the space to Sean to use. Thanks for the breakfast. We'll talk soon."

He gave Dita a hug.

"And, please, don't start thinking of me like that jerk Mankawicz or those other jerk bankers. I'm still me, just your old friend Teddy."

"You're not going to join the summer cocktail circuit with the upper classes?" Dita asked.

Teddy gave her a look.

"I'll know if you start combing your hair," she said.

He touched his hair and pushed it back. "Why, do I need to?"

"Not," Sean said.

Tuffy followed Teddy to the door. He stopped, turned back and directed a request to Dita.

"Before I leave, I have a favor to ask you too."

Uh oh, Dita thought, here it comes. *What does he really want from us?*

"You're friends with Rachel, right?" he asked.

Dita nodded. She held her breath.

"How about having me over to dinner some night and inviting her too? I'd like to get to know her better, but with the Lorelei closed for the winter, I have no opportunity to bump into her. She doesn't go to the Washashore, except for that one time at the Halloween party."

"Sure," Dita exhaled, relieved that's all he wanted. "I'd be happy to."

And, recalling the Halloween party when she'd seen them flirting, she really was happy to have them both over.

"I'll call her and set it up for this week."

Dita and Sean watched him cycle off, and then they let loose. Sean grabbed Dita and twirled her around. They both woo-hooed at the top of their lungs. It seemed they weren't going to have to move after all.

"And honey, I won't have to be married to a cop. I hear it ages wives. Besides, I am not equipped to care for uniforms," Dita said.

"Not to worry. George withdrew his offer this morning. Told me it would be inopportune given the open investigation," Sean said.

Dita was surprised. "Hmmm. I didn't shoot at anyone. Why are we being punished?"

"Great as this deal sounds, it's not a good time for me to leave you alone on the island. What if the 24/7 wants me to work hours that don't match up with the ferry runs? You did almost get shot last night, and who knows, they might try again."

"Until George catches this person I would either have to go

with you, or maybe I could stay with Loretta, Rachel, or Addie."

"We can't wait for the police to figure this out. You can't go alone anywhere on this island until whoever was out there shooting at you is caught. You need to use your sources at the paper and I need to spend a little time at the Washashore with the guys to hear some gossip about it. We have to solve this."

Far from acting as an obstacle at this point, he was going to help. Dita couldn't believe it. This was already turning out to be a better day than yesterday.

"I'll hang at the Books and Bakes. That's safe."

"Dita, be low key with your investigating, please. Actually, let's go to both places together. At the Washashore, though, don't sit at the bar with me. Find someone at a table or play pool."

"I'll get Loretta or Addie. You must have forgotten. I can't stand on one leg and play pool."

"Oh, yeah, duh," he said. "Get Loretta. Don't bring Joel's family."

"Right. Loretta and I will likely draw others to our table."

Sean thought for a moment, stroking his chin a few times again. Dita caught him doing it. She wondered if this newly acquired tic arose from his anxiety about her.

"You thinking of growing a beard?" she asked.

"No, why."

"Just wondering," she lied.

"I'll try to be like you and not ask questions like I'm grilling people," he told her. "Somebody's bound to bring you up. If not, I can just say something like, 'Fine thing this island's coming to when hunters shoot at people instead of deer.' That's likely to get the guys' ire up. They'll defend the hunters and maybe drop some names."

"And," Dita said, "you'll let them go on and maybe ask how they know that or who do they think it was then? I'll do the same."

Sean nodded. "Let's hit the Books and Bakes for lunch. See if some people come in. I can stop in the post office while we're waiting for our orders to come up, see who's got gossip there."

"Me too, I want to go to the post office too. I can hobble in."

Nor'easter Island did not have home mail delivery. Residents needed to pick up their mail at the post office, either at general delivery or by applying for a numbered box.

"It's a plan," Dita said. "Let's go."

Sean looked at her. "Not only is it too early, I'd say you aren't ready."

Dita looked down at herself. "Guess a robe and pj's won't make it even on this island," she said, and she disappeared, limping up the staircase.

"Take your time. No rush. We just ate."

They decided to go to the post office first, together as Dita wanted. She hopped in holding on to Sean's arm. A few islanders waited in line to mail packages. Sean and Dita skirted around them to the section with postal boxes, and took their mail from theirs. Having to go to the post office for your mail could be a bother, especially in summer when all the streets in town were clogged with traffic, but it did have some advantages. It was one of the few places to run into other people in winter, and there was a long table with a big trash bin next to it where everyone thumbed through their letters and immediately recycled their unwelcome advertising circulars.

While they were sorting and discarding, DeDe Schultz came in the side door. "Heard about last night, Dita. Who would've done that?" she asked.

Dita shrugged. "Who told you about it?"

"Damien. He stopped by to talk with Ed this morning. Said he was at the firehouse and heard it on the scanner. Then he was in early this morning for something and heard Chief Gomez."

"What did the chief say?" Sean asked.

"Not too much. Just Gomez is furious about it. Thinks Karl and that new guy Dave should have picked someone up that night."

"So do I," Dita said.

"Well, I'm glad you're okay, Dita," DeDe went on to the package line.

"Something doesn't feel right about Karl, does it?" Sean asked.

"No. I said he should've chased that car coming off the beach right away, even if he took our car to do it," Dita said.

"He's a lazy s-o-b. I think he didn't want me on the police force because I work too hard. Sometimes I think he has a real drinking problem," Sean just about growled.

"Hmm, you think?"

Sean laughed. "Okay, he does. Ready to hobble down to the café?"

They went out the side door and made their way to the Books and Bakes. Dita looked out toward the harbor.

"Is the dolphin still there?" she asked.

Neither of them could spot it, but even without it, the water was beautiful today. The sun sparkled on a surface so flat it looked like you could skate on it. Commercial fishing boats floated way out beyond the harbor, trawling for catch with their arms down, looking spectral in the distance.

"Almost looks warm out there," Dita said.

"I can tell you from clamming yesterday that it is not."

The Books and Bakes was unusually full today. Looking around, Dita noticed there were a few tables with summer people. Then she realized it was a school holiday on the mainland. The island would be busier than usual. She heard someone call her. It was her editor, sitting with the paper's co-publishers, her bosses Lawrence and Candice.

"Join us. Sean, too."

They had already heard what had happened to her, but they hadn't been aware of her sprain. As they got settled, Dita noticed people turning to look at her. The summer people leaned in and whispered to each other. She'd met some of them, doing stories, but today they chose to talk about her rather than to her. Her bosses looked at her leg.

"I tripped over a charred bonfire log that either was left over from a campfire up there or floated up from the beach in a storm," Dita explained. "Not as bad as a bullet wound, right?"

Sean went to the counter to order their lunches. Dita wanted a tuna sandwich and he chose ham and cheese. They made small talk at the table until he returned. One of the summer people, Thelma Goodwin, strolled over. Perhaps she'd been chosen to represent the others. Thelma was an older woman with a smooth face that shouted cosmetic treatments. Her veined neck and hands, however, gave away her age. She wore loose capris, almost a uniform among that crowd, and wedgies. Lawrence greeted her with his usual bonhomie, and answered for Dita when Thelma asked how she was. He supplied just enough information so that she backed off. When Sean returned, Lawrence cleared his throat, then announced to the table that the newspaper wanted to help discover who was responsible for ambushing her.

"We're offering a reward," Lawrence said. "We discussed it with George Gomez. Anyone who provides information that leads to an arrest and conviction will receive a $500 reward from the paper. The information can be relayed to George, or in confidentiality to us by phone, email, or a letter to either me or Candice. It will not be seen by anyone else except you, though we'll pass the information along to George.

"I'll announce it in an editorial on the front page. A threat against one of our reporters who's working on a story is not to be taken lightly."

Dita was pleased that the paper would stand up for her like that. It was a generous offer. On the island, a $500 reward in the slow season would pay some bills or buy needed groceries. And she thought someone would be more likely to pass the information on to Lawrence or Candice than the police.

"Thanks to you both," she said, standing on her good leg and reaching out to hug them both.

"Careful, there," Sean warned, reaching out to steady her.

"Let's hope it helps," Lawrence said. "We'll get it into the on-line edition right away."

"I wish I had gotten a look at whoever it was, but the night was foggy, no moon, no stars," Dita explained.

"Until we find him, I assume you won't be covering meetings. I think you could do telephone interviews," Mary said. "Especially with your leg. How long 'til that heals?"

"Oh, Dr. Bennett told me a few days. Just a light sprain."

Afterward on the drive home, a family of three deer jumped into the road and crossed.

"Is that where you spotted the doe you hit?" Sean asked.

"No, it was further up."

Sean was now on the subject of deer. "It's a nice day. I think I should pull the fur out of your bumper. Unless you want it as a souvenir."

"No, I do not."

"And I'll take a good look at the fender. The car's getting older, so I'm not bringing it to a body shop. If Mel's around, I'll see if he can come over and help me pound it out a bit."

Dita thought Mel was around. "If he can come, you could talk to him about staying on the mainland sometimes for work."

"Yeah, I will. He has a room but it's not near the ferry harbor. He works about twenty miles away. It wouldn't be a good option for me."

When they got home Sean texted Mel, who came within the hour. Dita went into the house and took her place on the couch, propping her leg up to rest it. Between cat naps and her book, she glanced out the window to see how they were doing. To her surprise, and a bit of dismay, Karl drove in and stayed for a while. She hoped he wouldn't come in with them when they were done, and she was glad when she heard his SUV leave the yard. When Mel and Sean came in to wash up, she asked if Karl had had any news. As expected, the answer was no.

Chapter Eighteen

By 4:00 p.m. a Canadian cold front had moved in. The sun couldn't even pretend to warm the air, and at 4:30 it set. By the time Dita and Sean were getting ready to go to the pub, it was 8 degrees Fahrenheit. Woolies weather. They bundled up, scarves, hats, boots, the works, and went out the door to their truck with Dita wishing she lived on a tropical island instead of a would-be iceberg. But then she looked up at the sky.

The Milky Way spiraled across the heavens, its stars glittering against the white ghosts of more distant galaxies, resplendent, reminding them how small planet Earth is, how tiny a dot we are in our universe. Dita stood and gawked like a teenager at the wonder overhead, Sean right next to her, seeming equally dazzled. She hardly noticed her fingers turning numb in their mittens. When they finally got into the car and drove off, Dita was in a decidedly different state of mind than when they had closed their front door.

Despite the frigid cold, Dita thought she was a lucky person to be able to live in a place where she could see the Milky Way. In cities, the buildings and ambient light obstructed star gazing, especially unplanned random sightings. The beauty of the night put her fright on ice for at least a few minutes, until they approached the pub; then she felt it return. Truth be told, Dita was terrified. Thinking about going into the pub almost brought on a panic attack. She talked herself out of it, believing no one would hurt her in such a public place. She steeled herself to hobble through the door, where she leaned on Sean, both to help her balance and to ward off any would-be attacker.

Inside the Washashore business was brisk. The summer people whom they'd seen in the café earlier were now partying in the pub. The regulars were drinking, eating and chatting; but when they saw her, she noticed they all looked up. Their interest seemed borne of curiosity, not a plan to attack, she hoped.

Dita and Sean stuck to their plan. He peeled away from her to a barstool; she found Loretta at a table close to the bar. She could hardly hear her friend's voice over the din. Loretta moved her chair closer to Dita to talk and she ordered their hot, spiced-rum infused ciders. It was Brenda who brought them. Brenda was built like the bar women in Dutch paintings, with a round, doughy face and a padded body. Dita could almost imagine her in a medieval round cooks cap and white apron. She had piercing blue eyes. Her tongue was sharp, the opposite of her body. She was not a happy soul. She was petty and complaining, but, as Harry said, a damn good cook and bartender. Tonight she was really in a snit. She slammed their drinks down on the table, drops of the rum and cider shot out.

"How come you're sitting here with Miss Newsy Know-it-all instead of working, Loretta?" she asked.

"The boss didn't call me in," Loretta answered. She had on her best ripped jeans and the same sweater she wore almost every day, but with a gauzy, green scarf. When she rested her feet on the rungs of an empty chair, Dita could see holes forming in the soles. She thought Loretta could use some extra money.

"Heard you almost got shot." Now Brenda was addressing Dita, one hand on her hip, the other pointing at her. "Best watch yourself, dear. Who'd a thought on this island?"

She turned back to Loretta. "If you can tear yourself away from your chit chat, carry some food out for me. I'm swamped."

She tried to smile but it ended up as a scowl. Brenda scooted away from them, back to the bar and then disappeared into the kitchen.

"Yeah, Miss Newsy Know-it-all? What's going on back there in the kitchen?" Dita asked. "Not my favorite person; but, Loretta, she is working her butt off."

"Notice she never said please? I would go help, but if Harry wanted me work, he'd let me know. I won't get paid if I volunteer, and Brenda sure as heck won't pay me. If she doesn't stop scowling, she won't get any tips." Loretta laughed.

It hadn't seriously occurred to Dita before, but Brenda might have been working in the kitchen that night. Could it have been Brenda shooting through the fog up in the dunes? She wasn't the most agile person to be running around up there. And why, Dita wondered, would Brenda want to kill her?

Loretta drummed her fingers on the table. "She's never acted this angry toward me before."

"I don't even know if you should eat food that she cooks."

"Maybe I should go help her. That way I can watch your food too." Loretta said.

"Very funny."

Loretta relented. She scooted behind the bar and carried dinners out of the kitchen to the tables. She made two trips, each with two full trays, and then she sat back down with Dita.

"That should get some of the scowl off her face," Loretta said.

"Did she say anything else about me?" Dita asked.

"No, she was just grousing. Forget about her."

They weren't alone for long. Carol joined them. She was table hopping, holding her glass of white wine.

"Good to see you," Dita said.

It hadn't been long since the funeral for Joel and even less time since Dita's visit to Carol. Dita asked how she was doing. Carol told them though she was recovering, she still missed Joel terribly.

'But how are you, Dita? I heard about your scare."

Dita mmmhmmmed.

Carol lowered her voice. "Some people think maybe Harry followed you out of the pub."

"Harry?" Dita asked. "Why?"

"I don't know. That's just what I heard. He may think you blame him for Joel disappearing when he left here."

"I don't. Who's spreading that?"

Carol named a couple of people, including Brenda.

Loretta seemed surprised, "I know I don't paint Harry in a good light to you, Dita, but he's not a killer. Why would Brenda say that, Carol?"

Dita thought to herself, *why would she say that?*

Carol got up. "I don't know. She seems unsettled lately. I need to get back to my own table. Come visit me at home again. We'll talk more," she mouthed as she moved away.

"Ordinarily, I'd bump back to the kitchen to give Brenda more of a hand, but I'm not going near her again tonight. I hope this isn't a permanent slump she's in," Loretta groused.

Dita noticed Sean trying to catch her eye. She smiled, and he got up from his bar stool and came over.

"Time to eat?" He asked.

Dita had lost her appetite. As she looked around the barroom, it struck her that someone, or some people, sitting nearby could have shot at her. Maybe Brenda, maybe Harry, maybe one of the guys eating pizza at a back table, or the father at the pool table showing his son a special shot, or the loud carpenter with his mistress next to him at the bar, grabbing her breasts, showing off for his buddies while his wife gave his kids dinner at home and put them to bed. She had struggled hard not to be consumed by fear, but that wasn't working. Sean, however, was hungry ,and he was waiting for her order.

"Get the specials for us," Dita said.

Loretta sipped her rum and cider. "Not to change the subject, but I will change it. Maria's going to open the Beach Dune next week. Did you decide to work a shift or two with me?"

"I don't think so. For one thing I'm still limping on my ankle. For another, Sean doesn't want me roaming the island alone until we find out who stalked me; and I think he's right, so you'll be waitressing on your own. Sorry."

"I hope they catch someone soon," Loretta said.

"Yeah, me too. I was just looking around the room imagining every person I saw as my killer. I can't do this forever. Every time someone says hello, even Carol, my stomach bounces and I wonder if a knife is going to come out of a pocket. I miss my solitary walks on the beach with Tuffy. I feel tethered."

Sean brought their food from the bar and sat down with them. It was nearly 10 p.m. when the pub began to clear out. It was time to go home. Loretta stayed to talk to Harry for a few minutes so they left her sitting at the bar, and bundled up to go outside.

The night was still stellar. The air was too frigid to hold any moisture, providing a rare clarity. They could see the Newburgh bridge on the mainland, often shrouded by fog and clouds, its lights strung across the channel in a graceful arc. Sean pulled over at a break in the dunes and they watched it glow in the distance. Dita wished the two of them weren't separated by a center console. Those old cars with their cushy bench seats allowed for snuggling. She'd love to be able to snuggle up to Sean right now. She wondered if a lot of modern designs made for more separation between people. In summer, she'd have dragged him out of the vehicle to sit together on the fender or in the truck bed. But for now, she settled for the view and the conversation.

"Do you think we'll get through this?" she asked.

"I hope so," he answered.

"Sean, the island gossip is that Harry stalked me. But you know who is spreading that? Brenda."

"You heard that from her?" he asked.

"No, Carol. She stopped in for a while. Doing better, by the way. But she heard that from Brenda."

"The poison tongue," he said. "I heard you're making Happy nervous."

"Happy? Never!" Dita laughed. "That's ridiculous. He wasn't even on the island the day Joel disappeared."

It suddenly occurred to her that his absence may have been the reason someone picked that day to send Joel off into the drink. She told Sean, and he agreed, adding that that was the most important insight the day had yielded.

"The only gossip I heard," he said, "is that we are not the only ones wondering why Karl didn't pursue the car that came up from the beach. They should have at least gotten the license plate. That's really bad policing, even if Karl was off-duty."

She thought, but kept it to herself, that she had never really liked Karl. He'd bellied up to Sean, but there always had seemed to be an awkwardness about his friendship.

"We need to talk to the chief," she said.

Sean agreed, and promised to call him in the morning.

"And call that 24/7 gym about the job," Dita said, giving him a little verbal shove.

"Yep, will do."

Chapter Nineteen

On Mondays and Thursdays, ferry runs to the mainland were scheduled so islanders would be able to spend the day there, with the first sail at 8 a.m. and the last one back at 5 p.m. Sean set up an interview at the 24/7 Fitness Center on the following Thursday, so Dita reserved a spot for the car on the boat, but only one way. The car would live on the mainland in the parking lot across the street from the docks, which was free of charge in winter. Sean could use it when he went to work, that is, assuming he got the job. Dita assumed he would.

They would have to share the truck on the island. It was too expensive for them to bring a car off and back onto the island twice a week. Dita was more worried about her life right now than having her own vehicle. She could still do very well without a car most of the time, especially with her ankle back to normal. Many a time she'd chosen to hike to town or to town hall, just to enjoy the exercise.

On Thursday morning Dita drove Sean to the harbor in the car and pulled it into the boarding line for the ferry at 7:40 a.m.

While not in a suit, Sean wore slacks and a collared shirt. He looked good, Dita thought. She didn't have to dress for any events, but since Sean looked good, she had decided she would, too. She wore her herringbone skirt with leggings and a black turtleneck. She copied Loretta today, wrapping a red wool scarf around her neck.

Dita was glad her ankle had healed just like Dr. Bennett said it would. She could walk without holding onto Sean.

When it was their turn to load onto the ferry, Dita pulled up in front of it and turned the car around. The crew always had the vehicles back up onto the boat. She followed the hand motions of one of the crew, who guided her backwards over the gangplank and into one of the four parking lanes on the boat. It was a feat of prowess for both the driver and the crew, who packed the vehicles as close to each other as they could. In summer, sometimes a passenger had to crawl over the center console to get out. In winter, there were runs when the vehicle deck wasn't full. Today it was.

"Good job, Dita," Sean said. There were drivers who turned their vehicles over to the crew to drive them onto the boats. Dita was not one of them. They turned the engine off and squeezed their way between the parked vehicles to the stairs, which were open to the elements.

"Brrr, it's cold," Dita complained as they headed up to the cabin. Her cheeks were numb. Sean opened the door and held it for Dita. A blast of warm air escaped from the cabin with a burble of chatter that rose above the engine noise. The crew always ran the diesel engines for a while before departing. The cabin was half-filled with islanders going grocery shopping, keeping doctor appointments, meeting mainland friends. Some were travelling to cities like

Boston or New York. On the hour ride to the mainland, they usually caught up on local gossip that wasn't carried in the newspaper.

The boat got moving soon after Dita and Sean boarded and went upstairs. They had stopped to talk to one of the contractors Sean sometimes worked with. He wanted to know if anyone had been charged with illegal hunting the night Dita almost got shot. Dita didn't correct him as to who was really being hunted. He didn't have a clue about the actual events, in part because he was a family man who didn't frequent the pub at night. He stayed home, accompanying his wife to pot lucks at his sister's house. He was a nice guy, and she was glad she could check him off her list of suspects.

One to two-foot rolling waves swayed the boat like a cradle in a comforting, rocking motion. Dita had no trouble balancing, and she thought she'd go to the concession stand when it opened for another cup of coffee after they found seats. But then she spotted Loretta.

"Look, Sean, Loretta. Let's sit with her."

"Go ahead, I'm sitting here," he said, sliding into a picnic type table with two benches. He sprawled out, his head against the wall and his feet hanging over the other end. With that, he closed his eyes and slid back to sleep. This was a common way of catching some zzz's while taking the ferry in winter.

"Don't muss up your clothes," she warned. She left him and slipped in across from Loretta at her table.

"Hello," she said with a smile.

"Well, hi there," Loretta answered, yawning.

"Where are you off to today?" Dita asked. "I didn't see your car."

Loretta always took her car when she left the island. She had no second vehicle to leave in the lot near the ferry.

"I need to do some shopping, but my sister Marion is going to meet me and drive me around. I'll spend a little time at her house too. We haven't seen each other in a while."

Loretta had dressed up for the trip. She wore one of her nicer silk scarves, a yellow one with small white birds in flight; and instead of her ripped leggings, she wore an intact pair of jeans and a fisherman knit sweater.

"Maybe we'll have lunch somewhere," she said. "Did you and Sean put your car on?"

"We did. It's getting more expensive. I think we'll leave it in the lot over there and share the truck on the island from now on."

"What's your plan today?" Loretta asked, yawning again.

"Sean has a job interview," she said. She saw the surprise register on Loretta's face. "But we're not moving. It's a part-time one. He can probably go back and forth for a while."

"Do you know the Chapmans? They live up on the hill," Lorraine said.

Dita nodded.

"They rented a place near the harbor and they let out rooms to people who need a place to crash. If he needs to stay over sometimes, he might be able to make a deal with them."

"Good to know."

Dita thought it was great to know, but Loretta looked like she didn't feel like talking much today.

"Hard night?"

"I worked until closing at the bar," Loretta said. "I rushed to make the boat. Barely got here when the gangplank went up."

Dita got up. "I'll let Sean know about the Chapman place. Get some rest and enjoy your visit with Marion. Say hello for me."

Dita had never known Loretta to be seasick, especially on a day like today when the boat was running on almost flat seas. But she looked a bit green, Dita thought, and there were dark shadows under her eyes. In the middle of her sentence saying 'see you later,' Loretta pushed herself off the bench, mumbled an excuse, and almost jogged toward the ladies' room. Dita ran after her. Grasping her friend's arm, she asked, "What's wrong?" Then, lowering her voice, because the ferry cabin was a microcosm of their village, with eavesdropping islanders scattered about, she asked a more personal question, one which crosses almost every young woman's mind when she is nauseous in the morning. "Are you pregnant?"

Loretta seemed to unclamp her jaw and she laughed, though Dita thought it was a forced laugh. "Not," she said as she shook herself loose and resumed her race to the head. "Must've caught a bug."

She looked back and added, "I'll be okay. I'll call if I need you."

Dita followed, but stopped near the door to the ladies', sitting on the closest bench facing it. Loretta ran in. Dita was just as glad to wait outside. The ladies' smelled dank and felt cloying on the nicest of days. It was painted the same green tinge Loretta's skin had turned. There were three small sinks with mirrors and three stalls, all built to hold svelte teenagers. Dita had trouble turning around to use them; she often wondered what overweight women did. She heard the clang of one of the metal doors as Loretta entered a stall. At least, she thought, her friend had made it to the toilets. Some women only got as far as the sinks. She twisted to look out the windows, and watched the wind turbines in the distance struggle to turn on this breezeless day. Joel often fished around them. The structures created an artificial reef under the water that attracted sea life. She wondered whether that was where Joel had spent his last day.

She waited, and she waited. She took out her cell phone and opened a game app. She played for a bit, looking up whenever someone went in or out of the ladies' room. She looked at the time and realized it had been over eight minutes, so she texted Loretta. There was no notification that Loretta received it, so she decided to poke her head in.

"Loretta, are you okay? Are you still in here?"

There was no reply. Dita wondered if she could have missed

Loretta leaving while she was focused on her game. Only one door was not swinging with the movement of the boat. She went over to it and banged.

"Loretta?"

She tried to push it open, but it was bolted shut. The space on the bottom was too small to crawl under. There were times being a tall, athletic woman was a disadvantage for Dita; today it was an asset. She pulled herself up on the door and looked over the top. What she saw made her gasp. Loretta still sat on the toilet seat, but was slumped over, her long hair dangling over her face, the tails of her silk scarf puddled on the floor next to her legs. Dita could not see her face to tell if she was still breathing.

She could almost reach the inside bolt. She tried twice, then dropped down and ran out for help. Brad, an island EMT, was nearby. She motioned for him to go in. Then she ran for Sean, who also was on the rescue squad. Brad was inside the stall by the time Dita and Sean got back. The two guys picked Loretta up and carried her out to the cabin. Dita was horrified. What could have happened to her?

The guys laid Loretta out on the floor in seconds, pulled her dripping wet scarf off and handed it to Dita, who tossed it onto the bench behind her. Then Dita noticed what she had missed earlier. Loretta's jacket was half off, her sweater sleeve rolled up and she had a needle in her arm.

"Oh no." Dita felt sick herself.

She knew they only had a couple of minutes to revive her. Brad shouted to the lady working the concession stand to grab the Naloxone spray from the first aid kit, and Dita swooped over to get it. The woman located it quickly. it seemed like forever to Dita. They should, she thought, have that right on the wall where someone could grab it just like the fire extinguisher. Sean did CPR until Dita returned.

"Is she breathing?" Dita asked, as she handed Sean the spray. He squirted it into Loretta's nostrils. He didn't answer. He watched Loretta.

"Wake up Loretta, please wake up," Dita chanted, and she watched for Loretta's chest to move.

"I have a pulse," Sean said to Brad.

Loretta opened her eyes, they turned her on her side and she vomited. She looked around, and Dita thought maybe she didn't know where she was.

Dita moved closer to listen.

"You're on the boat, Loretta," Brad explained. "We gave you Naloxone. You must have overdosed."

Dita's stomach turned, in part from the stench. The cabin air was close when the windows were closed. Sean opened one, letting cold sea air flow in.

"Does that help, Dita?" he asked.

She nodded. She could not believe Loretta overdosed. She hadn't even known she used, and Loretta was one of her best friends. By then a small crowd had gathered and were murmuring to one other. A crew member arrived with a mop and a bucket full of disinfectant, ready to clean as soon as they moved Loretta. Sean gestured for the onlookers to back up to give her breathing room. And the two guys lifted her onto a bench.

Brad told Loretta, "We'll have an ambulance meet the boat. It's another half-hour before we get in. You should be okay until then, but we have more Naloxone if you need it."

"I feel like crap," she growled. "But I'm not going to any hospital."

Brad looked Loretta in the eye. "You need to go."

"I'll stay with her," Dita said, sitting on the bench next to her. She moved closer and Loretta laid her head on Dita's lap.

"Well, now you know," Loretta said, looking up at her.

"Now I know." She paused for a minute, then pleaded with her friend "Hang on, Loretta. Please hang on."

"I am. I promise." Loretta shrugged. "I thought about telling you. I wanted to, but I felt like you'd be angry and judgmental."

Dita nodded. Maybe Loretta was right. She might have been judgmental. She was horrified, but that was because Loretta almost died. She felt her face flush as she asked herself, how she could have seemed so critical that Loretta couldn't confide in her and ask for her help. Did Sean perceive her this way also? She felt her eyes tear up.

"I'm sorry, I'm so sorry I wasn't there for you." She reached over and tucked in stray strands of Loretta's hair. "I'm with you now."

When the ferry entered the harbor, the crew announced passengers would have to wait until the EMTs removed their patient from the boat. Not that there would have been a crush of people leaving anyway. Except for those who went down to their cars early, most islanders waited until they felt the bump of the boat against the pier. That signaled they were in. Sean went downstairs to the car as they approached, while Dita stayed with Loretta. She accompanied the stretcher down to the waiting ambulance, parked at the dock.

"Text my sister," Loretta croaked, as though the words were stuck in her throat. "She should be parked out on the street."

Dita spotted her car. "I see her. I'll just go get her."

She brought Marion to the ambulance, said she'd see them both at the hospital and joined Sean when he drove over the gangplank.

Chapter Twenty

Are you ready for your interview after all that?" Dita asked.

"I am. Shaken about Loretta, but otherwise okay," Sean answered. "You know how angry I was with her before this. Now, I'm livid. Dita you really need to rethink your friendship with her."

Dita did not want to argue with Sean when he was on his way to a job interview. Besides, part of her agreed. For now, her concern was for Loretta's recovery.

It was only a five-minute ride to the fitness center. It was located in an L-shaped shopping center with a large-chain grocery store and a discount women's clothing outlet. The downturn in the economy had forced the small shops that once filled the other spots out of business, even the dry cleaner and the marine store, a popular merchant in a town with both sport fishermen and pleasure boaters.

"Good luck," Dita said, giving him a kiss before he jumped out. "I'll text you when I'm done."

"I think I'll go over to the hospital to see how Loretta's doing," she said.

He threw up his hands and she drove away. The hospital was another five minutes, just outside the small town of Willington. Dita pulled into the emergency room parking lot and found Marion's car. She parked next to it and made a beeline into the waiting room. Marion was seated in a corner, fingering her phone. She was dressed in slacks and boots with none of the flourishes that Loretta used, no signature scarves, no blue in her brown hair. Yet looking at her face, had Dita not known her, she'd have recognized her as Loretta's sister. Dita took the orange plastic chair next to her.

"How is she?" Dita asked.

"She was awake in the ambulance. I haven't gotten an update yet. Dita, how could this have happened? I saw her only a few weeks ago and there was no hint of her using this kind of drug." She drilled her eyes at Dita's. "Did you know?"

"No, I didn't. I'm as clueless as you."

Dita wished she could have said she'd noticed her friend acting differently and tried unsuccessfully to intervene, but she hadn't known. Loretta's drug use was a well-kept secret.

Marion dabbed her eyes with a tissue. "We were going to have a fun afternoon. The kids are at school, Bob's at work, so I made a reservation for two at the Oyster Garden. Now, I'm sitting here instead."

Dita shared her frustration and concurred when Marion added, a tinge of anger in her voice, "What got into her?"

The doctor emerged from the treatment area and called Marion to follow her inside. "I'll call you," Marion said to Dita. "Don't wait. If they discharge her, you can come to the house. You never know how long these exams will take."

Dita threw her a kiss and left. She went to her favorite grocery store, an independent one that had great fruits and vegetables. In summer, they stocked local corn, tomatoes, squash. Then in fall the area's apples came in. She took a cart and started through the aisles, and the panic returned. She looked over her shoulder and peered over the vegetable bins scanning the room as she squeezed an avocado. She was still frightened, expecting to be accosted. Maybe this time it would be a knife instead of a rifle. She hoped Sean would call soon.

Within a half-hour he did, so she checked out and drove back to pick him up. She couldn't give him the lowdown on Loretta, but he gave her a report on his interview.

"I got the job," he said, as he jumped into the car.

"Wonderful!"

"Now we have to figure out the logistics. Let's go to The Chickadee and get some lunch while we talk."

If you had never heard about The Chickadee from a friend or stumbled upon it by accident, you would never know it existed. Located at the end of a nondescript strip mall with everchanging shops, it looked as though it was in hiding. A curtained window obscured the inside. Its sign, attached to the lintel over the door, was diminutive, with a drawing of a chickadee and the name in block letters.

The Chickadee's 1950's style laminate plastic-topped tables with bargain store chairs and a short counter with padded stools created a luncheonette ambiance. But this mom-and-pop stop was a culinary find. The owners, smitten with New Orleans, featured southern dishes like black beans with a dollop of spicy sauce on top, red beans and rice, grits, sausage with gravy. The sausage was homemade and the best Dita had ever eaten. You could get a regular American breakfast or a burger too. It was super friendly, a place islanders like Dita loved.

Dita and Sean both ordered breakfasts for lunch, making sure to include the sausage patties.

They often bumped into people they knew at The Chickadee. Today was no exception. Dita waved to a few acquaintances also grabbing breakfast after leaving the ferry, but they took their own table for two so they could talk to each other. Then she spotted Karl in a far corner, dressed in civvies today.

"Wouldn't you know. What's he doing here? I didn't notice him on the boat this morning," Dita groused to her husband.

Sean looked up and waved. "He'll be stopping here soon. He'll want to know why I'm all dressed up."

"Right," Dita said. "So, tell me about the job; but if Karl comes over, stop."

Sean told her he would start the following week. He would go two half-days that week to learn the routine of checking people in, and to make sure he knew how to run their machines. The following week he would go in another, longer day to learn the computer system.

"When do you start a regular schedule?" she asked.

He would begin in three weeks, working two consecutive days. But they were interrupted by Karl, who had lumbered over. He took a chair from an adjacent table, pulled it backwards and straddled it.

"Looks like a serious conversation," he said.

Dita looked down at him. "It was."

He seemed flustered for a moment, but then he regained his composure.

"The chief asked me to see Loretta. I witnessed what happened on the boat, and called to let him know."

Dita had not noticed him helping at the time, so she blurted out, "Where were you when she was being revived?"

He explained he was in the front of the cabin, and it appeared there were enough people to help her so he waited. He had no jurisdiction on the ferry. He said he had joined them when they left for the ambulance. Dita thought she'd missed him there, too, but maybe because she went to get Marion. She felt he should have been helping on the boat. Why hadn't he? His excuse was lame. She kept her mouth shut, though, and waited for him to leave, which he finally did.

"He's so useless," Dita said. "He never helps and always has a poor excuse."

Sean put down his fork. "Where were we when he interrupted?" he asked.

"Talking about your work schedule."

"Right. All day Friday, and Saturday until 3. That's one night to stay over, if you agree."

"Yes, of course, but if the weather is bad and there's no boat you could be there for days."

"I know. But at first, until they find whoever shot at you, you'll come too."

"If we have to get a room, you won't have any money left from working. Did you guys talk about pay?"

"Hourly. But Dita, that's not the point. I'll get the managing experience I need to run the gym at the Double Ender."

They looked at their check, left a tip and paid up. Dita drove them over to Pete's, an old-fashioned general store carrying everything from beach toys to dishes to air conditioners and tools. It was a favorite stop of theirs whenever they were on the mainland. Today Sean picked up batteries and some parts for the truck.

Then Dita drove across the intersection to the wine store, a shop stocked with alcoholic products geared to two age groups, college students and professors. It was here that Dita had been introduced to some of her favorite wines. About an hour into their shopping, Dita's phone rang. It was Marion. Loretta wanted to talk to them. She'd been discharged and was resting at Marion's house nearby. Dita checked the boat schedule. They had enough time if they didn't linger. Sean didn't want to see Loretta, but he agreed to because Dita insisted.

Marion's house was a white frame New England cottage on a tree-lined street not far from the state university campus. The neighborhood was populated by university people, and Dita imagined their houses reflected their departments. Multicolored Victorians were owned by art and literature professors, modern homes by those in math and the sciences, and New England frame farmhouses by historians and environmentalists. Marion worked as an administrator in marine sciences and her husband was a history professor. Their cottage was farm style. Dita loved this area of the town. If she had to relocate, this is where she would want to live. Marion was watching for them and opened the door as they pulled into the driveway.

"Come in," she said. "She needs to talk with you. That Sgt. Schultz was here and Loretta's terrified."

When Karl told Dita and Sean that the chief had asked him to see Loretta, Dita just assumed he meant he'd been to the emergency room. She was surprised he'd gone to Marion's house also. And she wondered what he did that terrified her friend. Were they planning to arrest her?

Marion ushered them down the hall and stuck her head in a doorway to let Loretta know they were there. Loretta called for them to come in. She was resting on a double bed on top of a coverlet with a deep navy-blue stripe in the middle surrounded by a lighter blue. The walls were papered with a tiny yellow flower pattern, reminiscent of Swedish designs. Dita assumed it was the guest room.

She thought Loretta looked worn; but then, why wouldn't she? She'd almost died that morning. Dita thought how odd it was that the two of them had had near death experiences of late. A shiver went through her.

"Oh, good. You're here," Loretta said. "Close the door. I don't want Marion to hear this."

Dita examined her more closely. Her usually upturned mouth

sagged, her hair lay limply around her face, giving it a blue cast, and her eyes seemed distant, unfocused.

"Come sit with me, Dita. And pull that chair closer, Sean." Loretta took a deep breath. "I need to tell you something, but you need to keep what I'm going to say to yourselves. Don't share with Addie or anyone, understand?"

"Okay," Dita agreed reluctantly. She who worked for a newspaper always seemed to be in the middle of a secret, sworn not to reveal the conversation to anyone.

"No, say you swear. Both of you."

They looked at each other and did as she said, though Sean rolled his eyes as he did. Dita felt her heart beat through her jacket. Loretta leaned toward them and whispered. "Karl didn't come over to get information or pressure me to reveal my dealer. He came to frighten me into shutting up."

Then she took another deep breath and asked for her glass of water which was on the dresser just beyond her reach. She sat up and drank some, then lay back on her pillow.

"He gets paid off when they bring the stuff in and also when they distribute. He's on the take," she said. "He came here to warn me I would pay if I told where I got my drugs."

Dita did not trust Karl, but she'd never dreamt he was sheltering a drug ring. She glanced at Sean, who had turned pale.
Loretta reached out to Dita, putting her hand on Dita's arm. "My life is in danger."

"My God," Dita said. "That can't be. I know Karl's a lazy cop and not a great human being, but I had no idea he was crooked."

"Karl may have been the one who shot at you, Dita. I can't be sure. Watch out for him," she warned. "Don't let him know you were here."

"Did you know this before he came here today?"
Loretta looked down. Quietly, she confessed, "I did."
Dita felt angry. "You never said anything," Dita objected.

"No."

"His hovering over me," Dita concluded. "It's not to protect me at all, is it?"

"Not at all," Loretta admitted.

Sean had been quietly listening, but now he weighed in. "George told him to shadow Dita to protect her, so of course he seems to be hovering. I'm not convinced, Loretta. He's a simple guy, but dishonest?" Sean asked. "I'm not so sure."

Dita had not trusted Karl from the moment he returned her car to the house. She'd had a nagging feeling about him. Now she was sure her instincts were right. She could see Sean was going to have difficulty keeping quiet and not confronting Karl since he didn't believe Loretta. He was already up and pacing, so she tried to calm him by acting neutral.

"Especially if you don't believe Loretta, you need to not talk about this, Sean. Let's watch him and keep looking for the dealers."

She turned back to her friend. "What about you, Loretta?" Dita asked. "What's going to happen to you?"

"I'll be fine if I survive Karl and his pals. I wasn't on H that long. Until a few weeks ago, I only snorted. I think Karl's friends tried to overdose me with some fentanyl mixed into my heroin though."

"No!" Dita said. "They tried to kill you?"

"They thought I'd be shooting up at home, alone. Even so, if you hadn't looked for me, Dita, I'd be dead."

Dita got goose bumps, but Sean was still not convinced.

"Loretta, people do O.D. by accident," Sean almost shouted. "Are you sure you aren't overdramatizing this?"

"Why would they try to kill you?" Dita asked.

"I guess I overheard too much when I was buying."

"Like what?" Sean asked.

Loretta shrugged. "I'd rather not say."

Dita caught an exasperated glance from Sean.

"That doesn't help," Sean retorted. "We need to know who attacked Dita."

"I can't," Loretta said. She picked up an appointment card lying on the small table next to the bed. "The hospital gave me a referral to the rehab clinic tomorrow. I don't really need it though. I can live without drugs. I only snorted until a few weeks ago for a kick."

Dita started to cry. She couldn't hold it back. "This is so awful. Seems like yesterday we were laughing together at the pub watching Jake's grandson compete. Do you think it's wise not to get help?"

Sean cleared his throat. "And is it wise to keep Dita, and yourself, in danger by not telling us who did this?"

"I'll be fine. Dita will be fine. It will get better," Loretta said. "I'm getting tired, now, guys."

Dita and Sean needed to leave if they were to make the boat, anyway, so Dita hugged her goodbye. Sean didn't even say goodbye. He just stomped out. They found Marion in the yard rounding up her kids as they came home from school, and waved good-bye to her. They sped back to the harbor so they would make the boat hoping no local patrolman would clock their speed

"Dita, I don't trust Loretta one bit anymore. I don't believe she just started using recently either. That's what they all say."

"I don't know Sean. I don't want to talk about it now. Let's just go home."

The entrance to the parking lot was not across the street from the ferry. It was a block away and the streets leading to it were all one way the wrong way. They had to pass the dock and then go around the long block to get there, a ride that could make them miss the boat. Instead of just passing the dock, Sean slowed for a second, Dita grabbed the groceries and jumped out. They'd done this before.

She asked Joe, the boat hand, to have the guys hold the gangplank for Sean, who gunned the motor and flew down the street and around the corner to get to the driveway to the lot. Dita stacked the grocery bags on the racks along the walls of the car deck, and she waited. Would Sean make it? How she hated these moments. Then Joe signaled to her. He could see Sean running through the footpath. When he leapt onto the deck, the crew got the chains going and raised the gangplank. The boat floated out into the channel.

Many were the times they had gotten to the ferry just as the blue water opened between it and the dock, and then there was nothing they could do but stay overnight in a hotel. Dita had heard a story about a middle-aged out-of-shape islander who was so determined to get home one day that he jumped that gap; but a sane person had to consider the consequences.

They went upsairs to the cabin, grabbed an open table and waited for the concession stand to reopen. The boat was emptier than it was on the trip over. The buzz of conversation was sparse, just a few voices floating through the air. Dita was glad. She didn't feel like catching up with anyone.

"A drink, coffee....?" Sean asked.

Dita felt cold from the weather and the bad tidings. "How about a hot chocolate? With whipped cream, please."

Sean joined the short line and ordered, adding a bag of cookies to their drinks.

When he returned, Dita told him how worried she was about Loretta since Karl was still on the mainland overnight.

"Dita, he can't do anything to her there without being found out. I'm not worried about Loretta anymore. She's part of the problem. I'm worried about you."

He leaned toward her. "I think we need to speak with the chief, despite Loretta swearing us to secrecy. If what she says about Karl is true, the chief needs to know."

"We promised though."

Sean drilled his eyes into hers. "And, so? A promise to a compromised drug addict is sacred? She didn't come to your aid when you were shot at, did she? She didn't tell us about Karl until today, but she knew. And she didn't tell us who sold her dope. Or what she overheard. At this point I think she's part of the problem, protecting her drug sources, much as you don't want to hear that. Don't invite her for clams anymore."

Dita had to admit he was right. And that really worried her. It seemed Loretta's concern had been her habit and her dealers, not Dita.

"I don't believe she's going to stay clean. She'll shoot up the minute she gets back to the island," Sean predicted. "You and I need to stay calm and watch out for any other attempts on your life. Write articles about the school children, please. I hope George can sort this out quickly. I think I'll call him at home tonight."

When they got into the harbor, they realized they hadn't left the truck at the dock for the ride home. That morning they had blithely driven to the ferry together in the car, which was now on the mainland, never thinking they needed to come home in a vehicle. Some days, Dita didn't mind the walk. A couple of miles in nice weather along the beach was fine. Today they were both tired and carrying groceries. Sean called Mel. He came right away and took them to their house, getting an account of Sean's interview and Loretta's OD. Tuffy was walking around the yard when they drove in.

"Did you let him out this morning?" Dita asked. "I thought we left him in."

"I thought so too," Sean said. "Did Danny come over, Mel?"

"No, he went to Rachel's after school. Besides, aren't you locking your door these days? You're supposed to."

Dita and Sean looked at each other.

"Didn't you lock the door?" Dita asked.

"Yes, all of them, maybe, I think."

Sean took the steps two at a time and pushed the front door. It was locked.

"Wait," Dita reached out and grabbed the back of his jacket. "Did you lock that gun up or leave it upstairs?"

"I locked it up. And no one but you and I knew about it."

"And Karl," she said. "He saw it last night."

She let go of his jacket and he opened the door. He looked in. Tuffy bounded past him and ran into the kitchen, aiming for his water bowl.

"See anything wrong?" Dita asked, hovering outside.

"Not yet," he whispered. He stepped inside, Mel behind him. Sean took the living room and back room; Mel, the kitchen.

"Looks normal," Mel added. "Dishes in the sink."

"Dishes!" Dita shouted. "We didn't have time for breakfast this morning. No dishes!"

She swept into the kitchen. There, in the sink, was a bowl with a spoon. An empty beer bottle sat on the drainer.

"This is sounding a little like Goldilocks, but someone ate my stew. We had leftovers we were saving for supper tonight. And Sean they drank one of your beers."

"We'd better check upstairs," Sean whispered. "Make sure no one is still up there."

Dita heard them walking into the rooms, opening the closet doors. Then Sean yelled down.

"Check your jewelry box."

She did. It was all there, the small gold and pearl earrings from her aunt, the hoop earrings, the silver necklace with the whale pendant, the turquoise Native American earrings and bracelet, and the costume jewelry she wore every day. She went to the corner of the room to her desk by the window with the view of the ocean out back, and that was when she knew what they had come to get. Her laptop. It was missing.

"Someone's worried about information you might have collected," Mel said. "Do you have that pass coded?"

"I do. Could someone figure it out? Maybe, but there's nothing of significance on my search for Joel's killer or drug doings in there."

Dita looked in her closet and drawers. "Either the thief is not my size or has a different fashion sense, because nothing is missing."

"Good thing I locked my gun back up," Sean said. "But maybe I'd better check."

"Ya think?" Mel asked.

Dita followed them down the two flights. Sean checked his gun cabinet. He turned to Dita, who was standing at his shoulder.

"Still intact."

She felt some relief at that. But Mel shouted back to them from the garage section where he had gone and told them to come look. "I found their way in," he shouted to Sean and Dita. "The lock that holds the doors closed is broken."

They could see for themselves, the barn style doors had been closed on the intruder's way out, but the lock on the latch was lying on the ground, its hasp cut.

"That sure shows us," Sean said. "I'll need to replace it with something harder to break."

"I have a good lock I'm not using. Take that for now, but I think you should install a slide lock on the inside," Mel said. "And lock the door to the cellar in the kitchen."

"Someone is really trying to frighten us," Dita said.

"They're doing a good job," Sean responded.

Mel started to the door. "I need to pick up Danny from Rachel's. I'll drop the lock off later. But call the police, would you?"

"Well, now we have a reason to call George," Sean said.

"Except he's probably gone home and the dispatcher will send that new guy, what's his name," she answered.

"Dave, his name's Dave. I'll call George at home."

Dita poured herself a glass of red wine. She looked out the window. The pond was dark. If the sloop was there, she couldn't see it, not even an outline. Clouds had moved in again, shrouding the Milky Way as though it didn't exist.

Dita turned away from the window. "They ate the stew right out of the bowl. Must have been a guy."

Sean emptied the bowl into the garbage and put it and the spoon into the dishwasher.

"Wait. Don't do that. Maybe there are fingerprints, or even better DNA."

"And matched to what. I doubt whoever did this has been fingerprinted."

Dita disagreed. "You never know. Washashores with criminal records? Yes."

He removed the dishes and put them aside. He was more concerned with his empty stomach. "I guess we can heat up some frozen pizza for supper."

Dita felt naked without her laptop, and she hoped her password kept the thief out. "I doubt whoever took my computer will be able to open it, unless they're really good at decoding. My password isn't 1-2-3 or my name."

"Unless they know you well and take some good guesses."

"There's nothing in there about any of this, even Joel. Just what's already been in the paper. I have no new articles or research."

Dita handed him his phone. He dialed the Chief, at home.

Chapter Twenty-One

The chief arrived at their house not ten minutes later. Sean met him outside to show him where the intruders entered.

When they came in, Dita led the chief into the kitchen and pointed to the sink. "They ate our leftovers. We didn't leave dishes in the sink. We were saving this stew for our supper tonight. Do you test for fingerprints or DNA?"

"We're not on a TV show, Dita," he said, smiling at her. "I doubt there are any prints except for yours or Sean's if you picked them up today. They've probably been rinsed."

Dita pointed out there were still traces of food on both the bowl and the spoon.

"Some businesses have their summer help fingerprinted," the Chief explained, "but not all of them want to pay the cost of having it done, and year-rounders are rarely required to do it. As far as the

DNA of islanders, the database for them is almost non-existent. Television police forces are fake scientifically far ahead of a small island department."

To Dita's dismay, he left the bowl and spoon in the sink.

After a walkthrough of the house, Dita filled him in about Loretta's overdose on the boat. "Loretta is staying with her sister. Karl visited her, and now she's terrified, George," Dita said, sitting at the kitchen table across from him. "For that matter, so am I."

Sean moved in back of her, his hands on her shoulders. "Karl didn't help us revive Loretta on the ferry," he said. "I didn't even realize he was on board until we talked at The Chickadee and he told us. How could he just sit up front and not turn around to see the commotion? Better yet, why didn't he help? I don't get it. Loretta said Karl is taking money from the drug dealers."

"You do know Karl pretty well, don't you Sean?" the chief asked, more a rhetorical question than one he expected Sean to answer.

He seemed to Dita to be quite calm, not as distressed about Karl as she would have expected. If she was Karl's boss, his job would be in jeopardy.

"He's not in any drug ring," the Chief said, furrowing his brow. "Karl's okay. That said, I know he doesn't work hard, Sean. He's basically a good guy, but he's lazy. I have to kick his keister to get him to do the minimum on the job. Just between us, I don't think the people selling drugs here would need to bribe him to keep him quiet. He wouldn't notice anyway. When I tried to recruit you, I hoped you coming aboard would light a fire under him."

"Oh, really?" Sean looked surprised.

Dita wondered how Sean would have energizee him. In her opinion, Karl would just have sloughed work off onto Sean.

"You don't think he'd take money if it was offered?" Sean asked.

"Here's how I look at it. I view it from the other side, too. Have you noticed any showy purchases on his property, Sean? No Maserati or a Mercedes in his driveway. Just an old American car.

He doesn't even have the money for a motorcycle. And no fancy vacations. His wife and kids dress in thrift shop jeans. If there was money coming in besides his salary, there'd be some showy evidence."

Sean could not disagree. Dita was somewhat surprised that the chief could detect thrift shop jeans.

"Loretta's a drug addict," the chief continued. "Categorically unreliable for information. Whatever you do, don't share what you told me with anyone else."

Again, Dita thought. Don't tell. Hmmm.

The chief was still talking. "Drop your investigation into Joel, Dita. Let people know you believe it was an accident. And write up the overdose, but stop snooping unless I ask you to. I'm on this. Do you have my cell phone number?"

He gave it to them and had each of them call him so their numbers would be in his phone.

"Call me on my cell instead of the station or home if you have any more problems or need me in a hurry. Otherwise, I'll be in touch. Don't let them think Loretta gave you information you don't have. All I can tell you is, as I said, I'm already on this. And, lock your doors, for crying out loud. This break-in was more to keep you spooked than to steal anything." And he left.

Sean locked the front door behind him and parked his truck in front of the garage doors so no one could slip in there. Dita locked the sliders. When Mel returned with the new lock, they would use it immediately. Then they heated up their frozen pizza and set it on the kitchen table.

"I'm scared, Sean," Dita said, taking a piece of the pie. "Whatever is going on here is worse than I thought. I just assumed I could report on Sonny and Joel and people would rally to push the police into finding out what happened. Instead, I'm the one being hunted."

Sean put his slice down. "Either George is in on it and already knew about Karl, or he has the best poker face I've ever seen. He didn't act shocked. He just denied Karl could be involved."

"Do you believe him?"

"I don't know."

"I still think he should have taken the spoon and bowl for testing," she said, almost pouting. "He could be covering for them." Sean shrugged.

"I have an idea. How about we go to visit your parents or mine for a couple weeks until this is over?" Dita asked.

"Besides the fact that then we'd have to tell them what happened, I think we need to sit tight. I want to start my job. Besides, George may need our help to trap them."

"That's even scarier," Dita said. "I don't want to be bait."

"It's too late for that. You already are," Sean got up to go to the door. Mel had returned with the lock.

Sean took it and went outside to put it on. Dita heard him move the truck, and then Mel drove out.

The next morning Dita was startled by someone knocking on the front door. She put her coffee cup down and let Tuffy bark at the disturbance before she went to open it. Then she saw Rachel peeking in the window. She waved, and Rachel came around the side to the kitchen.

"I got scared. I'm glad it's just you," Dita said. "Coffee?"

"No, thank you. Sorry I frightened you. I'm parked in the beach lot because I went for a walk. Then I thought, why not pop in to see Dita. I came in from there so that's why you didn't hear my car.

"Addie told me about the trouble the other night. I'm sorry if it was me who got you into this," Rachel said.

"It's okay. It wasn't just you. I got myself into it."

"Anyway, I finished packing up the Lorelei shop and I thought I would invite everyone who helped me with it for a get-together there this afternoon. You, Carol, Loretta, Addie and Mel, of course, and Danny. Sean can come too. Just some cheese and crackers, a glass of prosecco, the year-end. Not like it would have been if Joel--you know."

Dita knew. She also knew Loretta couldn't come, but she didn't say anything.

"What time?"

"Fourish."

"Right. We'll be there. Hey, wait. Can I invite Teddy? Sean may be working with him this summer. He's living here now, and maybe it would be good for you to get to know him."

Rachel smiled and gave Dita a sideways look as she pulled the door open to leave.

"Invite him," she said.

Dita followed her to the door, and locked it when Rachel left. "Now I have to remember to lock the door every time someone comes over," Dita groused. "Sean!"

"I'm right in back of you. No need to shout."

"Do you want to call Teddy and invite him to the Lorelei party or should I?"

"I'm on it right now," he said, tapping his phone. "And then I'm going upstairs to work on exercise routines. Maybe I'll pick up some private clients while I'm working at the 24/7."

Every once in a while he called her to come up and try a sequence. She liked that room, the future baby nursery they'd left almost empty for now, with just a few weight bars and plates, and kettlebells. And she enjoyed doing his workouts. She couldn't stop herself from glancing out the windows, though, watching for enemies every time she heard a car come up from the beach, or a truck drive by on the road out front.

Between vacuuming and laundry loads, and helping Sean, Dita started some bread. She wasn't much of a cook or a baker, but the lack of a good, solid, seeded New York rye bread on the island in winter had energized her to learn how to bake one. She used a book with recipes in easy-to-follow steps, and she'd had a mentor on the island, a woman who taught baking in her commercial kitchen.

The repetitive motion of kneading it by hand usually calmed her down so she decided not to use the electric mixer. She loved the feeling of the pliable dough in her hands, the thought of the gluten stretching under the heel of her palms. She set it to rise in a warm corner cupboard. It would need three risings, so it took the better part of the day until it was ready for baking. She could smell the yeast working. When it was ready, she divided the dough into two pans, and popped them in the oven. The yeast had finished its job, and now the house filled with the scent of freshly baked bread instead. Just before they had to go, she set one aside on the counter for her and Sean, and took one for Rachel. She was careful to leave Rachel's unwrapped, placing it in a woven basket for the trip to the Lorelei with a cotton dishcloth loosely laid on top. Otherwise the crust would get soft. She thought there was nothing worse than fresh warm breads packed in plastic and tie wrapped, their steam dissolving the crust into mush.

At four they headed to town in the truck. When they pulled up in front of the shop, the lights were on inside, and the windows were picked clean of merchandise. They could see the guests who had preceded them. Dita was happy to see that Teddy had come. And Trent was in there too. Dita hadn't expected Rachel to invite him. Sean couldn't remember his name. Dita had to refresh his memory. They opened the door, jangling the bell that Rachel never took down. Carol dashed over and gave Dita a hug. She took the bread and brought it to the table.

"Look what the talented Dita Redmond brought," she said. "And it's still warm. There are some tasty dips open already. I'll cut some rounds for slathering."

Trent wanted to know when Rachel would leave for India.

"I've decided not to go this year. I can reorder the rings that I had made last year, with a few more for you, Trent. The factory knows how I like them and what quality stones I want. We can consult over the internet. Instead, I'm taking Addie and Mel and Danny on a vacation to Central America, to Costa Rica, Guatemala, or Honduras. I'll search for crafts and they'll relax at beach resorts."

Dita thought that sounded grand. Rachel extended an invitation to her.

"Why don't you come with us?"

Sean laughed. "We might scrape through the winter with our jobs, but there's no extra for travel. Not this year anyway."

He told them, and especially Teddy, about his part-time job. Trent asked how Dita felt staying alone on the island given what had happened the other night.

"I read about the reward your publishers are offering. Any takers yet?" he asked.

Carol echoed him. "Yes, has anyone come forward?"

"Not that I know of," Dita responded. She was wondering how Trent knew about the break-in, but maybe he was talking about the night she ran for her life through the dunes.

Rachel offered a toast. "To all my good friends who helped me close up the shop and provided shoulders for my grief."

They all cheered. Rachel said she wished Loretta had been there, but she couldn't contact her.

"Do you know where she is now, Dita?" Rachel asked.

"You all already know she overdosed on the ferry yesterday, I'm sure."

Everyone nodded except for Trent, but Dita noticed his face gave away the fact he did know. He didn't look surprised. She thought to herself, "*You knew. Why not admit it, though?*"

Aloud she explained, "The captain called for an ambulance. It was waiting on the pier when we got into port. The medics brought a stretcher onto the ferry and brought her down from the upper deck on the wheelchair lift. We were fortunate it wasn't one of the older boats that only had stairs. She was rushed to the local hospital emergency room. Other than that, I don't know,"

"I did hear she overdosed. But on what?" Rachel asked. "I had no idea she used drugs. Did you? Dita are you sure this rumor that spread last night is true?"

"I'm sure. I'm the one who found her in the ladies' room on the ferry with a needle in her arm." She hadn't wanted to tell them that. She started to cry. How she hated to do that. For women it was a show of weakness, though for men it was a sign they could have feelings.

Rachel had clasped her hand to her mouth while she listened. Now she put her arm around Dita and said, "I'm shocked."

"And I had no idea either," Carol claimed. "Did you know she used, Dita?"

"No, of course not," she said. "But now I do and there's nothing I can do."

"We can't lose anyone else," Rachel uttered. "We need to help her. You don't know where she is, Dita? The hospital maybe?"

She couldn't tell them that she and Sean had visited Loretta at her sister's.

"I tried calling her and her sister Marion. I can't reach either of them," Dita said, and that part was true. Loretta was not answering her phone. "Besides, you know Loretta. Maybe she went into a treatment center, maybe not. She disappears for days at a clip all the time anyway."

Dita was feeling angry at Loretta now. "Sometimes she disappears with a new boyfriend. A jaunt off-island with Marion. Our friend comes and goes without telling us."

Trent made light of it. "Grown up and single, and popular."

Easy for him to say, not being her friend, Dita thought.

Teddy added, "and worrisome."

Amen, Dita thought. *Thank you, Teddy.*

Aloud, addressing Trent, she noted, "Single and popular and an addict who almost died. You left that part out."

Trent ignored her sarcasm and went on. "I've even seen her out on the pond with the sailors from the sloop. But I need to go now. I'm sorry about Loretta. Don't get me wrong. But there's not much you can do for addicts. When she returns, let her know my house is due for a cleaning, if she's up to it. Thanks for inviting me, Rachel." And Trent slipped out the door.

"Not too concerned for Loretta, was he?" Dita asked.

Addie had been quiet, taking it all in. Now she spoke. "We may need to start offering treatment at the medical center. That Loretta is using is worrisome. It's even more worrisome that none of us knew. It means we could have a cluster of addicts struggling with habits here, people we care about and thought we knew well."

Addie paused for a second, and then asked in a soft voice, "Could my brother Joel have been one of them?"

"Of course not!" Rachel shouted at once, angry that Addie had even suggested that. "Not Joel, right Carol?"

Carol agreed.

"Do you think you can help Loretta stay clean?" Dita asked, looking at Addie.

"I don't know. I have no expertise in addiction and I don't think Dr. Benett does either. Given that this is getting to be a problem, though, I'd say we need to get some. Or bring someone in who does."

Sean shook his head. "Like they say, you can't trust what an addict tells you. She's not quitting, Dita, and she lies about everything. I know she's your close friend, but she's an addict first, and that's how we have to think of her now. Trying to help her stay clean if she doesn't want to? That's not going to work."

Dita realized Sean would never get over his anger at Loretta. He would forever begrudge her for not helping Dita.

They stayed to give a hand to Rachel to close up the shop. Then Sean suggested stopping in at the pub for game night. Teddy asked

Rachel if she would join them. She told him she had already offered to go to Addie's to stay with Danny so Addie and Mel could go to game night at the pub.

"Might they bring him for a while so you could come?" Teddy asked.

"No, it's a school night. But come with me. If you're good at video games, he'd enjoy playing you," Rachel suggested.

"That sounds like fun," he said.

Well, Dita thought, at least something's going right. She tried to hide her smile.

They were setting up the games at the pub when Karl appeared. He was in uniform, and he strode directly to their table.

"I wouldn't get started if I were you, Dita," he ordered in a loud voice.

Dita did not look up. She ignored him. But everyone else took note and the room grew quiet. Harry stopped cleaning the bar top. Brenda, cooking in the kitchen, stuck her head out to watch.

"You need to come to the station with me," Karl demanded. "The hospital and Willington police called. They want us to question you as you were the last person with Loretta before she went into the head."

"Are you daft? I wouldn't hurt Loretta. They should question you. You didn't get up off your ass to help."

He walked away.

On the way to the station, Dita called the chief's cellphone. She hadn't expected to need the number so soon when he gave it to them. Now she was grateful he did.

The chief was packing up to go home, he told her, but he decided to stay when he heard that Karl had demanded she come in for questioning. He assured Dita that he would take charge. When Felicity let them in at the station, the chief was sitting in his office with his door open to the entry hall.

Karl walked in behind Sean and Dita, and when he saw the chief, he said, "I thought you went home."

"Catching up on some paperwork. What's going on?" he asked, lying.

Karl explained he was bringing Dita in for questioning.

"You were on the boat too, weren't you?" the chief asked.

Karl nodded.

"Then I better do the questioning and see how it jibes with your report afterward."

With that, the chief directed Karl to check the doors at the island's school. "Someone called in. They saw people trying to open them."

The school was located on the other side of the island, a good ten-minute drive. Karl grimaced, but he did as he was told.

"Now then," the chief began. "Let's run through the events on the ferry again in more detail. I'll take them down and I'll get Karl's distorted version afterward."

He walked her through her conversation with Loretta at the table when she first boarded the boat, Loretta's sudden sprint for the head, and Dita's wait on the bench. She grew distraught as she recounted finding her friend passed out in the stall, and then the attempt to revive her.

"I don't think she got that stuff on the boat, George," Dita said.

"I'm close to finding out where she got it," he said.

Dita wanted to ask him more, but realized he wouldn't answer at this point anyway. She had to hope this whole episode would end soon. Her life was in turmoil at a time when she should be celebrating Sean's promise of a steady income.

"This is getting worse and worse," Dita said on the way home. "Karl, our neighbor and once your sort of bar buddy, wants to put us in jail. And I still believe Loretta that he's on the take to the drug gang. He might even have shot at me."

"I don't know. I can't believe Karl would have hunted you down like that."

"And I can't believe Loretta took hard drugs, but she did."

Once again, she wondered, who else among their acquaintances wished them ill will.

"Actually, I think the chief is right. We're getting closer to the truth," Sean said.

Dita thought that he was much more optimistic than she was. Each new twist made her stomach do flips.

When they passed the pub, she asked him to stop for a second so she could run in and let Addie and Mel know they were going home. She noticed how it looked more dismal than ever in there. Harry hadn't finished clearing up from Halloween. There was still broken furniture pushed against the wall.

She found Addie and leaned down. "We can't play. Something's popped up at the paper. Talk to you tomorrow," Dita whispered. She turned to rush back to the door, but Harry called to her. "Wait a minute, Dita." He reached under the bar and pulled out a computer.

"This yours?" he yelled, holding it up. "Someone left it here." Brenda grabbed it out of his hand and brought it to Addie's table. She pushed it toward Dita. It was her brand. Dita opened it.

"Looks like mine," She said, turning it on and typing in her code. The icon disappeared and her screen came up.

"It's mine. Harry, who brought this in?" she shouted. She was shocked.

"One of those sailors out in the pond. Found it on the board-walk this morning. Since I heard yours got stolen, I stuck it under the bar for you.'"

"Thanks," she shouted, trying to feel grateful instead of slammed. It was hard to believe someone had graciously left it at the Washashore after stealing it from her house. She gave Harry a sideways glance in case he was gloating, but he already had turned to talk to someone on a bar stool.

"By the way," Brenda said, "is Loretta ever coming back? I'm cooking and doing tables. Nights like tonight are busy."

Chapter Twenty-One

"I don't know. You know what happened to her. You need to ask her, or Harry."

Dita cradled her laptop under her arm and ran back out to the car.

"Look what Harry gave me," she shouted. "One of those sailors out on the Pond found it on the boardwalk this morning when he was coming in o town, or so Harry claims, and they dropped it here. Why here and not the police station? Not a likely story. More and more, I am starting to believe Harry is at the center of this, even though I didn't want to."

Sean shook his head in agreement, and said, "Though I still really hope it's not him.

"I hate to think every time we're in there giving him our business, he's planning a way to kill me."

As they slowed to pull into their driveway, Sean nodded toward the pond. "Look," he said. "Someone from the sailboat is rowing to shore."

"Probably going to the pub," Dita groused.

"There's a car in the lot. Maybe waiting for them," he noted. "Looks like Brenda's but I can't really tell in the dark."

"Unless she left it for them, it's not her. She's at the bar. Maybe I should jump out and question them about finding my laptop."

"Absolutely not. Not here," Sean said. "Let's go in to the house and eat supper."

"I guess we'll have to heat up some soup.".

"With your bread," Sean said. "Not so bad."

Chapter Twenty-Two

When Dita heard Karl's car drive past the next morning, she felt a wave of relief that he hadn't entered their driveway. George must have put a lid on that supposed investigation from the mainland police. There wasn't much real reporting work she could do, so she wrote a short article announcing the Thursday evening trivia games at the pub, and started a blog about winter on Nor'easter Island.

Then Rachel called. Dita expected to hear about her evening with Teddy, but that was not what Rachel had in mind.

"Dita, I think Trent knows what happened to Joel," she said, without any hemming and hawing around.

"Trent," Dita echoed, wondering what brought on this abrupt insight.

"Yes. I don't believe they left the pub together by coincidence."

Dita had thought all along that Trent knew more than he let on, but why had Rachel called today to tell her?

"Why? I mean, has something else happened to make you think that?" she asked.

"He invited me out to his house the other day to see some of his art work."

Well, Dita thought, *you didn't tell me that yesterday at the wine and cheese get-together.*

"He's brought some items over to the island to sell in one of the shops this summer. Actually, he asked about me taking some. Did you know he's staying right on the water, Dita?"

"I know. I've passed the Bradley house, though I've never been in it."

"And he has a spectacular view. I could see the Montauk Point Lighthouse. He'd be able to watch people going out to fish or sail. In fact, he said he'd seen Joel's blue boat once or twice, so he knew who Joel was even though he told the police, and us, he didn't know the person who went out the door with him. Why lie if you weren't involved?"

"Indeed," Dita agreed.

"Since I was there, I know the layout of the house. So, this is why I'm calling. Do you think when Loretta is back we could ask her to let us in to search the house when she's cleaning there? She did say he leaves for a few hours while she cleans. If Joel went there with Trent the night you saw him, we might find something of his that he left behind."

"It's unlikely he did, but it's worth a try. I don't know when she's coming back, though."

"She's supposed to go to work at the Beach Dune when it opens. Maria postponed it, but she might be ready next weekend."

"Yes, but hopefully Loretta's in treatment somewhere and she might stay on the mainland with her sister."

"Dita, she called Marie to tell her she'd be able to start work."

"Oh." Dita was upset Loretta hadn't told her. In fact, she'd been unable to reach Loretta at all.

"When did she call Marie?" Dita asked.

"I don't know."

"I guess she decided not to call me because I told her I wouldn't take shifts there."

"You sound upset," Rachel said. "Remember, she's recovering from a near-death experience, right? Not herself. Try to cut her some slack."

"I've been so worried about her. You can't imagine what it was like to find her slumped over like that."

"I know, it had to be horrible."

"I'll try to call her again. Rachel, if we are going to do this, we're have to plan well so Trent doesn't catch us. Or if he does, we need good enough excuses for being there. If he did kill Joel, we'll be in jeopardy too. Come by tonight and we'll figure it out with Sean. He'll help."

"No, you two come to my house. I'll cook dinner. Come at 5:30 for the leftover wine from yesterday. Bring Tuffy, too."

"Okay. I'll try to get Loretta now."

She tried Loretta, and when the message came on right away as though the phone was out of battery juice, her blood pressure rose. She immediately tried Marion's phone. She let out a long breath when this time, she heard a voice on the other end. Marion's voice.

"Marion," she said. "It's Dita."

"You're looking for Loretta, I think."

"I am, and how are you?"

"I'm good. Let me get her. She's not using her own phone. We're trying to keep her from getting involved with that island crap again."

Dita heard her call to Loretta. There was a pause and then her friend picked up.

"Hi, Dita. I'm coming back next week. Doing well. Feeling better."

Dita was a bit puzzled. What did that mean? Was she in treatment with Methadone? Suboxone? No treatment? Using again? Should she ask?

"Umm, I heard you are still going to work for Marie?"

"Yes, I start next weekend."

"Are you up to it?"

"Oh, sure. I'm back to myself. Actually, I'm going to clean the Bradley house Monday, next week. I need the money; and really, I feel fine."

Dita felt uncomfortable, but she asked anyway.

"Are you clean?"

"Yes. I'm a virtual prisoner at my sister's house. Besides, you don't think I'd risk the kids seeing me stoned, do you?"

In truth, Dita wasn't sure at this point whether that would bother Loretta, since on the ferry, the whole island neighborhood had seen her. But she could hear the irritation in Loretta's voice, so she dropped her interrogation.

"I was wondering if Rachel and I could come into the Bradley house while you're cleaning."

Dita, so good with words on paper, was hard put to phrase why they wanted to do that in a way that would not imply they were looking at Trent as a murderer.

"She still thinks Joel went to Trent's house that day they left the pub together and she wants to search the house to see if there's anything Joel left behind there," Dita said, hoping Loretta would not catch on.

"So you guys think Trent had him killed?" Loretta asked. "But Trent couldn't have pushed Joel off a boat. He's not nearly as strong as Joel was."

Oops, Dita thought, wishing she could undo what she'd said.

"Well, I don't, but Rachel needs to be convinced, so can you let us in?"

Chapter Twenty-Two

"Sure. He's usually gone for a couple hours. He can't stand me."

Dita thought, neither can Sean anymore.

"I have to go, Dita. Marion needs her phone. I'll talk to you in a couple days when I'm back."

Or not, Dita thought.

She went outside to tell Sean. He was cutting some brush around the driveway.

"Is that snow on your jacket?" she asked.

She put out her hand. Several large wet flakes plopped down into her palm like snow bombs, then melted into cold droplets.

"The first of the season," she said. "Was this forecast?"

"I didn't check, but I hope it doesn't get too windy. I need to go to work tomorrow for my training."

"Right. We can check the marine forecast later."

As they stood there talking, the wind gusted and suddenly they were surrounded by a swirl of supersized snowflakes blinding them. She could not see Sean though he was right in front of her. They landed in her eyes and mouth, and covered her clothes, melting rapidly because it was warmer at sea level than in the atmospheric layer where they formed. Sean's hair was white and then it wasn't. And suddenly the squall ended like a symphony with a good conductor. They laughed and hugged.

"Let's go in," he said and he called to Tuffy, who was off in the dunes doing whatever dogs do there—sniffing a trail of some deer perhaps. When he appeared, his fur, not as warm as their skin or Sean's head, was white.

Dita told Sean about their supper invitation, and then more carefully, the beginning of the plan with Rachel.

"Bad idea," he said. "Very, very bad idea."

Dita had expected his negative reaction, but was determined to convince him. They were now in the house, where Tuffy shook his melting snow flakes onto the floor.

"Another bad idea," Sean said, looking at the dog.

"Here's a towel to dry him off, and the floor too." Dita said, throwing one to him. "Sean, let's try to figure out how to search the house and leave again without getting caught. I think we need to do it."

Sean was on the floor, rubbing down the dog. He didn't look up at Dita.

"Can't Rachel go alone?" he asked. "She's got a relationship with Trent. She could make up a reason to go while Loretta's there. She doesn't need you with her."

"Part of that's a good idea, Sean. She could say she realized she forgot something when she was there before and called Loretta so she could pick it up."

"But you don't need to be there."

"Sean, I need to help her search if we're going to go through the whole house. It's large. She could just say she brought me with her because we're stopping in at Carol's on the way home."

"I don't feel comfortable about this."

"Let's think about it and talk more with Rachel at supper."

Chapter Twenty-Three

Dita decided to stop in at the office for a while. Snow accumulation was almost never a problem on Nor'easter Island roads, so driving was fine. It was a rare storm that necessitated ploughing, especially on their side of the island, where the air was saturated with salt. In addition, the wind blew the snow into drifts, leaving bare patches and random piles. Not much accumulated into a blanketed cover.

Lawrence and Candice were alone when she arrived. Even the administrative staff were out, including Jane.

"Where's Jane today?" Dita asked, not that she missed the absence of that clicking sound of the woman's fingernails.

"She went to the mainland. She's having her nails done," Candice said, looking to see how Dita reacted. She knew how Dita hated those nails. "It's pretty slow, so we gave her the day off."

Dita was glad because they had some privacy. The open rooms the staff occupied were not spacious, so everything spoken could be overheard.

"We'll show you the responses to our request for information," Candice offered. "But don't get your hopes up. We haven't received many."

"Here, read this one first," Laurence said, handing her a typewritten sheet of embossed stationery. "I should have expected at least one from him."

Dita looked. It was from Old Ken Johnson, the former island physician, who wrote frequently to complain about everyone and everything; in particular, whoever happened to be mayor at the time. His writing was entertaining, so they always published his letters. Dita began reading aloud:

'To the Publishers:
It has come to my attention that you are seeking information about the disappearance and death of Joel Berliner, the young man who brought me, and everyone else, fresh fish. He is missed. I will present you with some clues to follow in the hope that you solve this heinous crime.'

Dita paused, put the letter in her lap and said to her bosses, "This is the part where he blames the mayor, right?"

Lawrence and Candice laughed. "Of course," Candice said.

Dita picked up the letter and began reading again:
"First, I would interrogate the mayor."

"Bingo," Dita said.

"They, Joel and the mayor, were observed at summer's end engaged in several clashes over Joel coming too close to some of the mayor's *precious bird nesting sites. As you know he spends more time birding than mayoring.*

Joel trampled too close, and once or twice he was with that dog belonging to Dita and Sean Redmond, the big, blonde shaggy one, which really frightens the mayor's feathered creatures.

The mayor and his birding pals might have followed Joel in a boat one morning when he went out fishing, caught up to him out on the water and slammed into his boat, knocking him into the water. Or one of them might have gone aboard, engaged in a frightful fight and pushed him in. They are an aggressive flock, when it comes to protecting their birds."

Dita commented, "A real page turner. No evidence. He didn't see them, and doesn't name anyone who did. Not to mention, the mayor is the gentlest person. How many murderers have you heard of who identified as birders?"

Lawrence answered, "Duck hunters, perhaps."

Dita continued reading.

"I don't blame the mayor if he was angry at the dog, but not Joel, who never hurt anyone. That beast chased my prized ducks when they were swimming in a puddle along my road and they ran in front of a car and were run over."

"My sweet dog! He thinks my dog is responsible for Joel's disappearance and for his ducks. Not the driver who mowed them down. Now he's going to pester me to pay for one of his show ducks too? I can't read any more of this. Just tell me who else he fingered."

"No one else," Candice said. "You've got to admit, as curmudgeons go though, he's tops. And everybody loves to read his diatribes, except maybe the mayor and your dog."

There was also a letter from someone who worked for a package delivery service. He thought he'd seen Carol driving around that night. Dita knew Carol wanted her to investigate Joel's death, so she hadn't considered her as a suspect. But if Carol had been out that night, she might have seen someone. Dita couldn't give serious thought to Carol as a suspect, but she could ask her if she'd seen anyone on the road.

One more writer blamed Harry. There were funny things going on in the Washashore Pub, he wrote. Dita did not disagree. Since the letter was not signed, she couldn't contact them to follow up.

And finally, one respondent blamed Dita.

"Nothing substantial yet," Dita said. "Someone thinks I could have shot at myself?"

"Wait, back up. What do you think about Harry? I did give you that one, didn't I?" Candice asked.

Dita nodded. She gave it more thought. Harry and his bar were at the center of suspicion every time she talked about the drug ring with Sean, but she hadn't figured out how he fit for Joel. Maybe Joel walked into the Washashore when a drug deal was going down, or while Karl was being paid off. He might have overheard a conversation going on in the kitchen if he sat at that end of the bar. Neither she nor Sean had wanted to think of Harry as a killer, but then again, they didn't really know him from anywhere but his barroom. Brenda knew him best. If she asked Brenda, the woman would bite her head off. And Loretta, who sometimes worked for him, had not implicated Harry. Addie was his friend, but in reality, she only flirted with him for fun.

"I think Harry might be involved," Candice said. "Joel was last seen at the pub. And you said you stopped there on your way home the night you were pursued."

Harry certainly had had the opportunity to follow her out of the bar. Would he have had time to get into the dunes and scare up the deer that ran into her car? Would he really be involved in killing Joel, or her?

"I don't know," Dita said. "It could just be that I don't want to think he could want to hurt Joel, or me. He works so hard at his business, he's always there. You know, he did a blood pressure clinic with Addie, trying to get those guys that never get a check-up to have a sit-down with her. That's pretty civic-minded."

"Right, you wrote that up; but I thought he did it because he has a crush on Addie," Lawrence said. "Well, he's my prime suspect, but I hope some more leads come in."

"How are you holding up?" Candice asked. "I thought that Karl was out of line the other night, bringing you to the station for questioning because you saved Loretta's life. Dita, when this is over and you're exonerated, you're going to get the assignment to tell your story."

Dita felt relieved that the paper wouldn't carry a report about her at the police station as the would-be killer of a family friend; but the fact that she was being fingered in public by Karl rattled whatever modicum of sanity she still held on to. She was beginning to unravel.

"Time to go home," she said, slipping on her coat and wrapping her scarf around her neck.

"Before you leave, tell us how Loretta is," Candace said. "Seeing you wrap your scarf made me think of her."

Dita had also. "She'll be back to work at Marie's next weekend. How is she? I don't know. She's evasive," she explained, hesitating for a moment. Then, since neither Candace nor Lawrence said anything more, she left. Talking about Loretta still upset her. She didn't want to except with Sean, Rachel and Addie. She rushed down the stairs and into her car, and drove home.

Dita and Sean pulled into Rachel's driveway that evening and knocked on the door as they pushed it open.

"It smells delicious in here," Dita said. "What are you making?"

"For you, Dita, I found those Jonah crab legs you like in the grocery store."

"Super! I love them," Dita said.

Jonah crabs were not nearly the size of dungeness crabs. They had thick, meaty legs though, more like warm-water stone crabs. The Jonahs lived all along the east coast of the Atlantic Ocean down to the Carolinas, and Dita really did love them, almost as much as she loved lobster.

When she looked around Rachel's house, Dita was surprised. She hadn't been there since Joel's funeral, and didn't know about Rachel's big clean-up. She'd had the place painted.

"It was planned before Joel disappeared," she said. "I decided to go through with it. I had already ordered the new rug and throws. Everything was done in one week. Except for Joel's room. I left that as it was, for now."

"The house looks great. Cheerful and clean," Dita said, admiring the light ecru walls, the new living room rug all beige, black and white, the new seagull-patterned throws on the couch.

"Come see the kitchen," Rachel said.

Not just the walls, but the old wooden cabinets had been stained so they looked fresh and if still what TV personalities called, 'outdated,' they were made from cherry wood and well-constructed. She'd replaced the worn countertops with a new, white laminate. Even the floor was retiled.

"In the spring, I'm repairing the outside. Maybe I'll sell, I'm not sure. Addie and Mel invited me to move in with them, but I don't think I should. I could retire though, close The Lorelei after this summer and go to the mainland. Maybe even go to Florida like everyone else who retires from their businesses here."

She led them to Joel's room. "Danny and I have been cleaning up, sorting through Joel's things, bringing his clothes to the thrift shop. I'm giving Danny all of the fishing gear, and anything else that he'd like to keep, like Joel's watch. It was my husband's. There might be insurance money for the boat. That would go to Danny, too. I think Joel would have liked that."

Dita felt sad for Rachel, and for Joel. She was able to forget her own problems for a moment and have some empathy for someone else. How hard it must be, she thought, to lose one's child, even a grown one. Rachel's grief was palpable.

"I still know in my heart that my Joel was murdered. Dita, did you know his ring was missing when they found him? It wasn't on the list of belongings. He always wore it. It was one I had made in India, with a ruby I chose. Just like a school ring, only a ruby not a garnet."

"Do you think the killer took it?"

"He wouldn't have taken it off to fall off the boat or commit suicide. He always wore it, even fishing. I'll look for it when we search Trent's house."

"Because they left the pub together, and Dita thinks she saw them in a group of people on the street earlier?" Sean asked.

Rachel replied at once, "Also because Trent spent so much time admiring my rings in The Lorelei. And even ordered some."

Dita had suspected Trent when Joel first went missing, but now she didn't know how he would fit in with Karl's drug ring, unlike Harry. The two crimes, drugs and Joel's murder might not even be connected, she told herself, though her gut told her they were.

"If we were to find something, we'd have to get out of there fast. We couldn't park a car out front where anyone going by would see it and know we're there," Dita said.

"Without a car, you won't be able to escape. I'll come and wait outside," Sean said.

"No, your truck is a dead giveaway," Dita said. "Everyone on the island knows it."

"Not Trent," he protested.

"We can't be sure."

Rachel had spent more time in that area than they had and knew it well. "There's a path through the nature preserve to Carol's house. I can park my car in her garage, and we can leave that way."

"That sounds good," Dita said. "But if Trent comes back and sees us, let's split up. You go that way, and I'll cut through to the road, the other way. We'll both try to call Sean when we're far enough from the house, just in case one of us is caught. He can meet me down the west side by the overlook if we split up."

"That sounds like a plan," Rachel sounded excited.

Sean disagreed again. "No, that's crazy. It's too dangerous. Rachel needs to go alone, and we can both wait for her at Carol's. Maybe we should let the chief know,"

Dita shook her head. "Sean, we can't involve the police until we have the proof. We already suspect Karl's involved. Maybe the chief's involved too."

"Then I want to come with you," Sean demanded.

"No, we couldn't explain you being there too. Better that you pick me up when I call, or if I don't show up in a reasonable amount of time, come look for me," Dita said.

"Chances are, Trent won't return while we are there," Rachel suggested. "Loretta did say he gives her a few hours alone in the house because he doesn't like her."

"I don't like this plan. They already tried to kill you, Dita. How about I run it by the chief?" Sean asked.

"We don't know if he's involved. We can't."

"I think you ruined my appetite," Sean groused.

"Speaking of which, let's eat," Rachel said. "Stop worrying, Sean. We'll be fine."

They sat in the newly painted living room after dinner. Like Carol, she did not have a sea view, but she did have a view of a meadow. It was too dark to watch the grasses sway, but Dita did spot a snowy owl swooping low over the ground as it searched for a rat or a vole to prey upon. Its white feathers were barely discernable in the dark. Once rare on the island, in the changing climate they seemed to be shifting their habitat.

"That's the first one I've seen," Dita said. "I've been told people have spotted them roosting on our chimney, but I haven't." For that one moment, she was lifted out of her troubles.

They talked for a while, and then Sean and Dita said goodnight to Rachel.

"It was nice to see you both. I'm glad we have a plan," Rachel said. "Don't worry, it will work."

Sean rolled his eyes. Dita could almost feel them going up into his lids for that second. He would see that the plan was a good one if he could stop being scared for her.

"It will be okay," Dita said.

Chapter Twenty-Four

Sean nudged Dita awake. "Time to get up," he said.

"I'm staying home. Not going," she whispered without opening her eyes.

"If you want the truck you have to drive me to the dock."

"Okay," she agreed, but she snuggled deeper into the covers. "Maybe I won't get dressed. I'll just drive you and go back to bed."

"Fine with me. I'm taking a shower."

She let out a large yawn, and sat up on the edge of the bed. "I guess I'll make you coffee."

"No need. I'll get it on the boat. We need to leave in ten minutes. Be ready." With that, he disappeared into the bathroom, and then Dita heard the water running. He was spending the day learning the computer accounting system at his new job on the mainland.

She guessed no one would notice she was in her flamingo pajamas unless they came right up to the truck window, so she stayed in them as she had said she would. On the way out the door, Sean reminded her to lock up. She grabbed the key from its drawer in the kitchen, the one she never used to carry. They called Tuffy to jump into the back of the truck.

"I let the chief know you'll be alone. He promised to have Dave patrol once an hour, not Karl," Sean said.

"Definitely should not be Karl," she said. "I feel like a little kid. Maybe I'll go to Rachel's after lunch."

The thought of needing protection ruined her mood. She drove up Founders Road feeling angry. She thought about her close escape, of running for her life through the dunes. Would she never know who tried to hunt her down?

"Wait, slow down," Sean demanded. He leaned over to her and looked out her window. "Look at that big guy taking that wave."

A gaggle of surfers were out on the water.

"That's Teddy," Sean said.

"And that's Rachel standing on the beach waving." Dita pointed to their friend. "But you're going to miss the boat if we don't go." She stepped on the gas and continued driving to the ferry dock.

"Are you sure you don't want to go with me?" he asked. "You look upset. You're frowning and clenching the steering wheel."

She shook her head. When she drew up to the ferry office in the harbor lot, she gave Sean a touch-kiss, her words for barely placing her lips on his mouth. He stepped down to the pavement from the truck, and she watched as he picked his way through the small crowd gathered outside the ticket window. She'd promised to go right home, so she drove back to the house, locked herself in and dusted the table tops before going upstairs to work on the piece her editor wanted, a blog about her favorite mainland stops. Maybe it wasn't such a good idea to let people know where she went. She didn't want to be knifed in the discount clothing box-store, or assaulted on the street in front of the second-hand furniture shop. She'd ask Mary to hold the piece until the drug ring was exposed and arrested.

The morning dragged. Usually, she'd love that space of free time to write and catch up with chores, but today just seemed tedious. She lay on the couch dozing, her lead suspects and victims circling round and round in her head, just out of reach of a solution. Harry, Karl, Trent, maybe even Brenda, and the victims, Joel, Sonny, Loretta. She couldn't force them into a pattern even in the semi-conscious state that usually led her to figure things out. And the chief? Was he in on it, too?

She cancelled her afternoon with Rachel and played computer games instead, trying to adjust her mood before Sean arrived. She didn't want to be all gloomy. That could become a habit too hard to break. On her way to pick him up at the ferry, she slipped into the Books and Bakes for a chocolate éclair to go. Chocolate always improved her mood.

She pulled into the freight yard to wait for him, and swooned over the éclair, savoring the dark chocolate coating. Then she licked her fingers clean so she could text Sean to let him know where she was parked. Brenda pulled in next to her and Dita wondered who, or what she was waiting for because people picked up freight packages there also. Brenda had a small family on the island. Her husband had left for the mainland long ago, but her brother lived with her, and her nephew. Over the years she'd been single again, she'd had several main men, but Dita didn't know if she was with anyone now. Though Brenda was an acquaintance, she and Dita had never crossed much socially. She hung out with some of the contractors and fishermen, and a couple of the women who owned shops. Dita couldn't say what Brenda liked or disliked as far as sports, movies or music. She didn't know how she spent the time she wasn't working in Harry's kitchen off season, though she did know Brenda managed one of the smaller summer restaurants during the season. Today she tried not to look over at her. Instead, she leaned back and concentrated on eating her eclair. But out of the corner of her eye, she caught Brenda shooting glances at her. She waved to be friendly. Brenda looked away. Dita slumped down in her seat, as far from Brenda as she could get.

At last, the ferry backed in, bumped the dock and lowered the gangplank. The cars drove off. And then the small stream of islanders marched out, scattering when they got to land. She spotted Sean walking directly to the truck, holding a bag of groceries.

He slid into the passenger seat with a big hello. It was not freezing, but the weather was brisk, and his clothes gave off a chill. He smiled, reached over to give her a kiss, a real one this time, and handed her a small box.

"Open it now, before we go home," he said.

"Chocolates! You went to the candy shop." She smiled. He wouldn't know she had just devoured that éclair, and besides, she always had room for more chocolate.

"Just for you." He rubbed his hands together to warm them. She opened the box and plucked one out for herself, and one for him.

"Open your mouth," she said, and she reached over and dropped one in. Only then did she restart the motor and put the truck into reverse to back out of the space. Brenda began to back up at the same time. Dita stopped.

"No sense getting her ire up again," Sean said, laughing. "Her brother was on the boat complaining about how moody she's been lately. It's not just you or Loretta. Or Harry."

"That's interesting."

"Yeah, Ricky wishes she'd find a new boyfriend. He said she'd been hanging around with the sailors who come in on that sloop that moors out in the pond. They're distant cousins of theirs, distant enough to be kissing cousins, but those two guys have been fighting over Loretta for romance."

"Really? Loretta mentioned them once the day Joel disappeared, but not since. She seems more interested in that divorced guy, Mankawicz."

He shrugged. She was far more interested in this kind of gossip than he was.

"I had a good day," he said, as they cruised down Founders toward their house. "I think this will go well."

"Hooray. I see money and children in our future, that is, if we have a future."

"We do," he said.

Not long after they got home, Loretta called.

"I'll be back Wednesday as I told you last time we spoke. I'll ask Rachel if I can sleep at her place for a while, just so those guys don't try to kill me again with their fentanyl."

"Right. I'm tired of going to funerals, Loretta," Dita said.

"Me too. You stay out of their way, Dita. Give Sean and Tuffy a hug for me."

"Will do."

"By the way, Sean," Dita said after she'd hung up. "Marie asked if you want to help tend bar at the Beach Dune Saturday night. I know you're anxious about me being there alone. I did tell Loretta I couldn't, but if you went you could keep an eye on things and that would be good. We could both work."

"Sure, we could use the money."

Though Marie had uniforms for summer staff, now in the off season, jeans and a sweatshirt with the name of the restaurant would do. Dita felt excited to be back working with Loretta again, like old times, especially with Sean at the bar. Marie was a fun boss even in the tension of the summer when tourists lined up at the door waiting for seats to open up. She never lost her temper or sense of humor, no matter how large the crush of people waiting to get their dinners.

Tonight's special was fish and chips, one of Dita's favorites. And

Marie always made slaw with it. She'd get to eat some when the diners left.

Dita noticed Loretta seemed to have recovered. Her mood and her energy level had rebounded. She was chatty and laughed at the customers' jokes. Some of the women fussed over her, advising her not to tire herself out.

The locals came in spurts, which was fine for two waitresses and two bartenders. It gave them time to serve without running between stations all night. Marie's cook was a friend of Dita and Sean's, a summer sous chef at one of the tonier restaurants. Marie, Dita saw, had not lost her touch. She helped in the kitchen and found time to come up front to chat up her customers. If Dita could have forgotten the disaster hanging over her, she might have enjoyed this evening, but even if she could have, the arrival of Karl would have ruined it.

Karl showed up with his wife, an unusual occurrence. Neither Dita nor Loretta wanted to wait on his table. Dita thought she saw Loretta shudder. They decided to flip a coin at the bar to decide who got to do it, but Sean stepped out from behind the bar and took the couple's orders. Dita threw him a mental kiss. She wondered whether Karl's wife knew about his kickbacks and criminal behavior. And his hitting on the local women. His wife was avoiding eye contact with Dita and Loretta, so Dita figured Karl had told her something. Before all this, they had been friendly neighbors.

Addie, Mel and Danny arrived around 8. Addie brought her brood to a table in the back, far from the bar, and as far from Karl as she could be. Dita took their orders. She was delivering their plates when Addie's cell phone buzzed. Dita saw her tense up. Then she asked if Dita could wrap her order to go. Dita took it back and bagged it. Addie was at the front door waiting for her.

"Emergency at the medical center?" Dita asked.

"Walk with me a minute, please," Addie ordered, going outside. "Dita, George had an emergency. He's on his way into the health center now. You guys take Mel and Danny home later if I'm not back, ok? I'll let you know what's going on."

'Oh no! I hope it's nothing too serious."

Addie grabbed her bag of food and ran to her car.

"I'll call you," she said.

Dita felt like she was outside of her body. She had not realized she was counting on George being around for backup when she and Rachel went to the Bradleys'. What if he was laid up indefinitely, or worse, what if he died? Karl would take over. And then there would be no backup. She willed herself to finish out her shift without unravelling. After all, George could just have a touch of flu, or an attack of vertigo, like she was having right now.

She went back inside the Beach Dune, but kept glancing out the window. She was watching for a medevac 'copter to fly in to take George to a hospital. Sean caught her.

"What's wrong?" he asked.

She shook her head. "Tell you later."

Should she let Loretta know yet? She didn't want to endanger her friend's still fragile recovery. She went through the motions of her job, wishing everyone would eat up and go home.

Loretta walked past with a tray of plates. "Where did Addie go? Mel and Danny are still there."

"There was an emergency at the medical center," Dita said, trying to appear unconcerned.

Loretta looked at her, waiting for more information; and when none was forthcoming, continued on to deliver her meals, but not before she gave Dita some advice.

"Smile, you'll get more tips."

It was only on her way back to the kitchen to pick up another order, that Loretta demanded to know what was wrong. "You keep looking out the window, like you're waiting for the helicopter."

"I'll tell you later. Let's get through this shift first," Dita said.

Sean was watching them while he placed beers and cocktails on the bar. Dita fetched a few for her customers.

"Hope we get done soon and can talk about whatever happened," he said.

"Me too," she replied, glancing over his head out the window to see if the lights of a helicopter were out there. "I think Danny and Mel will be riding home with us. Addie had to go to the medical center."

She took her tray and swung around toward the tables. Once in a while she kept an eye on Loretta. She worried she would tire easily after her recent medical catastrophe, but Loretta seemed to be holding her own. Finally, the diners all left, even Karl.

Did he know about George, Dita wondered.

As they cleared the tables and cleaned up, with Mel and Danny helping since they had to wait anyway, Dita told Loretta and Sean about George. Sean pursed his lips and said they might have to wait to go into the Bradley house. Dita told them the good thing was no med evac had flown in, so perhaps they were taking care of him and sending him home. Loretta asked Dita to call her first thing in the morning. She would be at Rachel's.

"But Dita," Loretta said, "if George is hospitalized or laid up, it's even more urgent that you search Trent's house at once for something that will prove Joel was there. You need to make your case before Karl makes his version official. Or, you need to drop the whole idea. I lean toward that anyway."

Dita realized she was right about the urgency. "I'll be ready when you think Trent will be out for a few hours."

They all went home. Dita expected she'd have a sleepless night worrying. Addie texted her around midnight.

"Did I wake you?" Addie asked. "I thought you'd want to know about George."

"Oh no, he didn't die, did he?"

"No, no. He has appendicitis."

"Oh my God, Addie. Did you send him to Willington Hospital?

I didn't hear the helicopter come in."

"Calm down," Addie urged. "He might not need surgery. We're treating him with IV antibiotics for 24 hours and then we'll reassess. We've been treating appendicitis with antibiotics for several years now, except for the most inflamed cases, and we've been pretty successful. He should be back at work once the IV is out and he's on oral meds."

"Stay calm?" Dita asked, gasping for breath. "This could blow our whole plan. I'm nervous about doing it if George isn't available to back us up, though Loretta thinks we should get in there immediately, or drop the whole thing."

"Breathe," Addie said. "George will be probably be going home tomorrow evening with his IV out. He's s sleeping now. In the morning we'll see how he is. I'm staying tonight, so I'll call you then. And don't tell anyone else. I'm giving you confidential information and I shouldn't."

"Duh, you didn't need to add that," Dita grumbled. She was probably the only reporter in the world who never reported anything she heard.

Dita turned to Sean and repeated what Addie told her. After all, she figured, not telling anyone did not include him. Sean wasn't an anyone, he was her someone.

"Dita, we've treated other cases this way, so George will probably be fine. He might be back at work in a couple days."

"Right, just act as though my life is normal, nothing going on, right?"

"Yes,"

"Got it."

Two days didn't help her and Rachel.

Dita called Loretta as soon as she woke up in the morning. She took a coffee filter out of the cabinet with one hand and put the phone on speaker mode with the other. She hit Loretta's number, then spooned in the coffee, and ran cold water into the decanter that attached to the back of the coffeemaker. Loretta still hadn't answered. The message recording came on.

"Where are you?" Dita asked. "Call me."

Two minutes later the phone rang.

"I was in the bathroom," Loretta said.

"Not doing what you're not supposed to, are you?" Dita still worried about her friend having a relapse.

"Of course not."

"Okay, then."

"Dita, whatever happens with George, you need to search Trent's stuff today," Loretta said.

"Today?" Dita asked. "It's Sunday. What if Trent doesn't want to leave? And, what if he catches us? We won't have George for protection. You said Karl is on the take. He'll be slow as the old ferries."

"We have to. What if George gets transported to the hospital in Willington? He might not be back for a week," Loretta said. "Sean will have to be your lookout, on the street."

"He can't. He's learning the computer system at the 24/7 today. They didn't finish the other day. He's leaving for the airport as soon as the coffee's ready. You know the Sunday boat schedule. There's none until later, so he's flying."

"Dita, you need to do this pronto. I'll call the Bradleys right now and tell them I'm back and ready to clean. Then I'll let Trent know. He hates being in the house when I'm vacuuming and banging around. I'll call you back as soon as I set it up."

"But Loretta. Even the police wait for back-up. We have none," she said.

Dita felt Sean's breath on her neck. She turned around.

"Wait one day. I need to be here if George is not able to help," Sean said. "What if something goes wrong? There's no one we can trust."

"Did you hear Sean, Loretta? Tell the Bradleys you'll clean

tomorrow, Monday, as planned. It will give Trent a day to find something to do out of the house. Come over here today and spend the day with me."

"Okay. Maybe you're right. Hold on a minute."

Dita heard a muffled conversation in the background. Then Loretta came back on. "Rachel wants you to come here if you're not going to the Bradley's today," Loretta said. "She needs help sorting through pictures. Carol is coming, too."

"After I drop Sean off at the airport. Then I'll be over. Can we go for a long walk on the beach with Tuffy?"

"Maybe we could slip through on the path near Rachel's and walk away from town. Shouldn't be anyone much up there today."

"I think that would be safe."

She hung up, and she looked at Sean.

"Take your phones to the beach," he said. "And take Rachel and Carol. Five's a better number. If it's just you and Loretta, whoever took pot shots at you could do it again. Don't make me have to worry about you while I'm trying to learn their computer accounting system."

"Of course not. I can call the mayor to come with us too," she said.

"Very funny," Sean groaned.

"Who's kidding? He loves a good walk looking for wildlife."

Dita did not call the mayor. She wanted to keep the walk as secret as possible. The five of them, Rachel, Addie and Dita, Loretta, and of course, Tuffy, with a tennis ball in his mouth, took the path to the upper cottage beach at 9:30 a.m. The weather had warmed somewhat and could be tolerated with just a jacket and gloves, and sneakers not boots. The tide hadn't yet turned, and there was a wide swath of sand on which to walk. Carol looked for beach glass. Storms like the one a few days earlier brought them in from the churned-up sea bottom.

They puttered their way a half mile to a mound of rocks and

scrambled over them to the next stretch of sand. Tuffy swam.

"So, we go tomorrow," Rachel said.

"You do," Loretta confirmed.

Dita wondered if either of them had heard from Addie this morning. She remembered Addie's promise that she would call, but it was now almost 10 a.m. and there'd been no word, not for her, anyway. When she asked, neither of the other two had gotten a call either. Dita decided it was time to find out how George was doing. She texted Addie. A few minutes later, Addie texted back, saying she would call as soon as she had a minute.

Finally, she did. George was responding to the antibiotic. He was feeling much better. The pain had subsided, and his fever was down. They would probably send him home around supper time with a bottle of pills for the rest of the week. They could talk with him later in the afternoon if they wanted. Right now, though, he was about to nap.

Dita felt better knowing that George was not going to be sent to the mainland for surgery.

Around noon, they walked back to the house. They passed Harry, who was fishing along the beach. He nodded to them.

"What's he doing here today?" Dita whispered to Loretta. "Do you see a gun?"

"Relax," Loretta said. "There are four of us. Besides, he's just fishing, he's not watching us."

Dita looked back, just to make sure. Harry was reeling in his line. He looked like he was getting ready to leave. And soon, he was walking with them, a large bass over his shoulder.

"Hey, nice day out here, isn't it?" he said.

Loretta answered. "Sure is. You serving that tonight?"

"You bet I am. You coming in later?" he asked.

"I am."

He began to pick up his pace, and left them behind. "See ya then," he called back, legging it down the beach. "Got to get this baby on ice."

"So, Loretta, did he sell you your drugs?" Dita asked.

Loretta looked away. She didn't answer.

"Leave her alone, Dita," Rachel said. "She's not well enough to be interrogated. Besides, that's George's job."

"So is searching Trent's house, but I'm going with you tomorrow to do it," Dita said.

Her cell rang. It was Sean, on his lunch break. The morning had gone well. He was checking on her.

"Speaking of lunch," Rachel said, "let's not fight. I have a nice pot of lobster bisque," John Moss brought them over yesterday. Everyone is being so nice to me."

When they got back to the cottage, Dita stretched out on a comfortable chair while Rachel heated up the bisque. Loretta, sitting on the couch with her feet up on the coffee table, began to talk about how good it felt to be free of the habit she'd been developing.

"I never thought I would get hooked like that," she said. "It was just fun at first, and it made working in the pub nicer, you know."

"I didn't know you didn't like working in the pub," Dita said.

"It's not like waiting tables for Marie in the Beach Dune, Dita. It's mostly the same guys all the time that hit on you over and over, even though you say no as nice as you can, because you need the tips. Even Karl, or should I say, especially Karl, who can't keep his hands off me when he thinks no one's looking."

Dita waited for Loretta to go on. She had said she would tell them all when the drug ring was in jail. But Dita hoped she would say more now. She didn't. Instead, she whispered, as though someone was listening to them, "I guess I shouldn't babble about this until they're all rounded up."

"Bisque's hot," Rachel called from the kitchen.

They sliced some bread and buttered it, dipping their spoons into the thick soup. This was a real bisque, with large chunks of lobster meat, not the soups that were served so often these days with ground up leftover lobster, and a mere one or two morsels of meat. This was a bisque as had been made in the old days, before lobsters became scarce and ultra-pricey.

"Mmmm," Dita murmured.

"Double mmmm, I say," Loretta responded.

Dita laughed and suggested Sean would be jealous when she told him.

"Not to worry," Rachel said. "I have plenty and I'll send some home for him."

Dita stayed until it was time to collect Sean at the airport.

Chapter Twenty-Five

Dita's fingers tingled as she thumbed through her drawers moving clothes around. Soon she would be going through Trent's drawers, and this felt like a rehearsal. She tried to focus her anxiety on choosing her outfit rather than thinking about what would happen if Trent caught them going through his belongings in the Bradley house.

She planned to wear all black: black tights, a black stretch long sleeved tee, black sneakers. She fished them out of her drawers and her closet.

It was another of those perfect fall days, too nice to be indoors rifling through a near-stranger's house. She grabbed a black fleece pullover. The wind was down to breezes that came like flurries. The sun was as high as it gets in November. But she still needed the pullover.

"Ready?" Sean asked. He was driving her and Rachel. Loretta would already be there to let them in. Sean would wait for them down the road in the second cliff parking lot.

"I'm having second thoughts," she said, "and third ones, too."

"Well, you know how I feel. I don't want you to go. If you want to pull out now, I'm all for that. I should go instead of you." He seemed more nervous than her.

"I need to see this through, Sean. I'll go. But, thank you for offering."

"Do you have your phone in your zip pocket?" he asked.

Dita patted it. "I do."

"Has Rachel come yet?"

"No, I'm watching." She stood by the window, her eyes on the street.

They waited until Rachel drove by. It was time to leave. They followed her to Carol's where Rachel left her car, hiding it in Carol's garage as planned. Then she joined them in Sean's truck. He dropped them both off at the Bradley house and continued on alone to Dita's fallback rendezvous point. Loretta was waiting for them and opened the door when they rang the bell, as agreed. They rushed in. They had less than two hours to search the 4,000 square foot mansion until Trent was due back. Loretta suggested combing through the rooms he used, the largest guest suite, the kitchen and the television den first.

"I never see any dirt or belongings strewn around any other areas," she said. "He's a slob. If he did use them, I would see socks or skivvies and candy wrappers lying around. Stay out of those other rooms. And stay out of the garage. The Bradleys store their stuff in there. I don't want any problems with them."

Dita looked at Loretta, one of her closest island friends, and wondered how she had missed the woman's habit. She hadn't spent a lot of time with Sonny, so she had come to accept not knowing about his; but Loretta's, no.

"Don't look at me like that Dita," Loretta demanded. "I've done my bit. I told George about Karl as you insisted. Look for whatever you think might be here, and go. I don't want Trent finding you."

But Dita wondered, not for the first time, whether Loretta was more involved than she admitted. Why had she urged them to go yesterday when George was in the medical center, and Karl would have been their only backup?

Loretta turned on her vacuum cleaner and pushed off the other way, trailing her scarf of the day, a yellow cotton print, behind her. Dita watched her, wondering if she should warn her that her scarf might catch in the vacuum. But, she decided, Loretta probably did this all the time, just as she had ignored the danger of injecting herself with narcotics. She turned back to Rachel and they began searching the room where Trent slept and the adjoining bath.

"This guest suite is larger than all three of my bedrooms!" Rachel was stunned.

The furniture was large also. The bed was a California king with rumpled sheets. Loretta was right about Trent being a slob.

"Do you know that a California King is longer but not as wide as a regular King? There must be some tall guests who visit the Bradleys," Dita said as she rifled through drawers, engaging in chit-chat to calm her nerves.

"How do you know that?" Rachel asked, as she opened boxes on the closet floor.

"Hmm, remember, I'm tall, Sean's taller. We notice bed lengths."

They finished, flipped off the chandelier switch, and left.

Loretta met them in the hall, ready to vacuum there.

"Be very careful in the kitchen. He uses it, and it's the one place where he knows where he puts things, even though it looks haphazard and sloppy to us. Remember, the garage is off-limits. And be quick. When I was dusting the front den, I heard a car out there and almost crashed into a glass table."

Loretta seemed more skittish than they were. If she was so worried, why had she said yes to them? Dita wondered just what she'd seen when she was with Trent and his pals. Maybe she was more involved in Joel's disappearance than she let on. If so, she and Rachel needed to power through the kitchen search.

"We'll hurry, Loretta. Come on, Rachel, let's do this."

She opened the door nearest the kitchen. She'd made a mistake. It turned out to be the garage she was supposed to stay out of. When she glanced in, she gasped.

"Oh, my, holy moley...."

Suddenly she was sweating. Her heart was pounding. There were no cars in that triple garage, just large make-shift boards on saw horses covered with brown burlap bags and a stack of wrapped blocks that probably were bricks of heroin.

Rachel was standing at her shoulder. "Come away to the kitchen before Loretta catches us here," she urged, whispering into Dita's ear.

"Do you think she knows?" Dita whispered back.

"I don't know," Rachel said as she pulled Dita away and gently shut the door. "Her vacuum sounded like it was in the living room."

They turned and quickly opened the next door, which this time was the kitchen. They went in clutching each other, and then Dita leaned on one of the counters to steady herself. Someone was cutting and bagging heroin in this house. Should they run? Maybe they needed to get out now. Dita glanced around the kitchen. It was the size of a ballroom with long stainless-steel counters and an island, probably used for more than food prep. Lots of drawers. Quick was not going to work for their search.

"Should we go?" Dita asked, her voice trembling.

"You should, but I need to do this. I need to know if Joel was here," Rachel said. "I don't care what happens to me anymore."

Dita could not leave Rachel there by herself. Against her best instincts, she decided not to run out the door.

"Okay, I'll stay too, but let's get at it," Dita urged. She didn't want to think about what would happen to them if Trent came home.

The kitchen was designed to resemble an operating room, white cabinets, white floors and walls, and long stainless-steel counters. The stove had enough burners to cook a banquet for an entire hospital staff, the cabinets could hold a year's supply of dry goods. And then there was the refrigerator. Rachel remarked that it probably used more electricity in a month than her entire house. In summer, when rates were jacked up to make tourists pay more so the company could charge less to year-rounders in winter, that would be an extravagant amount. They zipped through every drawer and cabinet to no avail. Perhaps they were wrong about Joel coming here. They hadn't found anything that belonged to him.

"Time to go," Dita said.

As they were leaving, she spotted a closet in the mudroom. She thought they should rifle though it though they were running out of time.

"Bingo!" she shouted when she opened the door and saw it was a walk-in crammed like the Lorelei Shop. This was where Trent stored objets d'art from his city gallery, along with paintings and collections from the island that he might take to the city.

"Let's be careful, go through everything, even the small boxes," Rachel said. "But hurry."

They rifled through a few of them; some held brooches, others lockets, and a few, rings. Then Rachel gasped.

"Dita, stop! This looks like Joel's ring."

She held up a man's gold ring with a flat ruby. Rachel peered at the inscription inside. The date matched Joel's high school graduation. The initials were his, RB. Rachel inhaled a scream as she realized it was definitely Joel's.

"How did Trent get this?" she cried out. "He had to have been with Joel."

"Take it. Let's leave," Dita said, worried Trent was due back. "We have what we needed to find, and more. Put it into your zip pocket and let's get out of here before Trent comes home."

She backed out of the closet and almost knocked Loretta over. "Loretta! I didn't see you, I'm sorry. I thought you were vacuuming over in the hallway."

The vacuum was still running there.

"I was, but I came over for a second to say goodbye. Rachel, let's see what you found," Loretta said.

Dita held her breath, hoping Rachel wouldn't tell her. Rachel reached into her pocket and Dita grabbed her arm.

"What are you doing, Dita?" Rachel asked, shaking Dita's hand off. She held up the ring and with her other arm, she gave Loretta a hug. "Thank you, it's Joel's ring." She put the ring in her zipper pocket.

Dita cringed. Loretta had been sneaking around in back of them, her vacuum in the other room, making them think she was there cleaning. She knew now that her suspicions about Loretta, which she'd tried to deny, were spot on. She pried Rachel out of her hug.

"Too late, Dita. I can't let you go," Loretta said. "I was going to, but then you opened the garage door. I'm sorry. I thought it was locked. I should have checked it before you came." She opened a drawer in a small curio table and took out a small pistol, which she pointed at them.

"Loretta, you wouldn't shoot us, we're your friends!" Dita exlaimed, backing away, holding Rachel's hand and pulling her with her.

"It wasn't me who tried to kill you in the dunes, but a lot is at stake here right now," Loretta told them. "I can't let you go, even if it means shooting you."

"You were selling all along, weren't you?" Dita asked.

"I was surprised you didn't figure out who I am. You're supposed to be a reporter. My last name, Crandall. Recognize it? Heard it before somewhere?"

Rachel said, under her breath, "Dear God. She's in that family. The one that runs the rackets in New England."

"The granddaughter. And, for your information, I don't sell drugs on the island. The dealers under me do. I run the whole show. I import from South America and distribute across the state. I'm a liberated woman, at the top. I capitalized on the fact that there's often a traffic jam for container ships trying to get into port in New York and New Jersey. They sail this way while they wait at sea. You've both seen them out there. I have smugglers crewing on some of them. Our stuff is bagged, and we pick it up at night. You wondered where that sloop goes, Dita. The two guys meet the ships. The bags are thrown overboard. That's what you saw in the garage. I told you not to open that door."

"It was a mistake," Dita said.

"I'll say, for you and for the person who was supposed to lock it," Loretta sputtered.

For a moment, she looked almost rueful as she explained, "I tried to convince you to come yesterday before our shipment arrived, but you insisted on waiting until today. Yesterday you would have found Joel's ring and thought Trent killed Joel. Instead, you uncovered my operation."

Dita tried to stay calm, but she was terrified. She knew she needed a clear head to think of a way to escape. She would keep Loretta talking for now.

"So obviously you're not poor," she said. "The holes in your tights are for show. But why waitress? I understand cleaning to use empty houses to package the drugs but you must have a lot money stashed somewhere."

"I needed to keep an eye on the local distributers, so I went to work for Harry. And, the Beach Dunes, where I met you, that was fun. It's not like I haven't enjoyed living here, and being your friend. I tried to keep you out of my affairs, Dita, but lately you keep prying into my operations."

Rachel, tears streaming down her cheeks, moaned. "Joel, you killed my Joel."

"I ordered it, but the sailors on the sloop did it. We had to. He knew too much. You don't really want to know more do you, Rachel?"

"I let you live in my house," Rachel cried. "You, you...."

"All of that," Loretta admitted. "And Sonny, too. Both of them. They overheard Brenda and me talking about a shipment coming in by freighter that week. We couldn't let them live. You were right, Dita, Sonny didn't use. Brenda followed him home, and got into his bed; then she shot him up after they had sex and he nodded off. And, Joel..."

"Stop! I don't want to hear it," Rachel shouted.

She broke away from Dita and pushed Loretta, who stumbled backward and dropped her gun. Dita saw that as their chance.

"Run, Rachel," Dita yelled.

She was already on her way out the door, Rachel right in back of her. They sprinted as Dita reached out for Rachel's hand to pull her faster. A shot rang out.

The back door slammed shut behind them, but only for a few seconds. Dita didn't look back, but she knew Loretta had reopened it. More shots, zinging past them. She knew Rachel would be out of breath soon.

"You head to Carol's on the back path. It's just ahead. Stay down so she doesn't see you. I'll go the other way, lead her away from you. Keep the ring in your pocket. Lock yourself in your car and call George. Stay there until you talk to him and he tells you to go. And text Sean I'm on my way."

Dita gulped a breath of the fresh sea air and sped up, reaching the trail and running in the other direction. She took a shortcut, leaving the path to run through the weeds. When she reached the road, she felt calmer. She knew Loretta was not in good enough shape after her overdose to keep up and she never could pace with Dita anyway. She would be a few minutes behind even in her car which, thank goodness, Dita knew she would hear long before it arrived. She ran along the street at a good clip until she reached the bluffs, where she paused for a second to take some deep breaths. She heard a truck pull into the parking lot behind her. She knew it wasn't Loretta by the lack of clatter. Lots of tourists stopped for the view. She was not concerned, but she should have been. The jog had lulled her sense of danger. She was so intent on escaping Loretta and her gun, that she never thought about the rest of the gang.

The clay cliffs rose there 200 feet above the ocean. There were steps going almost to the bottom, where a stony beach connected to the overlook. With a rough serf in the best of days and a rocky bottom, the beach below the steps was not a draw for swimmers or surfers, and was often deserted, as it was today. She ran through the parking lot toward the stairs, not intending to jog down the 190 of them to the bottom, where boulders formed the final ten feet of the drop, but to pass by and cut back to the road further up where Sean would be waiting. The crashing surf drowned out any other sounds.

She reached the head of the staircase, trying to text Sean while she ran, so she was unprepared when she received a hard shove from behind. She stumbled and another push hurled her down the steps. She tumbled and rolled until she hit a landing 15 feet down. Bruised, but aware and able to stand, she saw her attacker taking the stairs toward her two a time. Her lips formed the word, brute. She uttered it in a whisper. He had a weight-lifter's build, but was quick on his feet. She realized he might be the guy in the fright mask at the Halloween bash.

He was almost upon her. She crouched into a coil to repel him, and pushed her whole body against his legs and pelvis when he closed in. He stumbled back, but regained his balance like a dancer and shoved her off her feet again. She had no time to think. She reached out to grasp onto something and caught the bottom of his unzipped cargo jacket. When he catapulted her down the cliff again, she kept holding on and pulled him with her. He lost his footing. She clung to the jacket for her life. They both went down the staircase, and then they were in the air, twisting. She lost her grip. Her hands ripped free and she jerked sideways, falling faster. She watched him flip over her, and heard him scream as he somersaulted straight down the drop, taking a hard landing onto the boulders at the bottom.

Dita bounced sideways, careened over the railing and catapulted into a clump of rosa rugosa, a thorny but forgiving landing pad. She was conscious, but barely, and lay there in pain. She heard a gun go off, and then she lost consciousness before she could think of getting up.

Chapter Twenty-Six

A chopper whirred in the distance; Dita heard it as a staccato drone. She lay prone in the middle of a rose bush, vines with ripe red rose hips strung across her legs. A voice, close to her ear, spoke over the sound of the chopper, "Stay still. We're here to help."

Pain. She shut her eyes.

The drone grew louder, and then the chopper hovered overhead. Who were they picking up? She tried to move.

"Sean." She thought she was shouting but it came out as a croak. A man leaned into her and, spoke into her ear, his breath coming with his words.

"It's Kyle, Dita. We're flying you to the hospital. Sean will meet you there."

They secured her neck and lifted her onto a stretcher. A thousand needle pricks taunted her, and she slipped back into a black hole.

"Can you hear me, Dita?"

A stranger's voice. She struggled to wake up.

"You're going to be okay. You're in the Willington Hospital. I'm Doctor Peters."

She opened her eyes. She was lying on a bed, under crisp white covers. He was speaking, a somber man in a white coat with a tie. She tried to listen.

" ...lucky. One arm... concussion....

And she slipped into her black place again.

She felt his hand on her cheek. "Sean?"

"I'm right here," he said.

Then she woke up. He helped her sit a little higher against her pillows. She saw a woman near the door, dark hair.

"Rachel?"

"I'm here too." Rachel came closer so Dita could see her better.

Her arm throbbed. "Broken?"

Sean answered. "You landed on it. It broke your fall, though, so your back is intact."

She ached everywhere. Her head pounded. She put her other hand on her forehead. No bandage. She ran it through her hair. No bandage there either.

"Your head is healing," Sean said. "Or at least, that's what the doctor told me."

"That's what you all think," she said. "Hurts."

An orderly rolled in a tray of food on a cart, and Dita realized she was famished. Was it lunch or supper? She had no idea. She didn't care. She ate some toast first, and then uncovered her cup of coffee. She wanted to taste it before it got cold. She sipped it and forked some eggs with her functional arm the best she could. It was her right arm that was broken, the hand she used for everything. Maybe it was breakfast. Rachel and Sean waited until she'd eaten almost everything on the tray and was finishing her coffee before speaking again.

"Thanks for endangering your life to help me find out what happened to Joel," Rachel said. "If not for you, no one would have bothered to follow up. And thanks for saving my life."

Dita put her cup down for a moment. "Tell me, Rachel. What exactly happened to Joel? Did you find out?"

"Are you ready for this now?" Sean asked.

"I am. I want to know everything," she said, and she patted the bed, indicating Rachel should sit.

"Now that I know you're going to be okay, I'm going to leave for a while. I'll come back later, Dita. Sean will tell you. It's too painful for me." Rachel threw Dita and kiss and left.

Sean leaned in toward Dita and spoke in a calm voice. "The two sailors staying in the sloop across the street from us killed him. They told Joel they needed to pick up something important on Long Island, but their skiff, the one they usually pulled behind their sailboat, needed motor repairs. They asked him if they could borrow his boat to get to shore from their sailboat. And, they invited him along for the ride.

"He stayed over at the Bradley's with them until the weather cleared early the next morning. Thought it would be fun, I guess. On the way back, the big guy that pushed you down the cliff wanted to go fishing over at one of those famous fishing holes out there, so he and Joel motored over in Joel's boat and left the other guy, supposedly to sail back himself. They planned to meet up with the sailboat back at port, or so Joel thought. Somewhere out there, the guy shoved Joel overboard, and then motored back to the sailboat. He just let Joel's boat drift away."

"That's really horrible. The terror Joel must have felt when he knew they weren't going to rescue him," Dita said. "How cruel. And Loretta oversaw it all? No wonder Rachel had to leave the room while you told me."

Sean covered her hand with his again. "I want to go to their trials and see them sentenced."

"Loretta," Dita said. "Where is Loretta? I would have thought she'd have shot me when I was lying in the rosebush."

"Karl got there just as she was climbing down to shoot you. He saw her gun and shot her first."

"Karl?" Dita asked.

"He's not one of them, Dita," Sean said. "You were wrong about him. And, Harry's not either. He used now and then, he snorted H, and shot up a few times, but he wasn't an addict or a dealer. After he'd used with them a few times, they threatened to turn him in if he didn't let them push stuff in the Washashore."

"And Trent?"

"He's a victim also. They knew he dealt in stolen art sometimes, so they muscled their way into the Bradley house with Loretta's cleaning service. If he talked, they threatened to tell the police about him."

Dita had lost her appetite. "I've had enough," she said, and she shoved the tray aside, almost knocking over the vase of tea roses on the night table next to the bed. "Oh, who sent those? They're beautiful."

"Lawrence and Candice," Sean said.

Dita smiled, and then she turned back to Sean. "I suspected something wasn't right with Loretta that day at the Lorelei when Trent said she'd been to his house a few times, but I didn't really want to think about it. And after she OD'd, she came back to the island too fast. She wasn't in any treatment program. I suspected she was still using. She must've OD'd by accident if she was the boss."

"She did," Sean confirmed that. "If it weren't for you, Dita, they would still be operating."

He handed her the water glass. She leaned against her pillow and sipped, then handed it back to him.

"Karl and the chief are out in the hall waiting to talk with you. Are you up to it?"

"Sure," she agreed. "I guess I have to thank Karl for saving me from Loretta."

"I think they're here to thank you for cracking the drug ring."

"Feels more like they cracked me, my head, anyway."

Sean texted the guys to let them know they could come in.

Dita said hello and remarked that they were in full uniform.

"It's a salute to you," the chief said, with a grin. "Karl here complained all the way over on the boat."

"Thanks, Karl. And I hear you saved me from Loretta."

"I owe you an apology for acting like such a jerk. Some of that was my trying to get in with the drug crowd, but it didn't work," Karl admitted.

"Sean told briefed you about the drug cartel; that Loretta ran it and Brenda worked for her?" the chief said.

"My good friend Loretta," Dita grumbled. "What an actress. What a sociopath."

"A rich sociopath," Karl said. "She had millions stashed away in the Caymans."

"Yet she lived like a pauper. Holes in her tights, affordable housing, cleaning and waitressing. Quite an act. Do I sound bitter? Because, I am," Dita lamented.

She wondered if she would ever trust a new friend again. Loretta had been a work pal at the Beach Dune all those years ago when she and Sean had been summer workers on the island, They quickly became confidantes. Well, she realized, I confided in her, but she never really confided in me. Was Loretta in the drug business then, she wondered. Had her family sent her to the island even in her late teens, to set up distribution there?

"If Loretta is part of an organized crime family, why didn't they just buy her a house here to work out of?" she asked, and she answered that herself. "I guess they didn't want anything in their name. I can't believe I never picked up on that name."

"Don't beat yourself up. No one else did either," the chief said. "We made a few jokes about it, but no one really thought Loretta was connected. If she was a relation, we figured it was distant. There are a lot of people carrying that name without a connection to the criminal clan."

Then he told her that Loretta confessed because she was more frightened of going to jail for life than of her family getting retribution.

Dita had one more question. "Who shot at me in the dunes? Loretta said it wasn't her."

"Brenda," Karl answered. "She was in the kitchen when you stopped at the Washashore. She figured it would be a good way to stop your snooping even if she missed you in the fog, so she slipped out the back door while you were sipping your Tia Maria and scared up the deer to run toward the road."

"I'll be. Is she a good shot?"

"You're still here, aren't you?"

Dita was discharged, and Sean brought her home. When they reached the house, Addie, Mel, Danny, Rachel and Tuffy were waiting. Danny and Tuffy ran into her arms. Mel had a platter of lobsters, all cooked and ready to eat, and Addie had a salad.

"It's good to be home," she said, "and to know I no longer have to lock the doors."

The End

Acknowledgments

Thank you, thank you, thank you for the contributions of the following people:

Jean Taber, my meticulous editor and friend, for her comments and corrections, and for being such an enthusiastic collaborator. I promise to try to corral my commas in my next book.

Lara Andrea Taber, who placed my words onto the pages and designed the format with creativity and attention to detail, and for adding her joy to that work.

Elliot Taubman, Esq., who reviewed the manuscript for legal issues and gave it a thumbs up.

Rebecca Green, Thomas Smith, and Leon Wann, extraordinary writers who developed into an extraordinary writing group, reading and rereading my chapters offering critical suggestions and support over the course of two-plus years. I feel privileged that they offer me their drafts for my review as well. What a joy it is to share my writing life with them.

Elaine Beale, whose fiction courses at The Writing Salon stimulated the ideas for several of these chapters.

Rosemary Malario and Signe Rogalski, my first complete manuscript readers, whose feedback and enthusiasm made this a better book. To Ruth Worth for her feedback on the first chapter; and to my nephew, Gary Rubenstein, who read through an early draft and offered encouragement; and Steve Rebello, who helped format letters to agents.

And, to my family: Ron, who listened to me yammer on about this book and gave me space to write it; Kevin, who solved most of my computer problems and kept copies of the manuscript on his; and to Christine, who let me take my son's time away from her and the children.